ENDORSEMENTS

Adam K. Nelson takes a bold and exciting approach to the classic question of Jesus: "What if you gained the whole world, but lost your own soul?" This book flips the question, destroying one young man's world both literally and figuratively, and forces the reader to answer, "What if I *lost* the whole world? Would I *gain* my own soul?" Exciting and addictive from start to finish, you may actually find your own soul moving from suffering to surrender in this wonderful story.

—Paul White,
Pastor, Midland Christian Church,
Poplar Bluff, Missouri,
and author of *Revelation to Transformation:
How Seeing Jesus Will Change Your Life*

Adam K. Nelson is a masterful storyteller, drawing you into a complex world where losing your life may be the only way to save it. *Learning to Live* is a journey of great challenge followed by even greater triumph. This story brings us face to face with what looks like an excruciating end, but there is always a light and through it all, Adam K. Nelson's grace-filled heart shines on every page.

—Joe Schmidt,
software engineer, and Jill Schmidt,
vintage comic book specialist

Learning to Live is a memorable, unpredictable journey of a young man's survival and personal growth. It is a gripping read that leaves you wanting more.

—Jamie Altrup, school counselor and mom

LEARNING
TO LIVE

To Rob & Trey,
Rich blessings & favor!

Akeem K. [signature]

John 3:17

ADAM K. NELSON

LEARNING TO LIVE

TATE PUBLISHING
AND ENTERPRISES, LLC

Published by Tate Publishing & Enterprises, LLC
127 E. Trade Center Terrace | Mustang, Oklahoma 73064 USA
1.888.361.9473 | www.tatepublishing.com

Tate Publishing is committed to excellence in the publishing industry. The company reflects the philosophy established by the founders, based on Psalm 68:11,
"The Lord gave the word and great was the company of those who published it."

Book design copyright © 2013 by Tate Publishing, LLC. All rights reserved.
Cover design by Samson Lim
Interior design by Caypeeline Casas

Published in the United States of America

ISBN: 978-1-62510-338-3
1. Fiction / Christian / Suspense
2. Fiction / Science Fiction / Apocalyptic & Post-Apocalyptic
13.05.13

This book is dedicated to my mother and father, who taught me not only how to live but led me to the great giver of life himself; to the band Dream Theater, whose song inspired this book and its title and whose music continues to inspire a multitude of visions; and to Michael White, who led me to Christ and continues to lead.

ACKNOWLEDGMENTS

This book would not exist were it not for Dream Theater, the greatest band of all time. I want to thank John Myung for his haunting, beautiful lyrics.

As I redrafted *Learning to Live*, the message of Jesus' radical grace and its power to work rich blessings in our lives helped shape the book into what it has become. I give the Lord all of the credit, but I want to thank some of His spokesmen, namely Paul White, Joseph Prince, Lynn Hiles, Terry Bench, Kevin Short, and Gary Bruegman. Whether directly or indirectly, their guidance and inspiration as received from the Holy Spirit gave this book its heart.

I certainly would not have been able to push this novel on through without all of the encouragement of my dear, dear fans. These fans fall into a few subgroups, which I'd like to name here.

Thanks to all the folks at Christ Community Church who were so supportive with *A Night with St. Nick*, coming back annually for copies as stocking stuffers and generally just showing me the love I needed to keep believing in it.

Thanks to the Black Market Llamas and all their fans. We've made music together that has exposed God's heart to us, and it rings in my ears when I sit down to write. Tremendous thanks to all you folks from Poplar Bluff. While I have not lived there in quite a while, it's still very much home to me. I especially want to thank my Facebook fans, as they near six hundred in number. You have faithfully hung on my every update. Each one of you is very dear to me, and I love you more than words can express.

A special thank-you to every teacher who ever played a role in encouraging my writing (I fear I will leave some of you out, but feel free to write your name all over this page): Mrs. Potter, Dr. Willis, Dr. Fuller, Charlie Hungerford, Tristan Davies, Mrs. Jones, and Dr. Meidlinger.

Special thanks to Jill Schmidt, who provided a very helpful perspective on Ryan's first encounters with God and gave of her valuable time to an additional review of the finished manuscript. Thanks also to Patrick Dunnegan, who worked with me on a Santa short-short for the *Springfield News-Leader* by providing a captivating, breathtaking illustration that spoke more than words. He also gave me some guidance that will certainly feed me as I compose the follow-up to this book.

I want to thank my coworkers and colleagues, past (at Assemblies of God Credit Union) and present (at Global University). Your friendship and support over the years have helped me achieve tremendous success.

And now, my dear ones. Mom, Dad, Amanda—you three are so very dear and awesome. I want to thank you for all of your help in pushing *A Night with St. Nick*. You know how shy and modest I am. You counted that all as dung and sung my praises loudly. I can credit at least half of that book's sales to your support.

Thanks go to my boys—Asher, Levi, and Judah. A friend described *children* as an "app for laughter and joy," and I can think of no more fitting definition for you three. You bless your mother and me tenfold for every one blessing we try to speak into your lives. I cannot imagine taking on any adventure, great or small, without you boys along for the ride, so this book and its lasting legacy are as much yours as they are mine.

Diana-bear, you silly sweet thing, you. My prayer is that this book will bring such tremendous success that we can populate the earth with more children who are just as sweet and beautiful as you are. You're the template, woman perfected. You're my muse, my inspiration, my dearest friend. There is not room enough in all the hearts of the world for all the love I feel for you and all the love you deserve. You are a paragon of radical grace in my life and always have been, before we even stepped foot in Midland Church and put a name to the face of it. Here you go, hon. You enjoy this book. It was written out of *special* fondness for you. Again I ask you, SHMILY?

PREFACE

———⟫●⟪———

The band was returning by bus from a marching contest earlier that day in St. Louis. We stopped at a Wal-Mart for rest and refreshment. I needed neither but instead wandered to the electronics department on a lark. I had some cash in hand and wanted to check out a band named Dream Theater. A very priceless mentor named Josh Livingston had discovered them on my behalf. Josh, who graduated the previous year, was a die-hard Rush fan, loving them especially for their drummer. He often would copy Neil Peart's patterns, incorporate them into his playing. His exploration of progressive rock music had brought him to Dream Theater. He shared them with me. He didn't know quite what to think of them himself, and I admit, they were rather heavy for my taste as I was only just beginning to leave my hip-hop phase behind.

Dream Theater had two albums at that Wal-Mart, *Awake* and *Images and Words*. I was a little more familiar with the former; it was the album Josh had played for me. I wanted to buy them both but could only afford one. I opted for *Awake*, but the clerk put it behind the counter and rung up *Images and Words* instead. When I realized his mistake, I began to speak up, but I was worried I would offend or bother him by having him reverse the transaction, and besides, I was just a fifteen-year-old high school sophomore. What right did I have to tell somebody else how to do his job? I took *Images and Words* and thanked him for his help.

I listened to it at home later that week, and as with *Awake*, I didn't know what to make of it either. This was music on another level of consciousness, much more advanced in structure and sound than anything I was used to. It took several listens before I began to appreciate it, and when that moment came, oh! how glorious! I would never come back from it. This book is the result of a happy mistake from a clerk at a Wal-Mart in an unknown town in between St. Louis and Poplar Bluff, Missouri.

Later that fall, my sister and I stayed a weekend at my grandparents' house in a tiny town named Sedgewickville. She let me bring along one of my own albums, especially selfless considering she and I were diverging quite startlingly in our musical tastes by that point, and I feared Dream Theater would be too weird for her. It was a dull gray morning, and the foliage had already turned and fallen. The last song, "Learning to Live," had a gray *sound* to it that matched the sky, and as we listened to it on that drive, I began to see the world that way. This wasn't a despairing thought, but rather a *what-if?* What if the world itself was gray? I pictured a figure walking across a desolate, empty expanse as the haunting melody behind the opening verse unrolled. The story began to unfold in my mind from there.

Four years later, a sophomore in college now, I began to write it and got a hundred pages into it before I sent my computer off the following summer to be cleaned of viruses and various junk that got on it. I made the mistake of telling the technicians that there wasn't anything on there I wanted to keep, and my first official draft of *Learning to Live*, then titled "Vessel," was wiped away forever. I had *real* momentum on it, too, and I couldn't bring myself to return to it for five years. I'm glad I waited so long.

Something happened in between those drafts. I started to feel the viscera of this book, the atmosphere, the darkness, the blindness Ryan feels. Passages detailing his struggle for survival after the fiery blast would creep me out to the point that I'd have to get up and go do something noisy for a while. I had never felt that about my writing before. Still, I felt like the book didn't have a *point* and was only a futile exercise in minimalism, an attempt to find a story that literally could have no setting. I had no motivation for the character, no real development to give him. I couldn't figure out what this guy was supposed to do other than just describe the drab, gray expanse around him and cry over what he'd lost.

I realize now that the drive for me as a writer is to discover the metaphor. Many writers can be literal, can give you a play-by-play of their novel's events, can thrill you just by what happens, and can supplement events with expert authenticating details, but I'm not that kind of writer and perhaps never will be. I discovered with *A Night with St. Nick* that if I hack away at it long enough, God shows up in my writing and points me to what the story is really about. *A Night with St. Nick* was really just supposed to be about a kid who meets Santa Claus and finds him to be a very gentle, sweet soul. It ended up being about Jesus and nothing less.

As I was finishing up the first signing tour for *St. Nick*, I returned to *Learning to Live* and discovered rather quickly that the same thing was happening; yes, this was a novel about a college student who survived the end of the world, but more than that, it was a novel that would ask and answer the question, *Is it possible to find God when there's nobody around to lead you to him and literally nothing to hang a hope on?*

The answer, as you'll see, is a resounding yes, and God is a very creative person. The myriad of ways in which he can reveal himself to us are fun and surprising, and his method can reveal just as much about his nature as the substance of his message. His communication with us can take place against a blank physical (or, if you will, psychological) backdrop just as easily and effectively as it can in a world full of stuff and people, and his message is always gentle, always good, always uplifting and never, for a second, against us. This, then, is a book about hope. Hope fills every page, every word of it. I pray that's what you receive. I am after happy tears. And it's time we have a post-apocalyptic fiction that isn't about the survivors raping and murdering each other. Stephen King and others have that territory well covered.

Ryan's experience is very much like my own. No, I've never lived through the end of the world, but there have been numerous times in my life when it felt like the world was crashing down all around me. In those moments, I heard God much as Ryan does. Additionally, I hear God's message much more clearly when I'm willing to step out of the human constructs such as the legalistic doctrine we often use to put him in such small boxes so we can better understand him. The fellowship of other believers is a beautiful thing, but you need to understand that the whole of your experience in all of creation comes down to just you and God. Leave all else aside for a while, especially your busywork that you do to please and serve him, and just sit and let him love you and talk to you. You'll be amazed not only at what comes out but also how it comes out. It was the search for what can arise from this experience that led to some of my favorite passages in this book.

Learning to Live is written as a "found" document. It was always meant to be first-person, but I believe its point of view shaped its ultimate purpose—to offer hope as Ryan Sterling has come to understand it. While its fictional intended audience are survivors of a blast that decimated the world, its *real* intended audience is you, that you may know there are always boulders of hope rising up out of a desolately flat landscape of despair. In fact, although it may not always seem like it, God's creation is *full* of them.

THE END

First, take whatever provisions you can carry with you. There should still be a wealth of them here. I took everything I could, but I left more than enough nonperishables. They'll keep just fine. Then, take this manuscript and come find me. I can't wait to see you. Leave a note behind to tell the others. I pray for your safety, whoever you are.

My name is Ryan Sterling. To wit, I am the only survivor. I long for the day I find out I'm wrong, and I've found that it's okay to hope. It's important to hope. It's not only the best thing; it's the only thing. You hope, too. If you're reading this, know that I am still alive. Believe it. Say it to yourself as if it's so, and when we find each other, we will embrace as long lost siblings and sup together on cans of cold ravioli. A feast fit for kings and queens.

You witnessed the fire. I don't doubt that. You saw it coming, took shelter, and lived as I did, but not without your scars. In time, the ash made a healing paste over your open wounds. Such irony—the thing that wiped us out now salving our wounds. I like to think it's because there's someone greater than us who can turn this greatest of tragedies into triumph, and someday we'll see that promise fulfilled. Even our spiritual wounds will find their healing.

You see, I saw them deliver our destruction. I witnessed it with my own eyes on December 12 of last year, and over the ensuing year, I have had to deal with the aftermath as you have. What do we do with something like this? The fact you're still alive speaks to your strength. Perhaps you've found that thing as I have, that something greater that will lead us to the glorious future.

Will you bear with me? I would like to tell you what I saw and what my life has been like since, so that you may have the hope that I have. Perhaps you have been eking out your survival but now dwell on the frayed ends of your sanity. Each day feels like it may be the last, but you continue to breathe and you allow the next morning to come because it also may bring that glimmer of hope. Perhaps your past, all that you've lost, haunts you every day, torments you, raising more questions each day that seem to go unheeded. You think you've lost everything, but you hang on for answers from out of the thick gray silence. I have good news— your questions have been heard. The silence is broken. I may have what you're seeking. Walk with me.

Had the world not ended, I would have graduated college last spring. As of this writing, I am twenty-two years old. The end came after the first semester of my last year at Drury University in Springfield, Missouri, three hours west (in drive time, that is) of where you are right now, a town that was known as Poplar Bluff. I was pursuing an English degree with an emphasis in literature and a minor in creative writing. I hoped to become a professor someday. I had not decided on a graduate program yet, however. I was planning on doing that in the spring. My future was undecided but wrought with possibilities.

I woke up on Friday, December 12, at seven. I was not normally an early riser, but I was excited for the trip home. My last final had concluded at four on Thursday afternoon, but I stayed just to kick back and relax at the apartment rather than head home, despite Mom's protests. My roommates had partied to celebrate the end of their finals the night before. They invited me to join in, but I had forsaken that scene my sophomore year when I learned how empty and superficial the party life was. I had no moral repugnance for it. I just didn't see the point; if I had to drink to loosen up and meet girls, they wouldn't be relationships worth pursuing. Besides, I had been dating Sara for over a year. I never needed that lifestyle in the first place, and I definitely didn't need it now. The occasional can of suds after a long study session was all I ever wanted.

I packed all of the belongings I could fit into my car—clothes, my PC, toiletries, textbooks, papers, notebooks, and the nonperishable foodstuffs I hadn't consumed yet, like packages of Ramen noodles, chips, cookies, coke, and beer. Aside from the noodles and beer, I kept all my consumables in the front passenger seat for the trip home so I could binge at my leisure. My mom would have killed me for it, but she wasn't going to be home to see my junk food and trash-littered car when I arrived at midmorning. I called her before I left and found out she was going to be in Cape Girardeau looking after her brother who had broken his leg in a fall on the ice in November. He had never married and didn't have anybody to look after him, so she visited him once a week and took care of any items of business he had on the table like groceries and laundry. She was to arrive home a couple of hours after me, plenty of time for me to clean up the evidence that I had not yet begun nor ever intended to begin eating the way she raised me to eat.

Our conversation that morning was far briefer than usual. My sister Katie and I enjoyed recounting conversations we had had with Mom. They always had a particular cadence about them, not to mention length. You never "checked in" with Mom. You sat down, had a cup of coffee, ate dinner and dessert, and then watched a movie. I knew to expect the same when I called her that morning. I was pleasantly surprised by the result.

"Heading out, Mom. Gassing up and then I'm gone."

"Okay. Be careful, all right? You're probably not the only one driving home from school this morning."

Yes I am, I wanted to tell her. It was seven-thirty in the morning. *Nobody* was up.

"Gotcha."

"I told you I'm going to Uncle David's, right?"

"Yeah, you'll be back this afternoon."

"Mm-hmm. We'll catch up then. You have a nice drive."

Is this really good-bye? I thought. *No new territory to cover out of left field?*

"Will do."

"I love you."

That last caught me off guard. So far as I could remember, Mom had never told me that. Sure, I knew she did. Katie and I both knew her love for us was as deep as the ocean, but we never *said* it to each other. I stammered out the same, and then we were off.

"Huh," I said to the still morning air.

⋅⋅⋅

It was a mild morning, kind of cool. I could see my breath. It must have been in the upper forties, but it would warm up in time. The sky was clear and beautiful at the moment, but out west I could see the ingredients brewing for the rain we would get later. There would be two systems: The first was going to cross into southwest Missouri from Kansas. The second would come up from the south in Arkansas and hit Southeast Missouri sometime between ten-thirty and eleven. I had checked online to see what I should prepare for. I was leaving in a window of time that would miss both systems.

I left town by heading west on Chestnut until I hit 65, which I would take until Highway 60. I turned east on 60, and it took me the rest of the way home. Around West Plains, it entered the woods and remained in them until Poplar Bluff, at which point I got off onto 67 and headed north into town. A few more turns, and I would be home. The drive was always uneventful except if there was a touch of weather to worry about. I had no indication this trip would be otherwise.

I drove a Toyota Camry. Very easy to drive, very safe and dependable. I brought along several CDs to pass the time. They ran the gamut of my personal interests. Dream Theater was in my stash, but so was Norah Jones, Diana Krall, and Dave Matthews Band. If I needed to wake up, I would put in Dragonforce. Typically, my brain switched off regardless, and I would idle away the time thinking about my life and the people in it. Sara most often came to mind, especially at the Hartville-Mansfield exit. We had a fond memory there, although she didn't like to return to it.

She got carsick on the way to Poplar Bluff with me the first time I brought her down to meet my parents. It was our first Christmas together. Something she had eaten the night before hadn't agreed with her. We pulled over at the top of the off-ramp, and when I slowed to a stop, she burst out of the passenger side door and got rid of everything in her stomach. I won points with her when I burst into action, running around to her side so I could hold her long brown hair back from her face. That part of the story she likes, but she could dispense with the rest of it. We didn't have to say it—that was love in action.

Farther down the road, I stopped at the Mountain Grove McDonald's for a cold Coke. I preferred it at the moment to the warming cans of it I had in my floorboard. It was an unnecessary expenditure, but that was precisely why I did it. It would be the last liquid I would have for a long while.

I made the turn into the woods and enjoyed the drive over the hills past Mountain View. The traffic was sparse for a business day. I found it odd but enjoyed having the road to myself. I could drive at my own pace. If I recall correctly, my CD player was on

Dream Theater when I arrived at Van Buren. It was their second album, *Images and Words*, my personal favorite because it was the first one I had ever listened to and got me to fall in love with them in the first place. Might not have been their greatest artistic triumph, but it changed the face of progressive music forever. I knew all the lyrics and sang them at the top of my lungs as the drive toward Van Buren conjured up childhood memories.

I had spent many weekends on the Current River with family and friends. I went on my first float trip when I was three. I remember it. Wasn't on the Current, though. It was the Jack's Fork, in a canoe, but tubing the Current was how we did most of our floats. Get up on a Saturday morning, pack the van full of snacks and gear, make the hour trip to Van Buren yelling way too loudly for our dads' comfort and falling silent at their frequent admonishments to "turn around, sit down, buckle up, and shut up"—only to start back up once a safe amount of time had passed. Katie and the other big kids, brave as they were, usually determined when the interval of quiet time was over.

We'd spend the weekend at a cabin owned by Archie Dale and his family. We'd start a few miles upstream and float down to it, usually taking about four hours. Then we'd spend the evening swimming in the water hole out in front of the cabin, where the current was slow and manageable. We'd come in when our folks called us up for hamburgers, scarf them down, and get right back to it, coming up with games to play in the water or holding fiercely competitive races, adventures we could go on along the bank, digging up rocks and exploring what came running out from underneath, catching crawdads and trying not to get pinched. There was a large pasture behind the Dales' cabin, and on the Fourth of July, we'd set the heavens on fire back there. We were too little to do much more than roman candles, but the neighbors put on a big, loud, expensive show, and we would head over to their property to watch after our own appetite for destruction was sated.

We fell out of touch with the Dales as our family moved through time and got busier, but we still frequented the river. Rather than use our own tubes, which had long ago become deflated or torn, we rented them from the Gravel Bar, a hotel/restaurant/tube-canoe rental along the side of Highway 60. You couldn't miss it, and while there were other, smaller outfits, the Gravel Bar was the one everybody was used to for floats. On the morning of December 12, it was entirely vacant. The season was over, and I doubt if a staff of even ten people were there to keep it running, which makes it odd that *that* was where it all happened.

I didn't notice until I had already driven past it, and I wonder if it had been there before I looked. I was over the bridge and about to make the turn up the hill across the river when I looked in my rearview mirror and saw an object that was most definitely closer than it appeared.

I cursed and slammed on my brakes, throwing me against the steering wheel so hard that it bruised my chest. The reciprocal force threw me back into my seat, and I heard a metallic click as the seat adjuster was knocked slightly off its tracks. Thankfully, there was nobody behind me. I had gone from sixty to zero in less than three seconds, and I would have been crushed by anybody following me.

Hands shaking from the panic of my sudden movement, I pulled the car over as steadily as I could to the shoulder and got out. I can't be sure that there weren't more of them around the world and that you may have seen one too. Perhaps you even saw this one, and if so, I'd be glad to compare notes later. You understand that I was traumatized by the sight. I could be getting some details wrong, but the fact that it was there and that it did what it did is indisputable. If you didn't know what set it off, this is for you.

Hovering a hundred feet above the Gravel Bar was a spaceship. Its bow was elongated and narrowed to a point, but its stern was bulbous, and I assume its crew, if it had any, were stationed there and controlled the ship from that part. It appeared designed for the best aerodynamic performance possible, which wouldn't make a difference in interplanetary or intergalactic travel but would be an asset if inside an atmosphere. I couldn't see if it had windows because the entire ship was blacker than night. From my vantage point several hundred yards away, there were no distinguishing features in the body of the craft. Its sleek design was smooth and unbroken. It was a fearsome and beautiful sight.

Distances made it hard to judge, but it looked at least as big as the Gravel Bar lodge, maybe a bit larger. It hung motionless in the sky and didn't make a sound. There was not even a slight variation in its altitude to suggest that thrusters were firing continuously to keep it steady. I marveled at it, and of course I thought I was dreaming. While I knew it was a pointless and clichéd gesture, I pinched myself and rubbed my eyes, just in case that sort of thing really works, but there it remained.

I summoned the will to break visual contact with it and scan the road and the bridge behind me. There were a couple of cars that had stopped, their drivers standing outside to gawk as I was. I couldn't see over the walls of the bridge very far down to tell if any of the Gravel Bar staff were observing it too. Nobody panicked and peeled out to get away from it, which I found curious as I thought about it later. Perhaps they felt as I did, overwhelmed by the sight to the point that panic seemed nonexistent. I'm sure they wondered as I did if the aliens were hostile, but thoughts of self-preservation were blanked out by sheer awe.

I wondered if I should drive toward it, even approach it. Were they waiting for one of us to greet them? Were they perhaps shy and even a little afraid to get out and see us? Were they aware of Area 51 and all the government cover-ups, urban legend or not? Still aghast, I couldn't even lift a foot to go one way or another.

It occurred to me then and several times afterward that I could have been witnessing a top-secret government project that got away, but if that were true, I would certainly have seen military vehicles and personnel either then or shortly afterward to work on damage and rumor control. No, I hold firm in the conviction that this was the real thing, and regardless of what a government project gone awry might do, nothing they had yet discovered could so meticulously destroy a planet as this thing was about to do.

The ship began to spin. It was hard to tell if it went clockwise or counterclockwise because the unbroken blackness of it made it look as if it could be going either way depending on what your mind told you. It didn't matter. The spin got faster, much faster, until it was going several thousand rpm. That's when I started to turn from "mildly afraid" to "scared to death." I didn't know what was about to happen, and that scared me just as much as if I did.

From the flat bottom of the spaceship extended a long black hose. It whipped and snaked wildly, back and forth and around, thrown about by the motion of the ship, but when it reached its full extent—about ten yards—it settled into a circular rotation that matched the ship's. That was when the ship started to make a noise.

Until that moment, I could hear the wind blowing gustily past my ears as it began to usher in the storm that was coming into the region. I could also hear some distant thunder announcing its imminent arrival. The ship had been absolutely silent, but now it was all I heard. My mind cycled through associations as I had never heard such a sound before, and it landed on Richie Sambora's guitar riff from "Livin' on a Prayer"—*wow, WOW, wow…wow, WOW, wow*. And then came the crackling as the light show began.

Blue bolts of energy like lightning flashed outward from unseen ports around the perimeter of the ship. I didn't count them, but in retrospect, I estimate there were at least a hundred of them. They wrapped around the underside of the ship and disappeared through the open hatch from which the hose had emerged, tentacles turned inward toward the belly of the beast.

The hull-side connections for the bolts were severed, the last of the energy disappearing into that hatch, and the rotating hose became stiff like somebody had pushed a two-by-four into it. There was a loud ear-piercing whine and then a deep explosive sound that I felt in my chest more than heard with my ears, and a blue pulse brighter than the sun shot straight down into the top of the Gravel Bar. In a split second, the building was gone. A cloud of opaque gray ash, rounded on the sides and with soft edges but eerily maintaining the shape and dimensions of the building, stood in its place. It looked like those cartoons when Wile E. Coyote blew himself up with his latest Acme gadget, and there was only a coyote-shaped cloud left where it was standing. He'd reach an arm out of the cloud and sweep himself up, and we'd laugh because it was funny, and it *was* funny because it wasn't real and could never be real. Even if we were worried, the coyote would appear in the next frame busily working on some other scheme.

As I stood there continuing to gawk, I hoped for the absurdity of the next frame, when all would be restored as it was, and we'd laugh in communal schadenfreude. But there was no scene 2, and all I heard was screaming from the other gawkers and then from myself. A plume of ash billowed outward in all directions, but through it I could see a glow. It brightened and grew, and the gray was quickly overtaken by a blue flame that shot outward and immediately filled the sky. The screams of the others on the bridge grew louder, but nobody moved.

"G-g-get away!" I managed to shout against my fear, but not loud enough for anyone to hear. I screamed it, but they still couldn't hear me. The sound that filled the air was like some mighty exhalation of the gods. I jumped into my car, threw it into drive, and peeled out, spitting gravel from the shoulder where I had parked behind and around me and barely keeping control enough of the wheel to keep it on the road. I didn't check behind me to see if the other folks had gotten away or even gotten into their cars. I prayed they did, but I feared the worst.

My mind was in full-on survival mode. My heart raced against my sore chest so furiously it's a wonder I didn't have a heart attack in the middle of it. So often during the weeks afterward, I wished I could have had such a peaceful sudden death.

The flame stayed behind me. In fact, I actually put distance between us. After twenty minutes, it no longer filled my rearview mirror but rather just hung out in a small bottom corner of it. But it was still coming, like a zombie from a George Romero movie. You could outrun them until the end of time, but they would never stop. They'd get you, and to run only delayed the inevitable.

The roads were significantly easier to drive than they had once been. Yes, a few curves here and there, but it was all four-lane, and wide. I came upon only a few cars going my way, and they were all hell-bent as I was on outrunning the flame. I was easily the fastest of all of them. I gave them little thought, honking here and there for them to move out of the way or at least drive faster when they inhibited my progress.

My stomach was in knots and threatened to toss up everything in it. I wanted to do nothing more, in fact, but by force of will, I kept it from happening. Instead, it came out the other end, and the stench filled the car immediately. I didn't have time to react to the mess I had made.

A thought flashed through my mind, something my high school biology teacher had said about the body's tendency to get rid of everything it can in situations of extreme duress such as this one, when fleeing is of the utmost importance to survival, like when a building is on the verge of collapse or you're about to crash in an airplane. This, then, was one of those moments, although I fail to see how pooping myself was any benefit as I was depending on my car for a quick getaway and not my own body.

The flame continued to make a long exhaling sound. It was deafening even inside a fast-moving car that was putting distance behind it. Underneath it, I could hear my own quick breathing. I thought of Sara and worried for her. At that point, there was of course no indication that this flame wouldn't burn itself out after a few miles, but already I felt that I may lose her. The thoughts were fleeting, though, as I returned constantly to thinking about the flame and whether it had gained on me. After half an hour of driving a hundred-plus miles an hour, though, I had put it completely out of even the corner of my rearview mirror. The wall of flame was easily over a thousand feet tall, so it must have been miles behind me. Were it not for the noise, I would have thought it had burned out. But, oh! That noise. Even now it haunts my dreams.

I didn't know anything else but to drive home. Our basement had worked well enough as a tornado shelter over the years. I supposed it could work as a fire shelter too. If my life was going to end, I wanted it to happen somewhere that meant more than any other place in the world to me, a place full of memory and love. I wanted to be wrapped in those arms of comfort in my final moments, even if there would be no one there to share it with. More than anything, I wanted my dad. I had a need to be home that surpassed any logic.

"Please, oh please, oh please," I said countless times as I approached the turnoff from 60 onto 67. There was no conscious object of my pleas. I wasn't even aware I was saying it at the moment, but it came out of my mouth a thousand times a minute. Tears spilled down my cheeks. I thought for a moment about the few people inside the Gravel Bar when it went. They didn't even know what had happened to them. They would be the lucky ones, for all the rest would see and hear the flame for agonizing, eternal seconds before it claimed them.

I slowed down considerably on the on-ramp into the turn, then floored it. I merged into busier traffic than I had yet faced. Unlike the folks on 60, most of these drivers drove as if they had no idea. I saw a few driving erratically and crazily as if perhaps they had tuned into the radio and heard a report about the event the others had missed. At any rate, I continued honking and shouting directionless pleas.

I saw highway patrol and sheriff cars driving toward and away from town with lights flashing and sirens blasting. As I got closer to town, I saw fire trucks and ambulances doing the same, toward what end I didn't know, but they were definitely getting people's attention. Cars were pulled along the shoulder along 67, folks shading their eyes and looking around to see what it was all about and find the source of that deafening breathy sound.

The sky was dark with rain, flashes of lightning, but I couldn't hear the thunder because the sound of the flame was so ubiquitous. The drops started to fall. I turned my wipers on high and kept the needle on the speedometer firmly toward the right. The first sharp turn I had to make was onto Katy Lane. There was a red light at that intersection, but I floored the car straight through it, narrowly missing side-swiping a pickup whose driver actually had the wherewithal in the moment to flip me off.

Katy merged smoothly onto Evans. I kept the pedal planted on the floor despite the large hills and blind curves along the way. I trusted in whatever cosmic force that had kept me safe thus far to keep me from crashing into anything or anybody as I crested each one. At the top of the last, I glanced at the console in front of the gearshift and saw my cellphone. I hadn't touched it the entire trip, not even to call Sara when I set out from Springfield and tell her I was on the road and that I missed her and loved her. I had planned on doing it but was so caught up in my music and junk food that it slipped my mind, and so it also had while I was racing to beat the devil.

Why didn't I call her? I thought.

I screamed in frustration and grabbed the phone. I looked in my mirror and out my windows and could see the glow gaining on me and filling my view once again. There was no time to call or even flip the phone open. Folks were pulling over to the side of Evans Road now, getting out of their cars and looking on in stupid curiosity. Others were careening wildly across the center-line of traffic. They forsook their own safety or anyone else's just to somehow find the fastest route possible away from the flame. They already knew. I could see facial expressions as I passed that told me the ones who had stopped were resigned to the inevitable. I was not going to be one of them.

I peeled out around the corner onto Roanoke Lane and almost lost control of the car, but I steered against the skid and took the immediate right onto Grant Avenue. My house was on the left side of a cul-de-sac at the end of the street. Most of my neighbors were still at work, but I could see a handful of families in their front yards looking around, confused. Some would be inside, frantically flipping through channels to find news of it. Others were loading their cars and trying to get away. I hadn't turned on the radio. I had no idea what information they had heard. I was informed enough by what I had seen.

That loud breathy roar had grown exponentially in volume. Dad and I went to a Lynyrd Skynyrd concert at the Black River Coliseum a few summers ago. The acoustics were horrible there—no noise absorption anywhere—so "Freebird" sounded like the most awful mess we had ever heard, the guitars bouncing off on everything in the room. It wasn't music. It was an unwelcome assault to the ears, and the most hardcore metalhead would have agreed with me. The fire sounded like that now that it was upon us. It had grown stronger from what it ate, stronger and faster.

My drive down the street only took a few seconds. I had to slow down to keep from plowing over some of my neighbors who were running toward and away from the cul-de-sac in a futile attempt to escape the fire. I screamed at them to come with me, but my window was up, so they couldn't hear me. They couldn't have heard even if I had it rolled down. I couldn't hear myself.

I reached my house, turned into the driveway, and shot straight up the hill and into the garage door. I slammed on the brakes and braced for the impact. The door came off its tracks and crashed on the roof of the car, caving it in but leaving me just enough room to climb over the gearshift. The passenger door opened the tiniest bit, and I squeezed out with no room to spare. A hook in the door caught my shirt and ripped it, slicing the skin over my ribcage shallowly in the process and quickly drawing blood. I cried out of panic more than pain; for a second, I had thought I wouldn't make it. I then had to squeeze out from under the edge of the garage door. I was pinned between it and the car, and I pleaded with my anxious, directionless prayer for help again. I was doubled over, my shoulders pushed up against the door, pressed so tightly that I almost couldn't breathe. I gathered all I had in me and pushed up against the garage door. It budged an inch, and I slipped out from underneath it.

I left the car running. There was no reason to turn it off, and I would have counted it a blessing if I *were* able to come back later and kill the engine. The sound of the fire was amplified by the acoustics of the garage. I thought I would go deaf and wanted to clamp my hands over my ears.

Some wallboard and shelves had fallen off with my crash into the garage. Nails, screws, screwdrivers, toolboxes, wrenches, bottles of carwash soap and wax, and various other jetsam littered my short path from the car to the laundry-room door. I slipped and slid over the debris, once catching myself against the sharp corner of Dad's workbench along the wall. It dug into my right shoulder, and I cursed at the sudden pain.

I reached the stairs to the laundry-room door in one piece and willed myself in that *one* moment to look out over the mess and take the last fleeting glimpse of the world I would ever have. It would forever be burned into my memory.

They were a family of three who lived two doors down, the Brents. Ed and Linda and their five-year-old little girl, Lacy. They were one of the families I had seen moments ago trying to get away in their car, but for some reason they had forsaken the effort and instead had run to the cul-de-sac, unarguably the most beautiful spot on the street. It was a grassy area that Dad kept mowed and properly seeded throughout its active season and well-kept in dormancy besides. In the middle was a flowering dogwood, now dormant for the winter, but you could imagine its glory just by its framework. Lacy liked to play there and climb that tree, and Mom and Dad liked to sit on the porch in the mild summer evenings and watch her. I'm sure it made them think fondly of the times Katie and I did the same when we were her age. Now, Lacy and her parents were there to die. It broke my heart.

"Come up here!" I screamed at them as hard as I could. Of course they couldn't hear me. Linda knelt on the ground. She held Lacy tightly against her with Lacy's face buried in her chest. Linda's face was twisted in anguish and fear. I could see the awful blue glow of the fire casting it in a doleful, morbid pale hue. The blue glow was growing to cover everything in sight. It was surreal. It looked like a blue sunset out there. It changed the color scheme of the entire visible world. Ed's arms were thrown around his wife and daughter, and he looked sad. He wasn't hiding his face at all, nor was he crying. He just looked lost. He didn't stand a chance against the beast. He was a man denied the right to fight for his family.

I felt the heat then. There was no way to go out and grab them. The fire had come, so I turned from where I had been standing at the laundry room's door to the garage and ran. Behind me, it devoured the house. I was vaguely aware of the entire structure crushing in on itself in a hellish cacophony of groaning and cracking in one moment and then disappearing into ash the next. Pieces of plaster from the ceiling rained down on me. Chunks big enough to take me down fell all around and just behind me, but it was only a few giant steps from the garage through the kitchen and into the hallway where the basement door was. Had I tarried, I would surely have been crushed, then burned away.

Tears of desperation streamed from my eyes. My bladder and bowels relieved themselves again, my body dropping weight involuntarily to aid my escape. I grabbed the basement door and threw it open. Thirteen steps descended steeply into the darkness of the basement.

When I was a kid, Katie and I would slide down them on our stomachs. We were small enough at that time to race side by side. We had to stop when Katie became a preteen and her body changed in sensitive areas. It wasn't fun anymore without her, and I never said anything, but it had always hurt me, too. The thought crossed my mind to do it now, but the unbearably hot blast of the fire hit me then. I heard and smelled the skin on my back cooking an instant before I felt it, sudden heat followed by searing and indescribable pain.

Without a choice in the matter, I jumped headfirst down the stairs and the fire turned my childhood home into fiction the instant I cleared it. I flipped once in midair and landed on my back; my head hit the floor a moment later. The carpet in the basement was thin, and underneath was bare concrete. My back took the brunt of the impact; had it not, I'm sure the sudden and brutal knock on the back of my head would have killed me instantly. Instead, it knocked me out, but just before I swam into the darkness, I saw the last of the fire sweep overhead and take existence with it, and the world turned black.

AWAKENING

I slept without wanting to. I had never experienced that before. In the moments before taking the plunge into the basement, I couldn't have been more awake. I had enough adrenaline coursing through my body to keep me awake for a week. But it was all shocked out of me by the head trauma, and so I slept. And I dreamed.

Dreams are different when you're knocked unconscious. I had always wondered. Katie had her wisdom teeth taken out several years ago. They put her completely under for it, and she told me that she was still aware of the tugging and sawing they were doing on her mouth to extract the teeth, but she also thought she was lost in a gigantic labyrinth where the walls, floor, and ceiling were made of neon lights bursting with beautiful psychedelic patterns of color. But she didn't appreciate the pretty colors because she was frustrated that she couldn't find her way out. When she came to, the labyrinth was suddenly lit up with a blinding white light, and the walls, floor, and ceiling fell away, and she was safely back in the surgeon's chair, slightly reclined.

"It wasn't pleasant," she said. "I felt like I didn't go under. I just went somewhere else."

I went somewhere else too, but it wasn't a place as active as her tripped-out maze. Thank goodness for that. But it was still unsettling. I was in a dark place, but it was dark because it was night. I was a baby in this dream. I think I was a baby. I was small enough to be held by someone. Or something. It was massive, but because it was dark, I couldn't make out its features. I sensed that it was strong enough to crush me if it wanted to, and I was picking up vibes from this hulking thing that made me feel the outcome was uncertain. For the moment, it just held me against it and carried me. I tried to look around and see if I could get a sense of where I was, but I woke up.

When I woke up, I didn't know at first that I had. My floor, ceilings, and walls fell away just like Katie's, but there wasn't a blinding white light followed by a doctor's chair. It was a sound, first, the sound of wind blowing past my ears and nothing else. The wind was warm, sluggish. The air was thick. My ears felt stuffed with cotton, the long slow recovery from a loud rock concert.

Because my dream had been so enveloping, I struggled to remember what had happened. I was slow to come to completely, so I lay still and listened to the wind. *Am I outside?* I thought. *Am I camping, maybe sleeping under the stars? But that can't be. It's winter. Maybe a window's open? I don't feel cold air. Did I travel someplace warm?*

No, something warm traveled to me.

Oh no, oh please no.

I opened my eyes and saw nothing. I put my hand up a foot in front of my face, but I didn't see it. I brought it slowly closer, but it never resolved. *Am I blind?* I thought. I very well could have been. There was no source of light anywhere, not even the blinking time on the VCR lighting up its little hole in the entertainment center across the room from where I lay, but I didn't know at first where I lay anyway. I went over the fall in my mind. It was an unpleasant memory, but I remembered how I had fallen and what my immediate surroundings should be. My feet would be a few inches away from the opposite wall, the top of my head pointed toward the stairwell.

And then I remembered the last thing I saw—the fire going overhead, sweeping my house from its foundation. I suddenly felt very vulnerable there in the impenetrable darkness. If I wasn't hallucinating there at the end, if what I saw *really* happened, then there was nothing above me but sky. I had no protection, no shelter from whoever did this and whatever further destruction they would unleash.

My breathing increased rapidly, my heartbeat pounding. I could smell my sweat and body odor, and the residue of my waste filled the air with a putrid stench that would certainly mark my position for any sensitive alien nose. I was petrified and couldn't will myself to move for several interminable moments. Nothing passed through my brain but the compulsion not to make even the slightest noise. Even my rapid short breaths became silent, but as I inhaled the air, I could feel something coming in with it, a bitter powder coating my throat and making me need to cough. Ash.

I tried the best I could to keep it from happening, but my body was wracked with spasms and I coughed so violently that it forced me to sit up and double over. As I did, I heard the sound of Velcro and felt a long peel from the back of my head all the way down to the backs of my feet followed immediately by a tremendous sting that surged throughout my entire body as if a strip of duct tape had been ripped away and took my skin with it. I screamed, vomited a glorious sick mess somewhere in front of me, and then fell back against a wet mass in the carpet where the charred back of my body had lain and passed out again.

———✦———

I dreamed again, went somewhere else. My mind transported me and let my body shut down and lie dormant for the time being. This time, the dream was a memory, and had it not been such,

I would have thought I really did go somewhere else. It was so vivid as to seem much more real than the world I had awoken to.

Dad and I were fishing in front of the Dales' cabin in the deep swimming hole. It was early fall. The water was cold. There hadn't been another boat on the river except one, a lone elder fisherman in a short johnboat at bass rock far upstream who gave us a nonchalant wave as we passed. I saw him catch a fish. He threw it back in. Dad and I were keeping ours. We'd have a good mess later, more bones than flesh, but it made Mom and Katie proud.

I was twelve. My friends' voices were changing. The subject matter of their locker room banter and strutting indicated that other things were as well, including an interest in girls that had begun to border on pornographic. I had no such interest, and I didn't want to talk about it either. But Dad did.

And so we had the awkward talk right there on the fishing trip. I felt like I had been ambushed. I should have known it was coming. And he didn't approach the topic indirectly. He went straight in.

After my second fish, half an hour into fishing at the deep hole, Dad said, "Proud of you, son. You're a good kid, and I'm going to do my best to teach you how to stay good in the middle of all the crazy junk that's coming down the pike for you."

I remember feeling sick to my stomach. He had actually started this conversation before but trailed off, and Katie warned me that he was wanting to have the sex talk but would probably find the right time to do it. She had overheard Dad and Mom talking about it. Katie was a notoriously crafty spy.

I hoped he would trail off, but out here in the still quiet there wasn't anything to interrupt or distract him.

"Like it or not, pretty soon you're going to get interested in girls. So much that you won't be able to take your mind off of them; even if you wanted to, it'd be impossible. But you won't want to. If anything, you're going to get curious, and curiosity's okay. It's okay for you to be curious and interested, okay?"

I didn't say anything.

"You with me, son?"

"Yeah, Dad, I'm with you."

"I know this embarrasses you, but hear me out. I'm just opening a door between us, Ryan. Wouldn't be doing my job right if I didn't."

He sat at the back of the boat with the worms and crickets. He set his rod down and grabbed his pipe from his shirt pocket. He only smoked it when we were on the river or sitting on the porch swing. Never at any other moment did I even see it in his possession, and I never knew where he stored it. It was some magical object that only showed up when he needed to be poignant and wise.

I got the feeling he was looking at me as I talked, but I kept my head dipped, eyes on my bobber several yards out from the boat. I didn't want to get into this with him.

"I'm not stupid, Ryan. I know you already know how it works. Your school jumped the gun on me."

In fourth grade, we had an unannounced sex education course. The boys had their class in the art room with the principal. I don't remember where the girls went. The parents were not informed and got in an uproar about it, but the school district held firm that they were allowed by government mandate under the current presidential administration to proceed without parental consent. At three in the afternoon, with no precedent or formal announcement, our class was split up into groups of boys and girls, and we were given the clinical discussion of how babies are made. That's the first I had ever heard about it, and we all came away with terms and points of discussion on the playground that transitioned us into premature adolescence. I'm not sure now that it was the best idea.

"I was going to have that particular discussion with you sometime that year, but they made it unnecessary, so I was waiting for the next milestone. I think you're old enough. Pretty soon, you're going to be going through all those changes that you learned about back then. Some boys you know are already there, and it probably seems like the girls have been there for a while. You need to know that it doesn't make them any better than you. To tell you the truth, there's something about puberty that makes *both* boys and girls stupid, like their IQ drops out of their brains and goes south."

"Dad!" I said. I knew what he meant.

He laughed. "Sorry to be so blunt, but it's true. In twenty-five years, you'll look back on your younger days and you'll know I was right. It'll happen to you too, so I want to catch you before it does. Like I said, it's okay to be curious. If you have questions, you ask me. You can ask Mom too, but she'll probably send you to me.

"I don't want to get technical here. You know enough about that. I want to talk to you about choices."

"Choices?" That was an interesting concept. My life until then had been about following directions, it seemed. There were always lines to stand in, procedures to follow in the lunchroom, places where we were allowed to play and plenty more places where we were expected to shut up, but choices?

"Yep. When your interest starts to peak, you're going to have to decide what you're going to do about it. When you're curious about a girl, will you ask her out? Will you risk possible rejection? Or are you going to turn and run the other direction? She *could* be the girl you marry."

I looked at him then, but he was looking away now, wistful.

"Let's say you do ask her out, and you two start dating. What do you do with your time together? Do you go to the movies, go out to eat, go to parties? What are people doing at those parties? Is it a place you want to be? If it's not, what's your contingency? Will you go to a different party, or will you find a place to be alone together? When you're alone, will you be able to stay within your boundaries? Can you trust yourself enough? You're going to find yourself faced with an infinite variety of tricky situations, and what you decide to do with those situations will affect the course of the rest of your life."

"How do you mean?"

"Are you aware that most of the boys and girls you know will be having sex with each other by the time you're sixteen?"

I blushed again and sat low in my seat, turning my attention back to the water. I thought I felt a tug, and I jerked at the line a little, but there was nothing. Just a fluctuation in the current. A cloud passed over the sun. It got cooler. I felt the chill on my bare arms.

I didn't answer him, but he went on, "Some of them are going to get pregnant, and all their hopes and dreams for the future will come to a crashing halt because of split-second decisions they made when they weren't thinking with their heads. People are too often ruled by their passions, and the next ten years might be the most important in your life. You'll be setting the stage for the man you will become. I can't protect you, and I can't pretend that you're always going to make the right choice. I'm not always going to be there to guide you. It's best for you if I'm not.

"But I'll tell you who *will* be, if you'll let him."

Up until then in my dreamy abandon on the basement floor, I had been observing this memory from a distance and wondering why it was coming to me now. I had considered it merely a diversion, synapses firing in response to the awful pain, shutting down my system and rebooting. Not so, now.

His face suddenly filled my vision. I could smell the acrid tobacco odor on his breath. It stank. I hated it when he smoked that pipe—not on principle but because he always found a way to breathe in my face when he was done. But the pipe was nowhere to be seen, and in the next moment the odor was gone. Residuals of the memory as it spilled into a very purposeful dream.

"You remember what I talked to you about next, don't you?" he said, dialoguing with me now in my present state. This was one of those strange dreams you can control.

I did remember, but in the dream it didn't play out line by line like the sex talk had. Instead, I thought back over it and replayed it as he sat there in the boat looking intently at me, a memory inside of a memory inside of a dream. He had talked to me about faith and God. I remembered that much, but then it was growing hazy, and I could feel the pain as I started to come out of it. Fragments and shadows. Something about authentic manhood. Valleys. Darkness. And then a full sentence, clear as a bell: "He will be your light. Pray…pray *hard*."

Those were his words. His intense expression shimmered away. So did the boat, the water, and then the sky, replaced by darkness. My eyes were open, and I saw only the blackness. I could picture my pupils being dilated to the size of saucers, but I had to squint against the stuff that was billowing about me, the thick ash. I could taste it in my mouth and smell it in my throat. It reminded me of campfires, but not so pleasant. There were dead things in *these* campfires.

I could also taste the residue of vomit that remained. My teeth ground against each other unpleasantly. I needed water, and soon.

Tears dried on my cheeks, tracks of ashen mud down the sides of my face. I had fallen back mostly into the position I had been in before. I could feel the wetness on my back and buttocks, the backs of my legs and arms, but more than that, I could feel the searing pain that made me gnash my teeth. So much pain there. And the weight of my body pressed upon it, grinding it into the carpet, the movement of each shallow breath sending sparks through my blackened vision.

Panic-stricken, I felt I had to move. I needed more shelter than this. Was there a ceiling anywhere in this basement that I could lie under and have at least one side of protection around me? The pain was so tremendous that I feared to move. I didn't want to black out again. I felt vulnerable enough as it was.

"Please," I mouthed, not even a whisper.

Pray hard. The words rang. Bounced off walls in my head. I went for it.

"God, please help me," I mouthed again. The words scared me. In my position, everything threatened to scare me to death, even him. I pressed on. "I hurt," I whispered. "I can't bear it."

There was a strength in me then. I didn't recognize it as such because I had no perspective. It was the merest inkling of a determination to help my situation. I shifted my weight to my right side. The pain was less there, barely. It took an eternity, but eventually the movement took me over onto my stomach. Daggers on the edges of my vision, and I cried out into the carpet. I could feel clouds puff against my cheeks, but at least I was there. I had felt the urge to turn over, and I had done it.

The floor was dry where I now was. I scooted my right palm over the place where I had lain and felt the wetness, a puddle of sweat, bodily wastes, blood, and liquid skin. I gagged, but nothing came up. I wondered where I had puked and decided it was against the wall inches away from my feet, but the thought brought on more heaves. A little bit came up, but I was mostly out of material.

Warm wind blew against my back, more waves of pain, *oceans* of it, but it began to subside as if the tide was going out. I was still conscious, but I began to question it. Was I disappearing back into the haze? Would the dreams come on again? "Not yet," I pleaded in a hush. "I can't go back to sleep. Don't do it."

The desire to retreat into unknown sanctity governed my every thought, but I was immobilized with pain and fear. In the darkness were monsters. With each howl of wind through the openness of the basement, I thought I could hear them laughing as they anticipated their delicious feast.

The pain became an almost bearable throb, but as it ebbed, fear grew to replace it, filling in cracks, clouding my being. My heart was a jackhammer. Extremities became drawn up. My hands began to cramp. My face was throbbing and swelling. I was hyperventilating.

Pray hard.

"Protect me, God," I said. *Did he hear me? Is this hell? Is it too late for me now?*

That last thought threw me beyond the pale, and against my wishes, I disappeared again.

More glimpses. This time I was ten. At Tom Sauk mountain with my parents and Katie. Katie was bored and put out and didn't want to get out of the Explorer. Years later I realized she was dealing with something Sara referred to as "girl stuff," although Sara said that PMS is a myth for most girls and some use it as an excuse to be spiteful. I'm in no position to judge.

Mom, Dad, and I got out and climbed the dozen stories up a fire tower. Once we reached the top, we would officially be at the highest point in Missouri. I couldn't not do it. Bragging rights with the other boys at school.

On the seventh story, vertigo struck. I didn't know there was such a concept, but up became down, and I teetered as I rounded the corner to the next set of stairs. I gravitated toward the edge of the platform, and my left foot slipped off. Hands grabbed me before I even knew I was falling, and I was suddenly against Mom's chest. Her heartbeat enveloped my whole world, and enveloping her was Dad. His arms were bands of iron around us. In the blink of an eye, my parents had envisioned their son falling down and crashing to the roof of the car far below, and they acted to save me before their brains had processed the thought.

It hit me that I almost died, and I became weak. We sat down and caught our breath and our heads on the bottom step of that next staircase. We continued the climb after a few moments. Their love that day carried me for miles. We never talked about it afterward, but we didn't have to. It was written on our hearts, a moment for all time.

———————

I started to wake up, but it was long and drawn out, and I vacillated among memories, dreams, and a sense of awareness of my surroundings. Fragments of images, nothing concrete, and then Sara. It was our third date. We were eating at Cheddar's. It took an hour to seat us, but that was Cheddar's for you.

We ordered our food. I got a blue-cheese burger. I'm not sure what she got. I think it was a chef salad. She was pretty health conscious. She looked awesome that night, the best I had yet seen her—a black dress with a V-neck that only barely revealed the woman underneath. Downright chaste compared to most dresses I had seen girls wear, she had a way of filling it that made me have to consciously switch gears in my mind to keep on track. She had on a white-gold necklace with a faux-sapphire pendant and earrings to match. Her father got them for her the previous Christmas. I was relieved to know it wasn't a holdover from a previous flame. She wore makeup—touches of rouge and mascara, some deep-red lipstick I was hoping to rub off later that night with my own lips. A smile with the straightest, whitest teeth, ear-to-ear. While I didn't want to jump the gun, I thought she may be in love with me. There was no question *I* was smitten.

When we got the food, something threw us off. I took a bite, but she sat very still and quiet. I looked at her, and the words "what's wrong?" were almost to my lips before I saw her clasped hands, head bowed, and eyes closed.

She's praying? I thought.

My stomach closed off, and I thought I wouldn't finish my burger. I set it back down and trained my eyes elsewhere, sat quietly out of respect while she finished up. She was that way for at least a minute. She wasn't just saying grace and having done with it.

When she was done, she snapped right back to it as if nothing had happened.

The memory faded away, but I heard my father say one more thing that echoed in my mind before I came fully awake. It faded in and out, like the Doppler effect: "…light in the darkness…"

———⟡———

I was facedown on the floor. I hadn't moved an inch. My muscles were in agony from being tensed for so long. Tensed against the pain and against the danger that lurked in the dark. But the pain of my open sores was mild now. I had a feeling that if I moved, it would exacerbate it to torturous levels again, but I could focus on something else now. And that was trying not to be afraid.

I was so parched that swallowing felt like moving a mountain. My thoughts raced, and the need for survival finally began to outweigh the need to cower into immobility.

"God, get me to water," I croaked out, a raspy whisper that startled me. My tongue was probably gray all over with the ash. It reminded me of the sugary dipping sticks we got at the pool, where you dipped it into the fruity powder and then let the stuff melt in the moisture on your tongue. This wouldn't melt.

I began to crawl then, short little movements that took me inch by agonizing inch across the ash-softened carpet. I could feel ash billowing in small puffs every time I put my hand down. I turned myself around fully over the course of maybe an hour so that I was facing toward the stairwell. I moved to the left of it. I touched papers in the dark from Mom's computer desk. A couple of pencils here and there. I had to bite my lip to keep from crying out of surprise. I had to think hard about every object I touched when I laid my hand on it. I fully expected to touch an alien foot in the darkness.

I almost went into cardiac arrest when I touched the feet on the stand of the crash cymbal in my drum set. I had forgotten that was even still down here. There was only a foot of clearance between the drum set and the opposite wall in that little corridor to the left of the stairwell. I wasn't going to fit without turning sideways, and so with much deliberation and steeling myself, I stood up.

The pain was instant and severe. I cried out in an agonized "ah!" that quickly got cut off in coughs as it irritated my congested throat. I hacked and tried to spit, but there was no moisture. I cursed quietly in between my barking coughs. I wanted to fall back to the ground in my army crawl so that the monsters wouldn't descend on me. In that horrible quiet, my noise was fit to wake the dead.

Pray hard, Dad said again.

"God, preserve me. I don't know if I'm in hell or not, but I hope that you hear me. Get me to water."

Slowly, like hiccups fading away, the coughs began to subside, becoming less and less. I snatched at the rags of shirt hanging off the front of my body, the clothed half. The remnants of my clothing clung to my sides and back, glued in place with all the pus and fluids from the severe burns. I dared not disturb their position. If I ripped them off now, I'd rip myself off in the process. Instead, I held the bottom hem of my shirt taut with my left hand while I tugged hard with my right. My muscles and burnt skin screamed at the strain, but I gritted my teeth and pressed on.

After a few seconds of self-created agony, I heard the satisfying rip of cotton blend. I pulled away a small patch of fabric. I felt no small victory as I held it up to my mouth and used it as a mask to take in the first uninterrupted gasp of air since the fire. Some ash still got through but only trace amounts. I didn't cough.

"Thank you, God," I whispered. I didn't smile, but there was a spark of a thrill in me at the small victory that sent a cold shiver across my skin. I breathed through my teeth as the shiver hit the burns.

I pressed on and took the few extra steps left to get to the hallway refrigerator. I still couldn't see a thing, and even if there was any light source, the ash was too heavy on my eyelids to keep them open more than the tiniest squint. I reached my hand to where the minifridge door should be. This would be my first test of whether I was in hell. If the fridge was there and this was hell, it would be empty. If I wasn't in hell, the water would be there in the unopened twenty-four pack of bottles Mom and Dad kept for the eventuality of the big New Madrid earthquake—a cataclysm that had been imminent for at least twenty years now. If it were to happen now, nobody but me would be around to notice.

I felt along the wall for the small alcove tucked back underneath the stairs. *Get me to water*, I thought. I felt the opening. My fingers crawled around the wooden framing and into empty space. There were a few inches of clearance between the side of the fridge and the wall of the alcove. Just enough for one of the smaller alien creatures to squeeze into and plan its attack. I braced myself for the feeling of hot fetid breath to waft across the back of my singed arm as it opened its fanged maw to clamp down. The fear sent waves of pain across my skin, adrenaline coming out my pores.

I darted my hand across that empty space, and my fingers jammed straight into the side of something hard. I could see sparks on the edge of the darkness from the pain. I yanked my hand back and put my fingers into my mouth to stifle my startled yelp and nurse the hurt. I put my left hand out, felt what had stopped the right. It was the fridge. I found the handle and pulled it open. I went to the floor, crawling around the side of the open door. I could feel the coolness of it. I had been unconscious for a while, but the fridge was still very cold. Mom kept it cranked. She liked it that way. It kept the white wine just where she liked it. It felt beautiful.

I wanted to cry. If this were hell, there wouldn't be so much hope. I was not in hell, and somehow my prayers were being heard and answered. I hadn't asked for the impossible so far, but I had asked for improbable resolve and received it. That was when it began—that thing in me that wanted to live. It was very weak, but it wanted to live.

I stuck my right hand in, throbbing fingers be darned. Waves of icy grace wrapped them in love as they searched, cans and glass and plastic bottles everywhere they touched—fully stocked.

A conversation with Mom a week ago—she said to me, "Dad's looking forward to having you around so much this Christmas break. He knows it might be the last time you call this place home. He wants to watch movies with you, practically live in the basement with you drinking sodas and watching blood-and-guts guy flicks, so don't be surprised when you see what he's done in the fridge and cabinets down there. I suppose he'll let me have you sometimes too." She sighed. "But it does give me a thrill that he's prouder every day of the man you're becoming and that he wants to kidnap you just to be a part of your progress."

I tried to cry, but there were no tears. My eyes were parched as well. I felt my face screw up from the emotion, and my hand shook as I felt for the plastic wrap on the package of water bottles. I clawed at it, squeezed through the hole I made. I found a bottle and jerked it out. It pulled the whole package with it, but I didn't care. I worked at it with two hands, widened the hole, then released it big as it emerged.

My right-hand fingers were yet too sore to clutch at the lid, so I opened it awkwardly with my left hand. I put it to my lips and could feel the freezing cold even before the water got into my mouth. I moaned as it trickled in. It was as if my tongue had been frozen in stone and I had discovered the magic incantation that would restore it to life. The layers of ash covering it, my teeth, the insides of my mouth were turned to mud. I should have spat first.

My traumatized stomach responded violently to the sudden intrusion. I could almost smell the color green as I retched and tossed it up in front of me. I cursed my stupidity and sat still on the floor as I waited for my convulsions to subside. The debilitating fear hit me again that I had disturbed creatures lurking in the darkness, and I sat stiff, my ears finely tuned to hear something sinister behind the lulling howl of the constant wind. But nothing happened.

My stomach felt better. My body craved more. I tipped the water back up and took some in, slowly. I swished it around and spat out the filth somewhere in front of me. I took another drink, swallowing carefully. It stuck a knife in the lump in my throat on the way down. Beautiful agony. The cold of it embraced me and blew kisses on my wounds. I thought I would die in ecstasy.

I polished off the bottle in seconds and craved more, but common sense took hold, so I decided to preserve the rest. I crammed the case back in its spot in the fridge and shut the door to keep the remaining cold in.

I was starving, but I didn't feel hungry. The pain was too intense to allow me to feel like eating, although my stomach protested differently. I would throw it up anyway, and I was getting sick of that. The hallway cabinet sat on the floor across from the fridge. I reached out and hit it before I expected to with the back of my left hand, the side that had gotten cooked as I threw my arms out in front of me and took a dive when the flame was passing over. I breathed through my teeth with the sting that jolted my entire frame and focused on maintaining consciousness.

When my world of darkness ceased its spinning, I gingerly felt for the handle to the cabinet door and pulled it open. The fear came again—more hands reached out from the dark to grab me, teeth suddenly bared and ready to feast. Hot, sick breath tainted with the stink of a thousand worlds and millions of light-years of travel. But again, nothing. *Small movements, keep moving forward, step by step, and pray hard,* I told myself. It sounded like my father's voice.

My hand landed on something plastic that crackled dully through the swirling ash. I could hear it through the clouds that still clogged my ears. *Pretzels, chips maybe,* I thought. *Large family-sized bags of them.* I felt cardboard boxes of crackers, cookies perhaps. Dad was a cookie fiend. It would make sense. I could also expect to find pork rinds in there, sunflower seeds, pistachios—I could feel their shapes through their bags. Small kernels of life. I smiled sadly. Dad and I were going to party until we puked.

I shut the door and felt satisfied. It wouldn't be nourishing, but there was enough there to keep me fed for two weeks at the most if I was really going to have to rough it. I mapped out the rest of the hallway in front of me past the microwave alcove. There would be a closet to the left with folding doors, and at the end of the hallway, a door to the basement bathroom. Turning to the right once I'm in the bathroom, I'd be in the basement bedroom, which used to be Katie's. In there, Katie's bed—downy heaven, the most comfortable place to sleep in the house. When I beat her home on the holidays, I'd steal her room just to make her mad. I'd have to relinquish it as soon as she got here. Dad insisted I be a gentleman about it.

If it was still there and I made it safely to rest while my wounds continued to decide if they were going to heal or leave me in misery, I'd have yet more proof that this place wasn't hell. I prayed that God would guide me as I slithered that way. There were more papers and basement debris along the way, but no obstacle I couldn't get past. I felt for the closet doors with my left hand. The left one was open and hanging off its hinges. The right was closed and didn't feel as if it had been touched by the fire, although I'm sure the top of it was singed, at least.

The bathroom door would be closed, and before I reached it, I began to prepare myself for the effort it was going to take to reach up from the floor and twist the knob. It took me some minutes to traverse the few feet remaining. I kept most of my weight on my left hand as I moved in a modified army crawl across the tough carpet. The back of my hand screamed obscenities at me as I put the burden on it. In my right hand, in an iron grip, was the patch of shirt I used to breathe through. I wasn't getting enough air and I felt light-headed, but I planned on passing out when I got to the bed anyway. The burns on my thighs made their presence known every time I shifted my legs. Like salt in my open wounds, sweat managed to seep through to the outer layers of the skin behind my knees as they worked.

I felt ahead of me for the bathroom door and found only open air. A startled curse erupted with the sound of demonic gravel. My fragile heart threatened to stop in the split second before I realized I was the one who had said it. The water had done nothing to heal my vocal chords, only modify the sound of their sickness.

Had I not gone far enough? The door should be there. Everything I had searched for in the dark so far had been where it should be. I grew up in this basement. I may be off by a couple of inches, but that door should be there, closed securely as always because nobody ever used it. We always went into the bathroom through the other door. Mom had used this part of the basement for storage before she and Dad finished the flooring in the attic and moved all the junk up there a few months ago. She figured that since nobody used this passage much, she might as well claim it.

Now that I was claiming it, the thought hit me that somebody else already had. So sure was I that something was lurking in the darkness that it wasn't a matter of "if" but "when" it was going to quit toying with me and reach out and grab me. I was tempted by my darkest thoughts to picture it as a physical presence, but it was too much to bear—debilitating, paralyzing.

"God, protect me," I whispered as that two-word mantra—*pray hard*—echoed in my mind again, the words burning themselves into my heart. I pictured them written across my forehead. The fear subsided very slightly and allowed me to move again. I cast about in the darkness to find a wall or the edge of the doorjamb. I found the latter, both sides. The right one was torn from the wall a few inches. I traced my hand over the cracks in the plaster.

I wondered if the fire had sucked the door fully off its hinges and into its maelstrom, but I slithered forward a few more inches and felt it hanging off to the left as it opened inward. I pictured the hinge at the top twisted, melted, and separated. I moved on, found the toilet, the stand-up shower, and the towel rack, all off to the left. Bath rugs remained where they had been, raised plateaus in the ashen desert. To the right, the sink. Above that would be the mirror.

I wondered what I looked like. I pictured myself looking into it and became frightened at the image I feared I would see, blackened beyond night as some awful minstrel figure, the bloodshot whites of my eyes glowing from within the darkness, and just over my shoulder were the others who dwelt in the dark and tormented me even now, coming out into sight to take me down. The mirror would be too small to see in full the horror that was about to eat my head.

Stop that! a voice said in my head.

Dad told me that once when I was three. I threw a fit because he went out the back door to gather wood for the fireplace, but the way I understood it, he was gone forever. When he came back in, I was a mess. He thought I was just putting on a show, and he was about to spank me before Mom got wise and told him, "He was afraid, honey. You didn't explain it to him."

He sat me down and told me he would never leave me. He told me I would never have to be afraid because he was always looking out for me. He worked my whole life to get me to trust that he knew best. It worked.

But where is he now?

"God, protect me," I prayed. Dad wasn't there, but I had to believe that God was. Even if I never saw proof, that belief was going to have to carry me. *The monster, carrying me in the dark— what was it?* I thought, that earlier dream coming back to me now.

I felt around in the darkness and put the thought of the mirror out of my mind, repeating "stop that!" under my breath as the images threatened to take hold again. I made it through the doorway and into the bedroom, sparsely furnished since Katie had left. A vanity would be to my left with a much larger mirror than the one in the bathroom. Oddly, it didn't scare me. Its view of the room was so encompassing that nothing could hide from view. All would be plainly visible, no possibility of anything nefarious. Against the far-right wall was a dresser. There was a small closet beside the dresser, but otherwise, only the bed and a nightstand.

I reached out for the bed and found it where it should be, intact. I used it to pull myself to a standing position. The pain was severe again, throbbing from excruciating to cataclysmic. I let myself fall face forward onto the bed horizontally from the side. My feet hung off, and I considered remaining that way before thoughts of things hanging out underneath the bed and waiting with delight to grab me sent painful shivers across my back, so I scooted my legs around and lay vertically the way the makers intended.

I felt the bumps and rises of the floral patterns of the quilt I lay on through ashen thickness. Mom made this quilt for Katie when she went to college. Katie left it here after she graduated and got married because it kept the room familiar. It kept it all *hers*. There was a lot of Katie in this room—posters, pictures hanging off the walls, clown figurines, and toys on the shelf set into the wall next to the bathroom. I oddly didn't fear the clowns maybe because there was so much of Katie's love and life in them that I could never picture them coming down to harm me, regardless of how much the clown in *Poltergeist* had scared me.

Past the mirrors and through the maze of fathomless dark, I finally felt comfortable. Fear had slipped away—for the moment. Exhaustion overtook my thoughts—rational and irrational alike—and I slipped into the arms of sleep again, hoping that I awoke to a healed world.

———◆———

The light in the darkness. Those words in the void again as my mind meandered through nonsense dreams, memories of childhood, and things my wise father had told me over the years. *When did he say that?* I became obsessed with pinpointing the memory, like finding the needle in the haystack and then trying to put it back exactly where I found it.

Then there was Sara, her face appearing first in the images of better times gone by, then the circumstance. Our first Valentine's Day. I took her downtown to eat at Millie's. I watched her pray over her food. This was our fifth date. We were growing closer but still had so much to learn. When she was done, she saw me looking at her. I had my spaghetti wound around my fork, frozen in motion, a thick spool building.

She cocked her head. "What?"

"You pray every time we eat."

"Mm-hmm."

"Why?"

"To give thanks."

"Do you *really* believe in God?"

"Of course I do," she said. "Do you believe in him?"

"Of course," I said. *Didn't I?* "But I don't pray in public like that."

"Do you *ever* pray?"

"Yeah, at church. Well, the preacher prays and we all bow our heads."

"Do you pray personally, though, like at bedtime or in the quiet times at church when the pastor allows for it? For meals or when you're facing stress? Is it just a corporate thing?"

Was this an inquisition, or was she genuinely interested in learning more about me?

"It's just corporate," I said and shrugged. "How often do you pray?"

"All the time."

"Wow."

"What?" She genuinely had no compunction. I was amazed.

"I didn't know you were *that* religious. You didn't seem that way when I met you."

"It's not a *religion*, Ryan. It's a relationship."

"Relationship? I don't get it. With who?"

The memory faded, and I began to slip back into consciousness, but not before the refrain echoed once again in my head— *light in the darkness...*

——————

As my heavy eyelids tried to open, something slipped in. Light.

"Mom?" I said.

A sudden memory of when I was six and lost a tooth. I believed in the tooth fairy. The tooth was under my pillow. I was so excited when I went to sleep. A quarter would replace it by morning, which I would cherish as if it were all the money in the world. It would buy me three lives on the Superman video game machine at Snider's while Mom bought groceries—my ticket to pixelated paradise. The tooth fairy was as important to me as Santa, the baby Jesus, and the Easter Bunny. I lumped them all together as the mythical figures that would be the harbinger of gifts at blessed moments of my young life.

But that night, something disturbed my sleep. The lamp by my bed was on. Somebody was lifting up my pillow. In the blurry glow of sleepy vision, I thought it was her, the tooth fairy. I gasped suddenly but didn't wake fully.

"Shhhh, go back to sleep," she said. The angel sounded like my mother.

Mom? I asked, but my lips didn't move. It came out sounding like a moan.

She repeated her directive. My eyes closed before my mind shut down. *Had they been lying to me?* I thought, but surely not. Mom and Dad loved me to death. I knew then, such a young mind, that they had kept up this charade because they loved me and wouldn't dare take the magic away from me. Instead, they fed it. Santa, the tooth fairy, the Easter Bunny, Jesus—they were all real. I decided to persist in believing the tooth fairy came to me. The next morning, I told Mom and Dad all about it. They shared an ironic smile. They had certainly talked about being caught and what to do if I brought it up, but I never did.

And now here she was again, years and years later, turning on the lamp, coming to visit me in my sleep, Mom/Tooth Fairy, harbinger of love and precious gifts. Selfless and beautiful.

But then things started to resolve themselves. I scooted my right leg over toward the edge, toward where she'd be sitting, and felt nothing there but more bed until the bed stopped.

"Where are you, Mom?" I whispered dreamily. "Where have you gone?" No answer.

Daddy! I wanted to shout. I wanted to shout all their names, but I knew that I dared not, for it would certainly wake hell up. How much more would I have to pray before my safety felt assured? I had not done enough.

"It's a relationship," Sara had said.

"What does that mean?" I whispered, my eyes still half-open and receiving that strange light. Was it the lamp?

No, it couldn't be. So dim, dark. Barely there, like somebody flicking a Bic on the moon. I opened my eyes to more than slits and tried to soak it in so that things might begin to resolve.

The nightstand was closest. I saw it slowly stand out boldly against the background darkness. I focused on it for several minutes, but it remained the only thing visible. I could barely make out a whiteness covering the floor, but it was darker than it should have been. The basement carpet was a brilliant ivory. This looked gray. *Ash*, I told myself as the cobwebs cleared and my thoughts became more coherent.

The fact that I could see now scared me more than the darkness had before. If the monsters and demons were as dependent on sight as I was, then if I could now see, even if only in part, they may be able to see *me* in full.

Pray hard—a song I couldn't get out of my head, but it worked. I prayed. Hard.

"God, protect me. Still my heart. Be my strength."

Where did that *come from?* It was no maxim I had ever heard. Not in corporate prayer, not in what Dad had said, not even in what Sara had said, but I do remember her singing a line every now and then that went like "my ever-present help in time of need."

I worked out what that light was, what it might mean. I assumed at first it was coming from an electronic source. I thought for a long moment as I stared at the gray below me. The only electronic light in the room would be from a bedside alarm clock, normally on the nightstand. I scanned the surface of the table for it but didn't make out its rectangular shape. I was startled. *Had something come in here and moved it?*

"Be my strength," I prayed.

My heart quieted. It wasn't worth thinking about. There was no room for immobilizing fear, however strong the temptation was. If it wasn't on the table, something otherworldly had come in here and moved it, or, hopefully and the more likely case, Mom had taken it out of the room or it had been knocked off by the tremor of the passing fire. It wasn't there, so it couldn't be the source. It was a plug-in anyway. If it had been there, it would have no power—unless a power line was miraculously still standing outside and transporting power to the house. Even in my delirious state, I knew that was highly unlikely.

There was no other possible source in that room, and the only other possible sources in the basement at all would be the computer monitor (provided it was on normal display), the flashing display on the VCR, or the green light of a power strip out in the basement den. The computer monitor was the only light that could normally reach all the way back here, but if that were the case, I would see the den lit up. It would provide much more light than I currently had, and again, it required a working socket. No dice.

The horrific reality began to strike me then. Had there been any doubt as to the current state of my environment, it was now completely shattered. The dim light, barely enough to equal that of an Indiglo watch, came from open sky above.

Do I dare turn over to see it? I wondered. I could feel the warm wind blowing the ash across my bare back and buttocks. I was completely exposed to the elements, and protecting my dignity was the farthest thing from my mind. Instead, I thought, *I'm already cooked. All they'd need to do is ask the blessing.*

I felt a buzz in my pocket. *My phone!* My heart skipped and then lit up with abundant hope. I waited a few seconds, and it buzzed again. I couldn't believe it. I was receiving a phone call.

I forsook any fear or pain-induced paralysis and lifted my body up so I could reach into my right pocket. I felt the familiar hard little square and jerked it out. I held it off to the side of the bed in my right hand. The white light of a message against the background of a picture I had taken of Sara and me at J. Parrino's on our first anniversary blinded me instantly, and it took long moments of squinting and waiting before I could read it.

"Battery Low."

I cursed. It buzzed again. The message repeated itself. That was what had startled me. I forgot I had put it on vibrate when I was moving out on Friday. Brian, my favorite of my two roommates, could be a pill in the morning if you woke him up too early, and he was a tremendously light sleeper. He lost it at Sara when she came over once to have breakfast with me and she was singing a Jesus song too loud. She tended to do that. I cleared the message. But another one popped up in its place, a previous message.

"Are you okay? You didn't call…" From Sara Butler, received December 12, 1:00 PM, just two hours after the spaceship sent the blast.

Frantic, I cleared the message. My cellphone operated off of satellite. I didn't know if hers did too. I hit Reply. The phone interrupted with its warning again. I saw the battery symbol flashing Empty again. I cursed at it, rocks grating against each other deep in my throat.

I turned onto my side, back screaming at me, to use both hands on the letters. Thank God for smart text.

"I'm alive. Reply," I said. There was not a moment to waste.

Instantly, a buzz. My heart fluttered. A text window appeared belatedly. The warning again. I screamed the foulest torrent of words I knew. As threatening as a mouse squeak. With the battery close to dead, the message I wrote would be all I could get off. Anything more would tax it beyond use. Anything I received would be the last message. I knew it.

I cleared the warning message and saw the picture of us. I stared at her and longed for her, lusted after her in heart, mind, and body. She had never been more beautiful, the picture of Eve at the moment of creation, God's template for woman. Her long dark-brown tresses. She'd had her hair done for that night. I took instant notice of it. She wore a strapless ankle-length black dress with silver sparkles. A sheen black wrap around her shoulders. A purse to match the dress. High heels that put her nose to nose with me when we danced later in the evening. We had our longest kiss that night at sunset on a walk through Nathaniel Green park. She took off her shoes, and we laughed as we tried to avoid stepping on goose poop in the grass. We shared the kiss on a bench. People might have walked by and seen us, but we only knew each other in the world. An hour of uninterrupted bliss. It was past closing time by the time we finally broke off, and we had to find somebody to open the gate and let us out. He was so amused by our amour that he lightly admonished us and didn't seem to mean it: "Don't get so carried away next time, huh?"

Please, God, let her text back.

Long, agonizing minutes, repeated warnings. Clear the message and gaze at her, heaven in her smile. I noticed the date: December 19. *The battery lasted all week? It's been a* week?

It was eleven in the morning if the phone was still receiving from the satellite accurately. I marveled the signal could make it through the ash, but I'd been able to use the thing in a tunnel once.

I faced an agonizing decision—do I give it any more time, or do I turn it off to save the battery to check later when she's had more time? I took a last lingering look at the woman of my dreams. I moved my thumb across the face of the phone to clear the ash that was collecting. It smeared and obscured her beauty, but I drew it up to my lips and kissed her.

A gasp hit me, hot tears cutting tracks on their way to the carpet. I could hear them hit. I held my thumb on the power button until it went off, set the phone on the nightstand, then curled up and cried like a baby.

My howls broke through the barrier in my throat and past that painful lump. I grabbed the pillow and screamed into it. Anguish that my heart had never known. When I gasped for air, I inhaled ash, adding insult to my grievous injury as I was set to gagging and dry-heaving from the sudden choke.

The violent heaves of my sobs and retching stretched the tight wounds on my back, and I could feel the cool wetness of fresh pus and blood seep through. Screams of pain now mixed in again. I slipped off the bed and fell to the floor, kneeling on all fours, then buried my face in the carpet. Tears and snot began to form a thick puddle around my head, but I didn't move.

I made a tremendous noise and found that I didn't care who stirred. She felt and looked so close with that picture, that text, the little communication I had been allowed. I wanted her so badly it was turning my insides out. I wanted her in my arms, pressed so closely against me that we might as well be one.

"Is she alive, God?" I shouted. "*Say something!*" I pounded my fist on the floor. Shards of glass up my arm. I cursed at the pain again. I slapped the back of my aching fist with my other hand out of spite, cursed at it again. I shouted at God again to speak to me but heard the incessant whisper and howl of the wind.

I stood and looked upward, full on into the dimness. The magnitude of it startled me. The anger fell away, and fear returned. Nothing above me but sky. I was adrift in a cloud of swirling ash, God drawing circles with it and then quickly erasing them. Beyond it all, somewhere up there, the sun was still shining, but small comfort; I felt like a dinosaur on the brink.

I fell back to the floor. *Pray hard.*

"What do I do?" I said.

Eat! I heard my father say with incredible clarity. I actually jumped. A nervous sweat broke out and set my teeth on edge.

"Dad?" I heard nothing. *Is he here somewhere?* I had actually thought I heard it, but a long moment of waiting brought nothing. No further directive, and I suddenly was starving.

A sudden courage, I stood up, swore at the pain one more time, and drew in a mouthful of ash through my teeth. I retched one last time. I turned and scanned the bedspread. I could barely make out the swatch of shirt I had used as a mask. I put it back to use and walked back through the bathroom and the left corridor to get to the cabinet. I felt my way through with my left hand. I could begin to make out the walls in the darkness. They used to be orange, gray now like the carpet, like everything. My imagined reflection in the mirror changed but didn't improve.

I opened the cabinet and grabbed out the first thing I could find, a bag of pork rinds. Barbecue flavored. I hated pork rinds, but I could chew and swallow them, and they were light enough fare that they sated rather than upset my engorged stomach. It growled as it instantly began to digest the food. I pulled another bottle of water from the fridge. I felt something warm pass over me as my body turned the food into energy. I felt…*provided for.*

"Why do you pray?" I had asked Sara.

"To give thanks." She had said it like it should be obvious.

"Thank you," I said now to the empty air.

The other thing she said: "It's a *relationship*, not a religion."

A month after Millie's, I asked her what she meant by relationship. We were cuddling up, Chiefs game on television. I turned down her invitation to go to church that morning for the umpteenth time, but she still came over to spend the afternoon with me, ever faithful and true. It was the kind of cold outside that grafted to your bones and wouldn't let you go until the fifth cup of hot chocolate, which she was now on.

"Relationship with whom? God?"

"Yes. Jesus, actually."

"How does that work?"

She told me a story of when she was seven and received Jesus as her Lord. Simple, sublime, perfect, like getting betrothed to the man of your dreams.

"You got born again?" I asked.

"Exactly that. Ever since, he's been Lord of my life. He's my everything, my help, my strength, my provider. It's something I can't fully describe. He's my best friend but also my king. My every breath is because of his grace at work in me."

"You make it sound like you're in love with him." Jealousy in my voice. She either didn't pick it up or looked past it.

She turned around and looked at me. She had a strange smile on her face. I had said something she didn't expect to hear. "I am," she said and laughed.

"Like you're in love with me?"

She laughed harder. I thought she was mocking me. I crossed my arms and pulled back.

"No, sweetie, it goes deeper. It's like he's my first love, the one that will be patient, true, and faithful through everything. He already has been. He's put up with a lot from me, probably a lot more than any mere man in my life would."

I gently pushed her away from me, got up, and went to the sink to clean out my mug. "Well, I suppose if that's how you feel, I should get out of the way, huh? I can't compete with that."

"Ryan, good grief! Are you jealous of Jesus?"

She had moved so that she was lying lengthwise down the couch. Her head was propped on her arms on the armrest. She was not the least bit flummoxed by my anger. If anything, she found it cute. I was so mad at her that I could spit. I did, in fact, into the sink, a clean pure wad of the stuff just like Dad had taught me. She frowned at me.

"Ryan, that's gross."

"'Mere men spit, Sara. Get over it. Jesus did it once, too."

"Yeah, but he did it because he was healing somebody, not because he was mad at his girlfriend for being in love with God. Are you really mad at me?"

"No, Sara. Gosh, it's a free country. Worship God however you want. I'm glad you're happy."

"Hey, come on now," she said. She got up and joined me in the kitchen, took the mug out of my hand, and placed it gently on the counter. She turned me toward her, put her arms around me, and kissed me. Her breath had the taste of unquenchable joy in it. It had never smelled so sweet. "How do you feel about me, Ryan?"

"I'm crazy about you," I said.

"I can tell. I find your jealousy very attractive, but it's directed at the wrong person for all the wrong reasons. I'm not going to force the issue because I get how you're feeling, but the one who lives in me wants to live in you too. You can be just as in love with him as I am."

I found the idea a little disgusting. My face reflected my feeling. *They know not what they do*, the thought occurs to me now, as I write this.

She laughed. "You silly, sweet boy. You don't get it yet, but you will. I am *sure* of it. Okay, enough preaching. Let's get back to the game. Cassel just threw another interception. He needs our support."

"Now you're talking." Our smiles split our faces in two as we kissed.

She kept praying over meals, and I saw her do it periodically as she did her homework. When we got fussy at each other, she'd do it then. Sometimes I'd see her bow her head after we broke off a long kiss. In everything, in all seasons, she prayed, and she came out of it looking content, sometimes beaming. She never forced the discussion again.

You don't get it yet, but you will.

Pork rinds filling my stomach, the growling started to settle down. My body was filled with internal warmth. Life. I felt the bag I held in my hands—half-empty. Maybe it was half-full.

"Thank you," I whispered again to God. I had another half a bottle of water to wash it down.

I had to urinate suddenly. I considered holding it, but to what purpose? I laughed at myself. Was I going to wait for the plumbing to come back on?

I weighed my options. *I could just pee in the toilet*, I thought. "If it's yellow, let it mellow," right? So long as I didn't put anything more solid in there, I was sure it would keep for a while. But it was clean water at the moment. *I might need that.* Every last drop of water I could salvage would be sacred, of utmost importance. I forsook the thought.

I certainly didn't want to just find a random corner of the basement to expunge, did I? I had already puked at least twice that I knew of, and there was a me-shaped outline of pus and other bodily fluids on the floor in the den besides.

The wastebasket, by the desk, I thought. I tried to take in my surroundings in that scant, almost nonexistent purple light. I could barely make out the hue of the walls and carpet, and there were blobs of objects in front of me, but nothing distinct. I still had to feel my way around. By this point, however, I was sure of what to expect as I reached out and hit things. If there were monsters, they'd show themselves soon enough. Meanwhile, I needed to use the bathroom, and I focused on that one thought, that one basic human need—to drive my next set of actions.

I felt my way over to the desk, found the plastic wastebasket with the bronze rim, and dumped its contents out on the floor—paper, mostly, scraps Mom had gotten every last use out of. She liked to print on both sides of the paper to conserve resources, but she ended up throwing most of what she printed in the can anyway. I wondered briefly if any of it would make good toilet paper, but the issue was a sensitive one for a burned butt as it was, so I tucked it away and decided not to worry about it until I had to.

Just pee, I told myself.

I unzipped and pulled my pants and underwear down without thinking about it first. I heard fresh Velcro and then felt the instant burn as a fresh set of open wounds was made around the side of my hips and thighs. The clothes tore away and took much of my skin with them. I screamed and fell straight to the floor. Before I passed out again, I felt a steady stream of urine hitting my stomach. So much for the trash-can idea.

—◦►◄◦—

My earliest memory. I was barely three, if that. I had climbed out of my baby bed (*was it a crib, could it have been* that *long ago?*), something I had never done before. I didn't remember the trip. I only knew that I had made it to the bottom of the stairs, and there I sat now, in my dream, while my body was resetting itself again back in the present. I looked down at myself. I was wearing yellow-footed pajamas, but the feet were actually duck bills, black eyes staring up at me out of the darkness. It was the middle of the night.

I turned my big brown eyes, all pupils, back up the stairs toward my parents' bedroom. I could hear Dad snoring. I could remember thinking that it must be later than time even allows if my folks were in bed because nothing stays up later than they did. My young mind was so full of wonder—I thought perhaps that I had fallen between the cracks of reality and reached a place where even Dad's fathomless love couldn't reach me. I had found a place beyond his protection, truly alone.

What's going to happen to me? I questioned the silent darkness, although if I had spoken them, the words probably would have come out much less evolved.

Across from me was the front door, painted dark brown and now blacker than the surrounding darkness. The walls were white, then. They were blue now. *Would* have been blue—that is, if they still existed. I began to resolve the shades and borders between things. The glow of a halogen streetlamp outside—it lit up the living room but cast more shadows than it revealed. In those shadows, I could see it, a great, big, arching beast, parabola of its shoulders heaving up and down. I thought, *It's the Tasmanian Devil, only much larger. And not Tasmanian. This is what he turns into at night when Bugs has gone home and the kids aren't watching anymore. This is what he becomes when Mom and Dad aren't around to tell you to turn the TV off.*

I whimpered but cut it off immediately. Even then, I knew that the slightest sound could wake hell up. The living room was off to my left; to my right, the corridor leading around the corner to the basement door. It was unfinished then, bare blue concrete floor down there.

I dreamed once that I had opened that door and could hear the Tin Man from *The Wizard of Oz* crashing around down there just around the corner. I knew it was him without having to see him or hear his voice. He was raising Cain, and he didn't care who heard. Even more terrifying, the lights were on. He didn't need to hide. I didn't stand a chance even if I could run, and now, in the dark, I knew he would make his ascent and come grab me and take me down there and hide me in one of the many corners that nobody would think to search out because, back then, we only used the basement for storage and storm shelter.

I was frozen in place between Taz and Tin Man, my every breath a painstaking study in utter silence so they wouldn't know I was here. My mouth went dry. I wanted to scream for Mom and Dad, but I feared that if I did, the devil or the Tin Man would get me before they even roused. Alone in the dark, I felt giant hot tears slip unimpeded down my face and soak into my duck-bill feet, but I didn't make a peep, not even the slightest sob. I was forced to be a self-reliant man at three years old.

I fell asleep in the midst of my fear. The adrenaline eventually wore out like it usually did when I woke up from a nightmare in the middle of the night and was too afraid to call on Dad. It was a disturbing and disturbed rest, for even as I slept, I knew the monsters would catch me unaware and eat me slowly. I could practically hear the clanking of the Tin Man's jaws grinding me down.

Then the feeling of snakes suddenly clutching me, wrapping me up in a death grip, squeezing the breath out of me. Their strength was so sudden and strong that they actually *lifted* me up in the air. I thought perhaps they were the Tasmanian Devil's tongues working in tandem to take this sleeping babe in. I jumped with fright and began to struggle, and then I heard the words.

"Sh, sh, sh now, I've got you."

I slowly opened my eyes, vision blurred much like it was when I awoke to see the first light after the fire. I could see dim light to the edges of my vision, and in the middle, something sort of a bronze color—tan, that is—with deep amber around the fringes of it. I blinked and rubbed my eyes with the backs of my tiny fists, opened them again, and the monster was looking straight at me, his eyes boring holes through mine, teeth bared.

"No, no, hey, Daddy, hey, Mommy! Katie!" I shouted.

The words again, this time the balm of Gilead. "It's okay, son. It's Daddy. I'm here. Easy now."

I blinked and then saw more clearly. He'd had a beard at the time. I had mistaken it for fur when I had looked through the glass darkly. His teeth were bared in a reassuring smile, not to eat me, and the snakes were his strong arms, wrapped around me, warding off the monsters. He had already vanquished them, even before picking me up, and I pictured him casting them out of the house—into the abyss, even, as if it were a foregone conclusion. That's who he was.

He sat down with me on the couch. He turned on the television there in the dawn light. I heard grownup voices talking about grownup things, and I felt again that they were in charge of the world and had it under control. There was order.

Dad's voice joined the choir and then sang solo. Well, he wasn't singing, not exactly, but his words were so beautiful, his voice so pure, that he may as well have been. Words came to me then as I revisited that memory there on the basement floor, words I had never thought about. I certainly remembered time and again that he said them, but they hadn't registered, not until now, when I was so broken and helpless, lying in a pool of my own urine.

"Dear Jesus," he prayed, "may my precious Ryan one day know that any time he is lost in the darkness, he can call to you and you will be his light, his light in the darkness, especially in those times like now when I tarried to rescue him. Do not tarry. Be his light. Stand at the door and knock…knock *hard*."

⸻⸱⸻

Be my light, I thought and woke up. But there was still darkness there. I could feel the sticky, acrid mess of urine on my body and the cold warmth of fresh pus and blood on my sides where the clothes had torn. The ash was quickly blowing in to cover the wounds. I searched for and recovered the patch of shirt that I needed to breathe through.

Throbbing there on the floor, I thought back to that fondest of memories of my father turning my most fear-filled moment into another opportunity to show me grace. And I realized, now that I had remembered his prayer over me, that he had spent my whole life teaching me as best he could but still only in part of the love that awaited me in the heavenly Father, and through Sara's testimony, through her faithful witness of God's love, I knew now in full what I must do in order to grab hold of that love that I had until now seen only dimly.

My lips trembling from pain and emotion, the warmth of fresh tears blazing new waterfalls into the pool collecting under my face, I began to stutter something that felt like a prayer. The words became sentences, and the sentences a confession. The pus and blood caked on my skin and exited my wounds, but it was milk and honey that began to run through my veins. I can't remember word for word, but it went something like this:

"Lord Jesus, I don't think I've ever spoken right to you, and I see now that I've always been wrong. You put Sara and Dad in my life to show me you, and I looked the other way more times than I care to count. But I can't look away now. I *won't*. Don't look away from me. I can't see you. I can't see anything. I feel I'm in hell, but I pray you see me.

"I've gone my whole life without you. I thought I knew what was best for me or could at least *get there*, you know? I thought I could at least be happy as long as I stayed close to the ones I love. But they're gone, and you're all I have. I need you now. I've always needed you. You've provided for me. You kept me alive this week, led me to water and food, sustained me through sleep and injury. By your grace, I'm alive. I don't know *why* I'm still alive, but I do know that I don't have the relationship with you that Sara talked about. That's a decision you've left it up to me to make. She told me that it's freely offered, but I must receive it. I receive your love now. Please, do like Sara said you'd do—come into my heart and make it your home. Teach me to see with your eyes, understand with your mind, to trust." I had never understood this concept of trust in the divine. I understood now. "I am a broken man. Patch me up. Teach me how to live. I am yours."

That wasn't all, but that was the gist of it. It comforted me to pray. Now that I was in Christ and he was in me, I felt I had a direct, unimpeded line of communication with him. Dark as it was, I had never felt more light in my heart. Hope stirred there. I pictured the phoenix rising from the ash. Fresh tears came to my eyes. But this time, they weren't sad. I don't know what they were, but they weren't sad.

LEARNING TO LIVE

The hours passed. When I got hungry, I returned to the cabinet and ate some more, but not until I was bursting or even until I felt full. I was barely satisfied, and it took tremendous control to keep from eating more than just a little at a time.

Mom and Dad sent me an allowance at college so I didn't have to work during the academic year. They either didn't know or didn't care that it was way more than I needed to get by, so I ordered pizza regularly, ate whatever junk came my way, and took Sara out to eat at least twice a week—and that didn't include my meal plan at the commons, which I took full advantage of as well. When the fire came, I had weighed two hundred pounds and was five feet, eleven inches tall. I don't know how much I weighed now, but just from feeling my ribs and hips beginning to jut out, I would say that I had already lost fifteen pounds.

I felt the need to use the bathroom again several hours after the first time. As I stepped across the floor, judging each step carefully, it occurred to me that I could feel the floor under my feet. I hadn't questioned it until now, but I was barefoot. I sat down and felt my feet. They were still shod on top, but there was nothing on bottom. *The fire*, I told myself. It had completely melted away the soles of my shoes and then burned off my socks. My feet *were* sore, but I hadn't noticed because the rest of me was so much worse off. They had been lightly singed, much like the tenderness after you touch something fresh out of the microwave before you realize what you have done. I couldn't imagine how unbearable the pain to my feet would have been had I already been barefoot when the fire licked them. I thanked God for the small but very important blessing.

That also meant, however, that I was bound to step in something unpleasant, and sure enough I did as I hunched my way over to the wastebasket to give it another go. A damp pool of urine. I could smell it, in fact. It smelled like the ash, reprocessed, like when you pee after having coffee and it smells like both coffee and pee.

It startled me when I stepped into the spongy carpet, a muddy mass. I cursed as I tried to hop off it, sure that I had stepped on something that was going to bite me. I stood still for a moment, catching my breath, ears finely tuned to something coming out of the dark to take me now that I had woken it up.

Pray hard, I now told myself, and I did. I prayed for protection, sure, but even more I prayed for confidence against the fear that threatened to paralyze me again, and within a minute's time, I had the confidence to keep going.

I will never leave you nor forsake you. Dad told me that once when I hurt my shin in a bike accident. It bled for hours. I told him I was too scared to get back on the bike. He gave me the promise that kept me going. I heard it echoed in his voice again now.

I grabbed the trash can and set it in front of me. There was much easier access to the things I needed to get to now that I had already peeled my clothing away from my skin. As I snatched at my underwear, though, it came completely off, and I pulled it out through the open zipper of my jeans. I laughed. *I might as well just go naked*, I thought, but then I knew from experience that I'd lose more than my clothes when I took them off.

I decided I would have much more success hitting my target in the dark if I knelt to the floor. I did so and found I was right. As the waste exited my body, I felt a chill, both physical and spiritual. I had done a good thing here. I was presented with a challenge, and I solved it. I had found success in a small thing. I was ready to try larger ones. As silly as this may sound, I was really looking forward to conquering number two when it came.

I flipped my phone on again briefly, barely long enough to find what I was looking for. The lack thereof, actually. Just the picture of Sara and me. Fresh tears, fresh prayers. It was six in the evening on the nineteenth. The scant light above me had disappeared with the onset of early evening. I thanked God for the brief amount of it I'd had. He was still at work, doing I don't know what, but that light was the promise of something. No atheists in foxholes? Try postapocalyptic basements.

I got sudden bowel pressure a couple of hours later. I hated that it came in the complete darkness, but when you got to go…

I used the bathroom wastebasket this time. It seemed only fitting as I would be near the toilet paper as well. My wounds continued to be nauseating, so before I did the deed, I took the initiative to search the cabinet just above the toilet. I found folded towels and washcloths, some packages of soap Mom and Dad had pilfered from hotels over the years, packs of toothpaste and little travel sticks of deodorant. *Aw, come on, Dr. Mom*, I thought. *There's got to be* something *down here.*

I found a bottle of extra strength Tylenol PM and some prescription Hydrocodone. I remembered Katie's wisdom-teeth surgery. She had rather enjoyed her recovery as her husband, Russell—her boyfriend back then—played nurse to her under Dad's and my supervision. They were pretty hot for each other, and we knew it was only a matter of time before Russell popped the question, but Dad wanted strictly-above-the-neck behavior under his roof. I played along just because the thought of any guy having it for my sister was simply disgusting to me.

A strange thought darkened my mind for a moment as I skimmed the labels for the pills in the light of my cell, just a fleeting thought. I pictured Sara, Mom, Dad, Katie, and other loved ones smiling at me, arms open wide, and I felt weightless, but underneath it all was a feeling that something had gone wrong. It left me as quickly as it came, but the strange soothing feeling remained. It wasn't right, but it was…lovely. *Death?* I thought, a dark cloud over the sun.

I took a couple of the Hydrocodone, lifted the lid of the toilet, and took a huge gulp of water. It was the first time I had drunk from the toilet, and while it felt weird to do it, it tasted almost as pure as the bottled water, just a slight taste of fluoride to mark the difference.

I set the wastebasket a couple of feet away from the sink and used the latter to hang on to and balance my weight as I positioned myself above the makeshift commode. The moment I pushed, I wished I had taken the Hydrocodone hours before. I spent the night panting on the floor, the pain shooting sparks into my eyes.

<hr />

No dreams that made sense this time around. They gave me the night off. I just drifted through thoughts and feelings, but even if they didn't mean anything, they still left me feeling upset and wrung out when I woke up and saw that my circumstance hadn't changed.

"Lord Jesus, make me accept the reality and move on, although it threatens to undo me."

I could smell the putrid odor from the wastebasket. I put a towel over it to mask it as well as I could. It worked tolerably well.

I had forgotten how much I regretted it when I binged on junk, but most of the time I had the comfort of plumbing to coddle me against the insanity of logistics.

It was still pitch-dark. I felt my way over to the bed and lay facedown on it waiting for the sun to rise. It would now be December 20. The light came up eventually. I didn't check the time on my phone.

The meds wore out. I left off on taking more. They'd only make me drowsy, and I didn't need to sleep. I prayed against the pain. It came on now with the irritation of the world's worst sunburn. Even thinking about moving exacerbated it, but I moved anyway, if only just to stumble around my environment and prove to the demons I supposed to lurk there that I wasn't afraid of them.

———

"You're not afraid or threatened the least bit by anything," I had remarked to Sara once as we watched the Panthers beat up on the Evangel Crusaders at Weiser Gym.

"Oh, I get scared, but it wears off," she said and smiled cheekily.

"Aren't you afraid of *anything*? In a way that doesn't wear off?"

Her smile disappeared, slowly. "Yeah, I am," she said reluctantly. "In a way that doesn't wear off."

"Of what? Snakes? Heights? Monsters in the dark?"

"Losing people I care about and never getting them back."

I glossed over this last. I thought it was just a woman's perspective—that tendency to care too much about their loved ones, something wrapped up in the need for security and stability. She seemed forlorn and lost there for a moment, so I took up the slack.

"What about monsters in the dark, though? See, that's one that bugs me that I've never gotten over. It's a fear worse than death."

She came back to me. "I used to be until my pastor growing up gave a sermon about it." She looked nervous after she said that. I knew why. I felt bad. I had shut this dialogue down before. I thought better of it this time.

"What'd he tell you?"

"I don't know how well you know the Bible, but there's several parts where Jesus casts out demons, and he tells his disciples they will do the same in his name. 'What makes you think we don't have the same gift?' Pastor Dan asked us, and then he went on to give a sermon about how nothing will stand against us when we are in Christ and call upon his name. It was very empowering. It hit me at an impressionable age. I started using what he taught that morning anytime I was in the dark, and as time went on and I got better at it, I learned to do it even before the fear set in. 'I can do all things through him who strengthens me.'"

"Is that in the Bible?"

She told me where, but I forgot. I got up to get some popcorn, which was really a ruse to end the conversation before she began to talk too freely. She didn't talk much for the rest of the night. We broke it off early, too. I'm not sure she meant it when she said she was getting too sleepy.

<hr>

Every time I made a noise in the dark as I walked about the basement, I cursed. That began to feel silly after a while. It didn't accomplish anything, nor did it bring me comfort. I cussed when circumstances got stressful or fearsome. It was second nature to me. I told Sara that once after she had remarked on it.

"Could you try your best to have a different 'second nature' around me, at least?" she asked.

I was flummoxed that it bothered her, but I assented—no cursing around Sara. It didn't change a thing in private, however.

But according to Sara and "Pastor Dan," that's not the way to get back at the monsters. *Give it a shot*, I could imagine her saying.

"Hey," I said out loud past the choke-hold the ash had on my throat. It startled me, and I shrunk, waiting. Still they toyed with me, circling about. I could see their teeth. They'd appear shiny white and sharp in night-vision goggles, daggers unsheathed, dripping with drool. I began shaking.

Stop it!

"Hey!" I tried yelling as hard as I could. A different kind of fear crept over me then, fear of what the one inside of me was suddenly capable of. I shook with a different tenor. The next words out of my mouth were so unnatural to me that even writing them down now, after everything I've learned, feels awkward. "I don't know if you're really there or not, but I can feel you there. I don't know if you heard, but I belong to somebody much stronger than me, than you, even." I was a kid standing up to bullies on a playground. "You have no power over me, whoever you are, and I command you in the name of the one who lives in me…I *command* you in the name of the Lord Jesus Christ to depart and torment me no longer. I'm telling you to leave. I can do that now."

The fear was completely gone. I pictured nothing—I *felt* nothing but love. There was peace in my heart and mind. I smiled. "Thank you, Lord. Give your angels charge over me. If the demons are out there, the angels have to be too. If the threat is physical, be they aliens or whatever, let my rebuke cast them away too, for they are also a great evil. Keep me from further torment or take me on home. I don't want to wallow in uncertainty."

Time went by. I flipped my phone open only once a day as soon as I could see light through the thick clouds. It kept me apprised of the date. Still no word from Sara. No word from anybody. I used the painkillers to help me sleep but got by on prayer during my waking hours. It wasn't the fear but the pain that robbed me of slumber. I found that the former would abate the more I prayed and the more I rebuked the ones that preyed on me and stole my peace. It seemed that when I spoke what I knew to be true about God, even with my limited, newborn spiritual mind, the dark cloud over my soul passed away. I felt warm and covered even though there was nothing over my head. I didn't know much about God. I had never read the Bible except for bits and pieces when I followed along with the pastor or Sunday school lesson. The words rose and fell back on the page. Too heavy for my mind to hold. But the little I knew from Sara and Dad's examples kept me fed.

My prayers were simple—for strength, for protection, for my wounds to heal, but more than these, that God would preserve Sara. I prayed for the ghost of a chance that she, my parents, and my sister were still alive. I threw in others as I felt led, but those four occupied any waking thought that wasn't governed by an immediate, pressing need. I prayed despite the uncertainty that they were still alive. God had not shown me otherwise, and Sara had once mentioned the power of persistent prayer, that sometimes it wasn't "say it once and then be still" but that God wanted to hear the cries of my heart. He wanted me to demand the fullness of his blessing, so I poured out the prayer, over and over, hour after hour. I persisted against the fear that I was getting on his nerves. One way or another, I expected him to answer.

He did on Christmas Eve.

I fell asleep in a Hydrocodone-induced stupor. It was the last of it, only one pill this time. The pain was beginning to slack off, and I didn't want to use more of the painkillers than were absolutely necessary. I still had the full bottle of Tylenol PM. I hoped not to need it.

No random memories this time. It was a bona fide dream. Sara and I were in my car, driving along a dark two-lane road. The terrain around us was flat—not that we could see much of it. Our visibility was limited to only a few yards. Along the edge of the shoulders, I could see patchy dry grass that made me think we were in the desert.

I had a deep sadness in my heart in this dream. Normally when I dreamed, I didn't feel what my dream-self was feeling but observed the action with an objective detachment. This time, I felt *everything*. I wasn't looking upon it with that uncanny valley in between. I was in it. And I had never felt such grief.

It was in the middle of the night. I even looked at the dashboard clock and saw that it was one in the morning. For the duration of the dream, the clock never changed. Nor did the sky get any lighter. We were stuck in time, driving into the west.

I kept my eyes on the road, but now and then I turned to look at her. She looked heartbroken. I felt that something external to us caused the pain. She wasn't sorry about anything, nor did I get the impression that I had hurt her. It seemed to have nothing and everything to do with us.

"I love you," she told me then looked down at her hands. Her bottom lip was trembling. I didn't ask her what was wrong, just listened to her moan softly, catch her breath, shudder. "I just wish we could have stayed longer."

So we were leaving someplace, going far away from it. We had no choice, but we burned to stay. We were afraid of what lay ahead. The wide open sky was black as if it were heavily clouded. There were no lights lining the highway, but we were in no real danger. The road stayed straight. We were blind, but we didn't need to see. Each time I tried to see beyond the sides of the road, I felt blocked. I could only look where I was going. All we had was road.

"I don't know why we couldn't," I told her.

"Because it was meant to be this way." She sounded authoritative but loving, like when she spoke of God. She knew what she was talking about but had compassion on me for not understanding. Ever patient, even in dreams.

I tried to move my foot to the brake pedal to stop the car, get out, and think, but it stayed planted on the floor and wouldn't move. We cruised at a hundred, but we had been traveling at that speed for so long that it didn't feel very fast.

"Who meant it, though?" I exploded at her. "Why does it have to be this way? Don't we have a say?"

"We always have a say, but there are things that are bigger than us, that we'll never understand."

We were silent for at least an hour, staring at the road in front of us. We had nothing with us, no belongings but the clothes on our backs. We didn't turn the radio on or put a CD in, and I wondered if we even could have. She reached over, taking my hand in hers. She felt warm, soft, smooth. Her long and slender piano fingers curled into mine, and she held me much more tightly than she ever had before. It hurt, but I didn't say anything. She took my hand and put it to her cheek so I could feel her tears.

"Baby," I said, choking on the last syllable. She took her seatbelt off and lay across the seat with her head in my lap. I stroked her hair while she cried against my stomach.

"I'm going to miss you so much," she said.

I felt like crying, and I let it happen. It was the most visceral sensation I had. I could feel the hot tears rolling down my cheek, dripping from my chin onto her face. She didn't wipe them away or sit back up; she just lay still, letting me drip on her.

"I don't want you to go," I told her. "I don't want any of it to change. It's not right. There was so much left for us to have together. I was going to ask you to marry me. We were going to graduate together, go out looking for jobs, be poor but happy. I *just* trusted Christ. It was only the beginning of our lives together. So much to explore now." I was thinking out loud.

Still crying—it hurt her to tell me this—she said, "God's plans don't always include ours, Ryan."

I didn't get angry. It was the response I expected. It made me sadder to hear it confirmed.

The car slowed down. I tried to lift my foot and put it to the gas, but once again, it was glued to the floor. The car pulled onto the shoulder. Sara sat up and wiped the tears from her eyes.

She sniffed and said, "This is it, my love." She took me in her arms and kissed me with her mouth open. Our lips held tight—hot, teary breath bouncing on each other's cheeks. It was our very last kiss, and she meant for it to be the best, the most passionate. We threw away our inhibitions with that kiss. Before, she always broke it off with superhuman self-control when she thought it was getting heavy. We fought several times about it. I felt jealous that she would save herself until God determined the time was right for sexual abandon after marriage. She felt hurt that I wouldn't even try to understand. Now, it was she who pressed for more. She was still virtuous and virginal. She merely kissed me like it was the last time.

We kissed for an hour, maybe two. It was too short. I wanted to consummate our relationship in the backseat if only to know her intimately before good-bye. I felt that we could do it and wouldn't ever regret it—a boy's foolish hope when lost in the momentary passions—but as she told me, God often has other plans.

Her door opened without her touching the handle, and she let me go and stepped out. "Good-bye, my love," she told me. Her eyes were still sad, but I could also see hope in them, and the faint impression of a smile curled the corners of her lips. *Is she happy?* I asked myself. The thought that she found something good out of this sent daggers into my heart.

My crying had grown into deep, heartfelt wails. Anguish ripped the tears out of me; my nose flowed freely. I didn't care that I was a mess, nor did I care that she saw it. It felt good to cry as a rebellion against what was happening.

She stepped away from the car without a final look behind her, and the darkness quickly swallowed her up. Not even footprints in the dirt marked her passing. I shouted her name at the top of my lungs, but suddenly no sound would come out. I strained my vocal chords, sucking in each breath and pushing it out with all the force in my body, but nothing would come, like I had lost my voice from yelling too much already.

My dream faded slowly away as I called silently into the dark void. Nothing called back, not even crickets or cicadas. As I started to awaken, I knew that I had just said good-bye to Sara forever.

"No, no, no," I said endlessly in a panicked whisper. I whipped my phone out of my pocket and flipped it on. There was an instant glow of our anniversary picture, then black. I screamed no, but like in the dream, I still had no voice, not enough to yell as hard as I wanted to, anyway.

I made the futile attempt to turn the phone back on, thumb pressed hard on the power button, letting the seconds tick by, turned into a minute with no results. I kept it firmly pressed.

"God, don't do this to me!" I snapped. "This wasn't my prayer!"

Five minutes passed, maybe. Nothing. The date had read December 25. My Christmas present was to hear from God that Sara and thus all I felt I had to live for were dead.

I threw the phone across the room, hearing it hit the far wall. Pieces rained down on the floor. Some hit the vanity table.

"*You killed her, didn't you?* It was your choice, who lives and who dies out of all this mess. You allowed it! You're the almighty, the power was in your hands to save her! You heard my prayer. You *knew* how I felt. You knew I needed her, and you took her. I *trusted* you, and *this* is how you repay? It was just *one thing*, that you give me the hope she's still alive. She's gone! All we had, gone! For what? Is it your good pleasure? Does it please you to see my pain? Have at it, then!"

With that, I scraped my lengthening fingernails across the sores on my back, opening them anew. I screamed out my pain, an endless stream of profanity directed at the hurt and my crea-tor. It threw me into a fit of nausea, and I vomited, another mess on the floor to try to step around without seeing it. I could have cared less. As far as I was concerned, it was over.

Not only did I curse him for Sara, but also I cursed him for Katie, Mom, and Dad, wailing at him for being so unkind, so unfair, to leave me here but take them.

If he'd have taken you, too, you'd be in hell right now, Ryan, a voice inside of me answered. I cursed it too. It sounded like something either Dad or Sara would have said, and it added insult to injury. They were in heaven now, probably never even saw this coming, and their lingering counsel is meant to comfort me?

"Shut up!" I shouted at the voice. "Just shut up! I don't want your sick platitudes."

Could hell, after all, be *any* worse than this place? I was utterly alone in darkness in a world that no longer existed. All I had was this hole, small mementos here and there to remind me of what I could no longer have, and I couldn't even see them clearly enough to take whatever small comfort I could from them about what we had together.

I scratched again at the wounds, hoping to cause enough pain to black me out, keep me from this conscious hell. It only woke me up more.

There was only one way.

I stomped into the bathroom, stepped in my puke as I walked fully upright, demons be damned, every last one of them. I cursed at the vomit. I stepped on a piece of the phone and heard it pop. I cursed that too. I opened the cabinet, took out the PMs, and threw a heaping handful into my mouth. I bent down to the toilet and took in as much water as my mouth would hold around the pills. I was going to swallow them all. I didn't care if I choked on them. I would embrace the misery and punishment of it rather than the coddling death I was planning on having.

Just before I took my gulp, I thought, *This is going to send me to hell after all, isn't it? Thanks for nothing.*

"I'm the only one with the power to do that, and because of what I did on the cross, you are righteous, even now."

I froze. A few of the pills hung at the back of my throat, ready to slip on down with one final flick of the tongue. Was that Dad again? It couldn't be. That sounds like something Jesus would have said.

Who's there?

I AM.

Who?

I AM is here.

That wasn't Dad! The voice was even more familiar than that, and it was as clear as a bell, the clearest thing I'd ever heard. I doubt I would have heard more clearly if he had spoken out loud for my ears to catch. It vibrated the lining of my heart. I felt tears come.

"Stop," he said. It wasn't the exclamatory command my father had made and I had been repeating to myself. I pictured big strong hands covering mine, holding them so they would be still. It was a heartfelt plea.

I began to cry, and pills, one by one, slipped out of my mouth, the water trickling down both sides of my chin. I sat back from the toilet, pills still coming out. There were at least two dozen of them. Arms embraced me in the darkness. I was in the presence of the eternal. I curled up into his wide hug, buried my face in his chest, and cried.

You can curse me, you can slander me, you can spit in my face if you think that's going to get it all out of you, but your life is mine, *you understand?*

I nodded. I felt so ashamed. *I'm sorry.*

There is no "sorry." You are forgiven, for once and for always. Everything—past, present, and future—is covered by my shed blood on the cross. You are pure, born anew in my likeness. When the Father sees you now, he sees me, and that is no small comfort, is it?

I shook my head, crying so hard that if he had spoken out loud, I surely wouldn't have heard him.

"Why, Lord? Why did you take her?" I jumped up and swiped clenched fists through the air in front of me. I jumped at him and tackled him to the floor. He yielded and didn't fight back in the slightest. He let me have at him.

"I thought I was going to have a new, rich, full life in you now. I thought the other day, when I gave you my heart, I thought that was the beginning of something good, and you turn around and take the thing that means the world to me. She was all I had left. Why?"

He didn't answer, but I could feel him putting his arms back around me, holding me, waiting for me to be still. I realized that I was really fighting against myself. He had already won.

"Where were you when I created the heavens and the earth, when I put the stars in their place, told the ocean when to stop, set the birds to soar in the air, the fish to swim, and breathed life into man? Were you present at the moment of creation, when I said 'Let there be light' and it was, and it was good? Where were you when I bled and died for you? Your greatest-grandparents weren't even born yet, and yet you especially were on my mind. If I know every day of your life, if I have numbered every hair on your head, would it be so difficult to believe, then, that I have gone ahead and know what tomorrow brings? And if I have been so gracious to love you and preserve you until now, when you didn't know me and stood against me, how much more gracious do you think I will now be to you? Will I not give you every good thing?"

I began to lie still.

"Ask and believe, and I will give it to you, and none of that 'please' nonsense. Speak boldly. You dwell now in the Holy of Holies."

"Bring Sara back to life."

"You don't know what you're asking."

"You can't do it?"

"I didn't say that. I said you don't know what you're asking."

"You won't do it."

"I didn't say that either. You don't believe I will do it. You want it, but you want it because you know you can't have it, and it burns you inside. Your faith is lacking."

"I can choose not to believe in you anymore since you won't give me what I want."

"*Don't test me!*"

I felt microscopic.

"Your faith is built upon the rock now, not shifting sands. Don't goad against the spurs. You have the fullness of Christ in you now. My spirit is with you, but you are a newborn, naïve in your faith. You drink milk when I would have you eat meat."

Fear filled me, as did the awe-filled wonder at this mysterious person who was speaking such truth to me now. He reminded me of my father, but there was much more here to explore than there was even with that great man.

I sat in stunned silence for a moment. I could feel his anger, but it was righteous and loving—and *merciful*. Grace abounding filled that voice even while it reprimanded me. I focused on calming my beating heart. I wanted to apologize, but that would only bring further admonishment. I remembered something Dad said: "You can tell me anything, son. Don't ever be afraid of what I'll say. I prefer you lay it all on the line than keep something important locked away and eating your insides, okay? And I will always love you."

When was that? Where *was that?* I remembered—just out there, at the computer desk. Dad found some porn I had downloaded. I had been sloppy about it. Normally, I deleted the history on the browser and all cookies just to cover my tracks, but it had been late—three in the morning—when I did it, and I just figured I'd do it later. He checked the history first thing when he got up and found it. He put a filter on the computer before he even told me he found out.

After I confessed, he said, "I have a confession to make too, son. I knew this was coming, and I did nothing to prevent it. I didn't talk to you about this because I hoped it wouldn't happen to you. I should have put the filter on the computer to begin with. I should have known better. I didn't protect you, and I'm sorry."

I was fourteen. I didn't have the heart to tell him that my best friend Joey's older brother had shown us a porno when we were eleven—the first images of a naked woman I had ever seen, even. Most guys started with *Playboy*. Not us. We went all the way. Dad would have killed Joey's parents if he knew.

Because of Dad's intervention, I now realized, I never again looked at porn, wasn't even tempted, and had made it even to this moment without ever going farther with a girl than a french kiss. That's grace. It covers everything. It goes ahead, takes care of the stuff we haven't even thought of yet. And that was just what Dad had shown me.

"Are you as gracious?" I asked the Lord. I didn't even need to speak this sudden memory aloud. He knew my thoughts.

"That and much more. Are you ready to trust me now?"

I hung my head, closing my eyes tightly. "I can't do this on my own anymore. Look at me. I'm a wreck."

"You are the righteousness of God in Christ. Say it."

"No, I'm not. I'm a sinner who is unworthy of you. I scoffed at you my whole life while those around me loved me with your grace, prayed for me. They pined for the day when I would wake up, but I never did."

"I don't know what you're talking about."

"Yes, you do, you know everything. You can't look past these transgressions."

"I can if I've completely forgotten about them. Your sins are as far removed from you as the east is from the west. What is left is pure and spotless. You are clothed in my righteousness. Now say it and take hold of this new life. Claim it. It's true."

"It doesn't feel right."

"That's your conscience talking. Forsake it. It doesn't have to 'feel right' or 'good' for it to be true. Truth is truth. Say it."

I could feel the fluids drying on my back. The stench of my vomit and feces filled the air. I could also smell my body odor. I was an inglorious mess of filth. The assertion sounded like the greatest possible contradiction, but I said it: "I am the righteousness of God in Christ." I sat silently for a moment then said it again, this time with more confidence. I felt a strength rising in me as I began to believe what I was saying.

Sara and I were eating in the commons on a Friday afternoon. We were talking about our vision for the future, what we wanted to get out of life. We were juniors and had just declared our majors. I was in English; she was in psychology. We sat at a table with friends, but they had to go, leaving us to get silly with each other.

Her eyes lit up. She had a clever question, chomping at the bit to get out. "If you were somebody else, and I asked you to describe Ryan Sterling to me, what would you say?"

"I'd say he's hot and you'd be an idiot not to go out with him. I'd also tell you to watch out because he's been giving you the eye from the moment he first saw you. Oh, and that he's going to be famous someday, so the two of you better get an early start on having lots of babies so the older ones can take care of the younger ones while you're out with him staying in four-star hotels on book tours."

"Ryan Sterling, you better behave!"

I flinched as she punched me in the shoulder, hard. She looked delicate, but she could put her full weight behind a hard smack if she wanted to. It hurt.

"Gently, babe!"

"I'm not sorry. Watch your mouth."

I had mentioned sex, the unpardonable sin, but I didn't mean it to sound as cheeky as it did. I genuinely loved her, couldn't wait to get married to her someday, couldn't wait to *ask* her, but at that point, we had been dating only six months and needed to finish college before we made too many plans in that direction. I knew better.

"Now really, tell me," she said.

"Well, he's a nice guy, still hasn't quite figured out what to think about this mess called life, but for an artist, that's not that bad. He's a moderately good writer—already has a couple of stories published in *The Bonfire* and got some good feedback from *The Missouri Review*. He's got potential. He's going places. He's also just good to hang out with. Easy to be around. You know, something like that.

"Is that more along the lines of what you're looking for?"

"Yes, very nice. You took my question seriously. I appreciate that."

"Is that an accurate description based on your experience?"

"Well, I'd have a few more things to add if I could, but that's a nice start." I wanted to ask her what she'd add. There appeared to be mischief in her eyes, and my heart grasped at the chance to hear her say I was sexy or something similar. But I left off, just in case she said something noble or poetic—something decidedly unsexy, in other words.

"What about you?" I asked her. "What would you tell somebody about Sara Butler?"

She blushed but also glowed. "Sara Kaye Butler is a beautiful daughter of God."

———

I smiled in the darkness, ash-covered teeth bared in all their glory. "I am a beautiful son of God," I said. I got it now. Grace warmed over.

"Now give me this," I said. "Take away my pain. I'm tired of hurting."

The warm wind blew around my back, bringing fresh ash to put on the sores I had just opened. It felt like fingers rubbing ointment over my wounds. I felt the ash turn into a paste against the moisture. Sure enough, the searing pain deadened, and I could take in a deep, back-stretching breath without any protest. I did so through the faithful swatch of cloth held against my mouth.

"Thank you," I said.

He was silent, but I didn't need him to speak. I knew he was there more than I had ever known anything. I got saved a few days before, but I felt like that Christmas morning conversation was the beginning of true heart-knowledge of who he was and who I now was in him.

The basement was still pitch-dark, but I felt like it glowed in his light. There wasn't a thing that could happen that morning that would disturb my peace. My wounds no longer a bother, I knelt on the floor unhindered and thanked him for everything that would come to mind, including sparing me from death so that I would know him, even though the rest of the world, so far as I knew, had burned away.

I turned onto my back. The ash in the carpet added to the layers already soothing my wounds. I could feel it cling to me there on the bathroom floor. I brushed away the temporarily sickening thought that the ash that coated my body and the inside of my continuously parched throat was made up of dead things, including people. *It is what it is. Accept it and move on.*

A vast black sky boiled above me. Light filtered through, turning the stew purple. I couldn't wrap my mind around it. The tumult that had passed over had wiped out everything from the Gravel Bar outward in a radius of at least two hundred miles wide—since Sara was dead too. If it had made a perfect circle, it would have also taken Mom out. Dad had been at work. Barring the possibility that the house or business he was currently working on had a basement and he had managed to take shelter in it, he'd be gone. Thoughts of the end of the world had already entered my mind. That fire had burned with seemingly unquenchable energy. It neither slowed down nor sped up from the moment it arose. Who would want to do this to us? Why would they do it? When will they come back?

Fear entered in. I prayed against it. The Lord was quick to comfort me. *Take it easy, Ryan. Live off the bread I'm giving you. Think only on today, on what's important to get you by. Leave the rest up to me.*

I spent the next week rationing out my food, living in near starvation, munching just enough to get by. I had been wrong in my estimation—because of how sparing I had been, this stash would last me three weeks, almost to the end of January. I sipped at the water in the toilet first. Particles of ash were blowing into it through the crack between the seat and the lid. It started to taste foul. Still, I wanted to hold off on the good stuff until I had exhausted the bad.

There was nothing to do but pray. Even by New Year's Eve, it was still almost absolute darkness even at midday. I enjoyed the prayer. God didn't talk back like he had, but he didn't need to. I knew he was there, and he provided what I needed. The pain came back here and there, but it wasn't so bad. It felt now like I had done too much heavy-lifting and needed to take it easy, but no more burning. The ash was caked on so thick back there that it started to act like a permanent skin. It was so strange, this make-shift skin graft. Could it be that God had turned great tragedy into a blessing for me? What manner of grace was this? I thanked him for it, but it reminded me of what was gone, and I grieved sorely. I remembered stories of Old Testament figures like Job and David tearing off their clothes and covering themselves with ash as they mourned. It certainly wasn't by my own design, but here I was.

When the tears were gone, I went back to that blessed basement cabinet for more junk sustenance. I would have liked to feast more abundantly, but that wasn't possible, was it?

Ask and believe, and you shall have it, he had said.

"How, Lord?"

He remained silent. I spent much time in prayer asking for long-term vision. I believed that he wanted me to live, now more than ever. My heart dwelt on that hope.

I spent hours near the bookcases in the hallway leading to the bedroom. I couldn't read a word of them, couldn't even see the titles, even on the hefty volumes of Greek and Roman history Dad liked to collect from a mail-order program. I felt the heavy weight of a Sherlock Holmes collection and a volume that contained *The Lord of the Rings*. Dad had thumbed through these pages countless times, getting lost in their stories. There was doubtless some Charles Dickens in the stacks somewhere, but I didn't know them by touch. Dale Carnegie's *How to Win Friends and Influence People*—I doubt I'd be needing *that* one, but it might be a good read if I ever found some light to read by. There would also be some children's works down here, a couple of collections put together by Clifton Fadiman—weird stories, but they engrossed me well enough as a kid.

I took mental note of them all. This could be the most important corner of my little hovel. Entertainment in the empty days to come.

As my fingers traced along the spines, they came across a leather volume, small and unassuming in the midst of a thousand-plus-page literary anthologies. Lettering was imprinted in the spine. I pulled it out. The cover was soft and flimsy. The first and last several pages were glossy and thick, but the pages in between were onionskin and felt fragile. *A Bible?* It made as much sense as the rest of it, I supposed. It was a bookcase, after all, but so far as I knew, Mom and Dad only kept two Bibles, his and hers, on their nightstands. Long gone now. Katie would have taken hers with her, along with most of the rest of her stuff. She was a slob and left things lying around, but not her Bible. She knew better.

Names were usually imprinted in the front cover, weren't they? I traced my fingers across the front, wishing desperately that I had some light, a match, anything. I felt the lettering, but it was in some fancy cursive script, no pronounced capital curve to the *S* on our last name, and it felt like the rest of the letters in that word were lowercase. I felt the slightest indication of a space between first name and last. I felt slowly along the first name but wasn't getting anything.

Good grief, I'm getting sick of being blind, I thought.

My fingernails were getting long and jagged. I was surprised they hadn't been burned away, but then again, they were always hardy. When I was a little kid and Mom clipped my nails for me, she would exclaim, "Quit drinking so much milk, for crying out loud! Clipping these nails of steel is wearing me out!" Then she'd tickle me to death. I found out she wasn't kidding when I started clipping them myself.

Now, I took that hard left thumbnail of mine and slowly moved it along the letters and spaces of the first name. I had my suspicions and wanted to make sure. It meant the world to me at that moment to find out who this Bible belonged to. Here in the dark, how could I have been so sure that's what it was in the first place? It could have been a pocket dictionary for all I knew.

But that was definitely a "Sterling" at the end of the imprint. You don't put names on dictionaries. And unless I was just delirious in that darkness, I wouldn't have felt it on one either.

I moved my nail slowly from one letter to another and felt the miniscule spaces in between. I was concentrating so hard then that I could have felt grass grow under my feet if I were standing on bare ground. One-two-three-four, space, then *S*. "Katie" has five letters, and "Mikayla"—well, that's obvious. It could have been "Gary," but that first letter was open on the bottom and rounded on the top. This was my Bible. I fell to my knees, overcome.

They got it for me when I turned thirteen. *What is this, a bar mitzvah?* I wanted to ask. I could barely conceal my disappointment. I had asked for a PlayStation, and this was *all* they got me.

"What were they thinking?" I asked Katie later when it was just the two of us, only I dropped a very foul word in there.

She gasped. "Ryan Travis, you watch your mouth."

"What, you going to go tell on me? Don't, they might take my Bible away!" I put my hands to the sides of my face in mock dread. "This is the worst birthday ever."

"I'm not going to talk to you until you settle down and quit swearing. You can just get out of my room!"

I looked into the dark maw of the bedroom doorway, remembering that night. My eyes watered. I had muttered a thank-you to my parents when I opened it. I remember Dad giving Mom a weighted look.

He said to me, "I know you wanted that video-game system, the PlayStation, was it? Maybe next year, bud. Or Christmas. Things have been tight for us this year. Folks have had a hard time paying the company. We've cut them some slack but have had to take a loss. I hate that we've had to do with less, but your Mom and I were thinking this might be an investment for your future."

"No, Dad, it's cool. I appreciate it," I said through clenched teeth. Only Katie could see the disgusted expression on my face. Mom and Dad were behind my back, looking over my shoulder as I read the inscription on the front page: "To Ryan, from the rest of us, may this be your Light in the darkness." Then the date it was given. I was enough of a wordsmith at that age to know that "light" was improperly capitalized. It added to my malcontent.

"Mom and Dad could barely scrape up enough money to get that, Ryan!" Katie told me in her room.

"How much did it cost?" I asked her.

"That is none of your business! And besides, I don't know. Eleven bucks, maybe."

"That would have been enough to go down to the Game Closet and get me a used game for the Nintendo, at least," I said.

Smoke came out of her ears. She had the last word before she pushed me out of her room. "That is the most important gift anyone has ever given you. They told me I didn't have to, but I put in a few bucks of last month's allowance because I knew how much it meant to Dad for you to have it. Don't talk to me again until you can figure out how to at least *pretend* to be a decent person."

I flipped her off with both hands as she slammed the door in my face.

I never read it, barely even touched it. I put it by my bed so that Dad would think I had read it. Over the years, it got moved into different parts of my room, put in with some books I had on a shelf, ultimately forgotten. Dad must have put it down here sometime after I went to college. That was when he got these floor-to-ceiling ornate mahogany bookcases. I had perused the volumes here several times and borrowed some that caught my eye. Never had I noticed the Bible was there.

Now, it was the most valuable, priceless gem the world had ever seen. The glossy leather turned slippery with my tears. I replayed the moment when Dad gave it to me, thinking over what I said and replacing it with what I now wished I would have said. I spoke it out loud.

"Oh, Dad, I asked for milk and you gave me meat. Don't be sorry. I don't know what it cost, and I don't care because never was money better spent than on this Bible. It's the greatest birthday gift I ever got." My mouth dripped with drool as I bawled and sputtered the words out. Lost in a sea of regret and innocence regained, I had forgotten to breathe through the swatch, but God who provides kept me from choking.

"I'm so sorry, Dad. I didn't appreciate it when you gave it, and I'll bet you knew I wouldn't, but you didn't know you'd never get to see the day that I would." *And it's so dark I can't even read it!* I thought. "I never read it before, but now I'll dwell on every word as if it's the last I'm going to hear. Jesus, give me light soon to see by so that I will learn more about you, plumb the depths of your mysterious love." I wasn't talking to Dad anymore. I had unconsciously switched from my earthly father to my perfect heavenly one. I remember that as an awe-filled child, I had thought they were interchangeable.

Teach me how to live, I had prayed.

He didn't say it out loud or even in the silence of my own mind, but I knew his answer now: "You asked, and I have given abundantly."

I literally did not let it out of my hands for the rest of the week. I didn't even set it down to the use the bathroom but performed the function with one hand. *If I can't read it*, I thought, *perhaps I can* absorb *the words.*

———

I had begun keeping score of the days on one of Mom's double-sided printer pages with a ballpoint pen. I had no idea if it had any ink left, but I had pressed hard enough to leave an impression, and so it was that I knew it was January 22 when I ran out of food.

At first, I was surprised when I counted up the tick marks. I had been marking them to the immediate right of the one before, going by touch. I hadn't bothered with the nonsense of slashing a set of four with the fifth mark. That wasn't very helpful in the dark. Regardless of how long I had made it on the small stash I had, the fact remained that I was out, and I had no idea where my next meal would come from.

———

Every once in a while, Sara went on what she called a "fast"—a strange word for what I considered insane voluntary starvation.

The first time she did it was a week after I met her at the ice cream social just before the spring semester started our sophomore year. We found out we had a political science class together and made it a point to sit near each other—strength in numbers, just in case things got too heated and liberal.

We became immediate friends, and I quickly asked her out. She told me she needed to think about it a little bit. I didn't mind her being hard-to-get. I could wait. She said she'd call me in a couple of days with an answer, but until then, don't bug her. Of course, she said yes, but I found the time delay interesting.

"Why two days?"

"Well, this might change your mind about me, but…here goes." She took a deep breath. Her voice was shaky. I understand why now. It's hard to come at an unbeliever like me with such boldness of faith. "I prayed about it, and the Lord told me to give it a couple days, pray again, then call you. I also fasted and prayed during my meal times instead of eating."

I laughed at her.

"I knew I shouldn't have said anything. This was a mistake. I'm sorry." I could hear a shuffling as she began to hang up the phone.

"No no no! Please don't! Sara, you still there?"

"Yeah." She sounded embarrassed.

"I'm sorry. I didn't know you were being serious. My friends and I bust each other's chops a lot, and we like to poke fun at religious folks. I knew you were a Christian. I'm sorry. I should have known better. I won't laugh at you like that again."

"It's okay. I don't expect you to understand, and don't worry—I'm not a nut. I just know how easy it is to make the wrong choice, and I need to know the Lord is in it before I do something."

"Is he in this?" I asked her.

Her voice softened, a sudden comfort and closeness. "Yes, he is."

"Why two days and the fasting and all that?" I asked her.

"It's a big decision. Fasting keeps me focused on what God has to say. When I go without certain comforts, I turn more to him. I can't do the right thing without him. Again, I don't expect you to understand, but when I'm stressed, facing a big decision, scared about things—uncertain times, whatever—I fast, and it brings me peace."

"It's cool. I can dig it," I told her. I had a huge crush on her. She was drop-dead gorgeous, and her joy for life got under my skin in all the right ways. I'd have approved of anything about her if it got her closer to me.

———

I hadn't eaten since midday on the twenty-first—the last of a bag of chocolate-chip cookies. I think they were Chips Ahoy! I hadn't brushed my teeth since the twentieth. The taste of the cookies lingered in my mouth, just a hint. I had begun brushing my teeth on January 2. I had held off for so long because I didn't want to waste water on the process, but I remembered the scene in *Cast Away* when Tom Hanks had to knock an abscessed tooth out with an ice skate. That was *not* going to be my fate. So I used a bottle of water, very sparingly, to rinse as I brushed once every three days. The feeling of an ashless mouth, even if for only a few minutes, had yet to find an equal.

Sara said fasting brought her peace when she was stressed, facing a big decision, or scared about uncertain times. I now faced all three in one. *And I'm expected to find peace by depriving myself? I couldn't be any more deprived!*

I lived in constant starvation. I must have lost another twenty pounds. I was turning into a human broom, but that memory had struck me for a reason. God has funny ways of telling us what he wants us to do, and I was growing accustomed to his use of memories as one of them.

I turned inward, searching my mind, trying to think of what else to do. Nothing popped in there. *Be patient and wait on the Lord, milk drinker*, I chided myself, and I did.

I had my answer the next morning before the light. I judged the passing of each day by when the light first appeared. Otherwise, of course, I wouldn't have known. That morning dawned more brightly than those before, just a shade, but it was enough to count. I could make out the bigger capital letters on the spines of the larger volumes and anthologies Dad had, giving me faith that the day may come down the road that I could read between the covers.

The answer to my problem came when I remembered that our next-door neighbors to the west, the Nortons, had a basement. They were a couple in their late fifties whose son and daughter had graduated a few years ahead of Katie, too old to ever play with me but nice in passing. They'd lived there my whole life and used to host neighborhood parties and getting-to-know-you affairs where Mr. Norton would make the sweetest, most vanilla-laden ice cream you ever tasted and Mrs. Norton would bake cookies every bit up to the standard of her husband's confection.

Their basement was mostly finished. They had an entertainment center down there, some video games, a pool table, a bathroom, and a guest room. There was also an unfinished concrete room with a washer and dryer and shelves for Mr. Norton's tools. The last time I was over there was the summer between freshman and sophomore years. I had just broken up with my high school sweetheart, feeling pretty bummed. Mom and Dad took me to a barbecue the Nortons were hosting. Nobody else was there even remotely close to my age. I went downstairs to hang out and play video games. I had had to go to the bathroom. Its door opened off that concrete storage room. Before I went in there, didn't I take a glance around and notice something different in there?

I had!

It wasn't a big deal at the time, and why would it be? It was just a fridge the Nortons had put in, and I remember thinking, *Huh, that's a big fridge.* Now, it glowed in my memory like the doorway to heaven, and my stomach was *screaming* to be filled. I could think of nothing else.

But that would mean crawling out of the basement. My clothes had begun peeling away over the past week, and with the sores on my back closed up and no longer an issue, I took them completely off and dwelt underground clothed only with ash. I would have felt quite immodest had my mind not constantly been occupied by just trying to survive. Now that I was thinking about emerging from the dark, however, I felt mortified. Yet the gnawing sensation in my gut, screaming for sustenance, would not be contained. I felt faint and dizzy, and nauseated. I hadn't felt that way the day before. I think the Lord was trying to tell my modesty to buzz off and go get what my body needed.

I hopped out of bed, prayed for a firm resolve, and then stepped down the corridor and began going up the stairs, intent on heading out the back door, walking across my yard and then theirs, and knocking on their door to ask.

I stopped midway up the stairs, my hand on the rail that was still loosely attached to the wall. I couldn't help it. I had to laugh at myself. The stairs were not attached to any foundational wall. The walls of the stairwell were still there, making me think it was as secure as it had always been, but if I walked all the way up, paying no attention to what I was doing, I'd have stepped entirely off and slammed my naked crotch and derriere directly into the top of the wall between the bathroom and bedroom, and that would put all thoughts of eating completely out of my mind for the rest of time.

I forsook the stairs and used Katie's bed to boost me up and outside onto the ground, and there I was, for the first time, looking at the world after it ended.

It was as I had feared. Trees, grass, structures, every living thing, everything itself was gone. Not even the dried-out husks of even the hardiest oak as a landmark. It was all gone. The fire had burned everything away. I couldn't see far in the dim light, but it was far enough. I could make out the rises and falls of small hills and valleys; the structure of the ground itself hadn't changed, at least, but otherwise there was nothing but nothing. A constant swirl of dust devils and demons rose and fell and swooped about and around, a vast maelstrom of desolate discontent. The world was a palette of purple sky and gray earth. Out of the basement now, the wind had a different pitch. It sounded like the groans and moans of hell.

I wanted to fall back into the bedroom. As my wounds had healed to more tolerable levels, I began using the sheets when I slept at night. It gave me a semblance of the old comfort, and now I wanted to bury myself in them and die of starvation rather than face the awful truth like I now did.

Keep going! I heard that familiar voice. He accented each word.

I was crouching low to the ground, afraid of something emerging from the darkness overhead and picking me off like some naked albino desert rat. Even though I was as gray as the rest of the landscape, it would be no problem for the aliens with their advanced technology or some foul beast they had unleashed from another dimension to pick me off.

They'd have killed you by now. Go!

I kept low to the ground and moved slowly across it. Directions and distances were near impossible in this world. I kept my eyes on where their basement should be, but it was set partially into a hillside and obscured. I was traveling blind, going on trust that what was supposed to be there would be there. I glanced behind me every few yards to make sure my hole in the ground was still there, but after only twenty feet or so, I couldn't see it anymore. Wind had picked up over the top of it, something fierce, and set a wall of gray where it should have been. I was in the open ocean between two uncharted islands without stars to go by.

I looked at the tracks I had made, quickly filling up with ash swirled by the wind, but I could see the straight line I had been traveling in. I kept at it, step by step, checking behind me to make sure I was still going straight. I wish I had had the gumption to make a rope out of the bedsheets and tie it to my waist before going out, but starved as I was, there wasn't time for invention however much the spawn of necessity.

The wind picked up even harder, blowing the ashen blizzard around me and taking visibility down to zero. I held a new remnant of my shirt to my mouth for the journey. Now that I was completely naked, I had much more material to work with. I was glad I did. It was cleaner than the old patch and thus kept more ash from getting in.

I slowed down to a snail's pace. The long journey must have taken a half hour already, each step labored, carefully considered, prayed out to the nth degree. I took little note at the moment of what the ground felt like under my feet. It was warmer than the surrounding air, like it was still cooling down from the flame. Other than that, nothing spectacular, just hard-packed bare dirt covered by a thin layer of ash. My mind, however, was completely centered on the task at hand and keeping my cool. It was providential I had slowed down and checked myself, for the wind stilled for a moment, and I found myself just inches from falling into the Nortons' basement.

I cursed and leaped back, my heart hammering so hard I could almost hear it against the wind's hellish crying that had started anew with fury. I put my free hand to my chest, focused on calming down, and prayed for fortitude—I received it.

From opening to floor, the distance was about seven feet, a hairy jump in bare feet, but not bad. It was dark. I had to stare a few minutes into the hole to make sure I was going to land safely. I stood above the southeast corner of the rec room. I could barely make out the entertainment center several feet across the room. A few feet away from the wall was the pool table. I sat down on the edge and hung my feet and legs over the opening. I was afraid to let go, slipping on down and into the unfamiliar. But the God I trusted was there. I had heard him. I could feel his spirit.

The edge of the top of the wall was rough and sharp. The fire had made as clean a cut here as it did in my own basement. The wall was a faux wood paneling on top of concrete. There wouldn't be any danger of splinters if I slid off, but that was a small comfort. It would still skin half my butt off. I propped myself up on the top of the wall with my arms, weak though they were, and swung out and down to the floor.

It was a smooth landing. The carpet was at least as thin as what was in my basement. I remembered it being dark blue before the ash, which softened the floor and soothed my feet as I walked.

I felt around with my hands out in front of me, scooting rather than stepping with my feet. I was sure of my immediate environment, but not sure enough. I touched the table, ran my hand across the smooth wood finish underneath the soot. The balls were all in the corner and side pockets. I remember playing a few games with Amy Norton down here. She was much too old for me, but I had a little kid's crush on her, nevertheless. I think she found it endearing. She was a much better pool player than I, but she let me win from time to time.

I'd let Sara win when we'd play in the basement of the Student Center, every time. She caught wise after the fourth or fifth time.

"Are you ever going to play this game like you know what you're doing?" she asked.

I laughed. "I never know what I'm doing around you. Pool is the least of my worries."

She shot me a look. "Rack 'em up and play it like you mean it. You're holding out on me."

I'm no pool shark, but I had sunk six in a row before I finally missed and she had a turn. She never had a chance. The game was over in less than six minutes, a record.

"You sorry you made me do it?" I asked.

If she could ever look at me lustily, she did so then. "I couldn't be happier. That was awesome. You should win more often. You look good doing it."

I smiled sadly in the dark. She was always pure Sara. The fondness of it had completely taken me out of the moment. Then, new pangs took hold, my stomach growling like an ogre.

With singleness of purpose, I pushed through the door to the mess room. It had twisted off its top hinges as well. The floor was clear, obviously picked up before the flame, but I found it odd that here, as at my basement, there was no debris of destruction from the rest of the house. The fire had been so clean, so thorough. Aside from knocking doors off their top hinges or shaking a few things off the shelves here and there, it had completely left these basements alone and preserved. So spooky.

Memory served me well. In the corner was a large steel box lit eerily and unnaturally from the sky above. The darkness was such that I couldn't clearly see into the basement from above. I would find this to be the case every time I looked down into a basement. The sky above grew lighter over time, but never light enough to see clearly from above before I explored. I always had to drop in and look for things on the level. So, having found the refrigerator, I threw open the doors and found paradise within. Like my refrigerator, it was cool—not cold, but still…good. It was fully stocked with everything one would expect from a fridge. I began eating without prejudice, thinking little that the stuff inside would have gone bad by now.

Luckily, my hands found lunch meat first. Of course I couldn't check the expiration date, but my stomach handled it well enough to tell me that it was still good. Sliced turkey, ham, bologna—

probably chock-full of preservatives that weren't in any wise good for me, but it was all I had, and it tasted like manna from heaven. There were two packages of the stuff. I ate one and a half before starting to feel the satisfying, sleepy effects of being well fed. I hadn't eaten meat in over a month, so it was glorious. I washed everything down with some soda I had found in the fridge. The sound of the fizz drove me to bliss.

I fumbled more discriminately after the initial stuffing and found a bucket of chicken from KFC. I could see the white letters practically glowing in the darkness. I sniffed at it. Much of it had gone bad. I could feel the fuzz of mold on a few pieces, but there were two drumsticks and a breast that were still good. I ate heartily and mightily of them and tossed the rest over the wall and onto the ground outside. If there were any creatures in the world left to scavenge such spoil, they could have at it. I'd welcome them, name them, try to take them in as pets if they'd have me. I'd enjoy knowing that I wasn't the only living thing left in this world.

I found vegetables and other packaged foodstuffs that were still, praise God, good to eat and might keep for a couple of days. I took as much as I could carry and set out to head back home. I had thrown all that food down in less than half an hour, but quick as that was, I felt like time had stopped, and for just a little while, I got to wander around in heaven again.

It was now time to leave. I tried at first to scoot the pool table over to the wall from which I had entered, but it was far too heavy. I settled for a recliner to boost me instead. I was almost up and over the wall when a thought occurred to me: *Are they here?*

I set the food on the pool table and turned back to face the rest of the basement. "Mr. Norton?" I called. It was barely a whisper. *Still with this fear of loud noises!* I chided myself. I forced the air past my strained vocal chords. It broke through the ash and found a tone. "Mr. Norton!" I shouted full-volume. It was like yelling in a blizzard. The sound disappeared. It sounded as dull in my basement, too. I just hadn't noticed until now because I had been too afraid to notice much of anything.

"Mrs. Norton!"

I waited, longing for the answer. I heard nothing. *And what if they come out and see you in all your pale naked glory? They'd die of shock or laughter. Which would be worse?*

I'll take my chances, I answered myself. If they were going to see me in the flesh, well, I'd cross that embarrassing bridge when I came to it.

I wanted so much to have done with it. They weren't answering; they weren't there. *Get on home! Before the daylight dies and then you do too.*

But I couldn't let it go. If I had survived, surely there were hardier souls out there who had done it too. Mr. Norton would be a good case. He had grown up on a farm in Iowa, *Field of Dreams* country. The guy was made of sinew and forged steel, but had a twinkle in his eye that betrayed a gentle and contrite heart. He was twice the man I'd ever be, merely half the man I now realized Dad was. He should be here...*provided he had gotten downstairs in time.*

I stood still, thinking for a moment. I had to check the other rooms. I groaned at the thought of exploring the space. I had searched my basement and known it was good. This place, I wasn't so sure. I prayed.

I'm afraid, Lord. You keep telling me not to be, but I'm not cut out for this—not alone. Find where I'm lacking and plug the holes with your strength. I don't believe you got me this far just to die by whatever lurks around the next corner.

Strengthened, I began to inch my way around the space. The rec room was in two parts. In the opposite corner of the room where I had entered was the stairwell. I could barely make out the door to it in the dark. On that side was the entertainment center, with a forty-something-inch television and whatever game system Aidan had left down here, possibly an older generation Nintendo. There would be movies over there too. A couch was in the middle of the room, centered in front of the television. The pool table occupied the other half, the half I was standing in. The cue rack was in the corner.

I went back through the door to the mess room. The other rooms would open off from that, along the left side. I marked their doors in my memory, two of them—the bathroom and the extra bedroom. If anybody was down here, they'd most likely be in the latter, unless they were having a particularly rough day on the toilet.

I had walked quietly, stealthily, my fears of awakening beasties from the dark renewed by the unfamiliar space, but surely the Nortons would have heard me anyway, wouldn't they? Provided they were awake—*or alive.*

Even if they were dead, I had to know. I tried the bathroom, the first door on my left and the less likely to contain living or dead bodies. Its door was still attached but swung open uneasily. I found nothing but the expected facilities: a sink, a toilet, a stand-up shower. I lifted the lid on the toilet and smelled the water—ash but nothing else. Nobody's naïve little kid left it unflushed before the flame. I marked it in my memory as a source of more water if I needed it, although I hoped I didn't.

I stepped on to the bedroom. Its door was also still attached but rattled when I swung it open. I did it slowly, praying as I went for safety and courage. The room was also lit poorly by the scant light from above. I could make out the shape of a bed and a dresser with a mirror. The latter was similar in size to the one in my room and would have offered a reflection of a large chunk of space had it not been coated with ash. I was thankful for that. I wasn't ready to see my reflection yet. I had managed to avoid looking thus far.

I was both anxious and afraid to make out any bodies there in the darkness on the floor or the bed, but I saw neither, just blankets and pillows. There were pictures on the walls. They were held in a glass frame, and because of the ash, I couldn't make them out. Above the bed, a thick wooden board ran along the wall a few feet. I stood puzzled by it before realizing it was a windowsill. The fire had swept the glass away, as it was aboveground, while the trim was *just* below ground level. I was continually astonished at how clean and meticulous that fire had been. The same thing had happened to a couple of windows over the computer desk in my basement.

I sighed. There was more than a bit of relief in it. My overactive mind imagined that everyone else might have turned into zombies or vampires and may wander the landscape taking care of whoever hadn't shared their fate, in which case I should count myself lucky not to have run into them. But I knew better. The God who was there was a loving God, a jealous God, and he wouldn't allow good people like the Nortons to go the devil's way, if such a thing were possible.

I noticed it was getting darker. I had been out for only an hour. I didn't have a clock to check, but by my estimation, the light first appeared at approximately ten and disappeared completely three hours later. My waking hours, the only time I could work on figuring out how to live, were very few. I lived the rest completely by faith. My quest for companions finished for now, I slipped out of the Nortons' basement and returned home with my booty.

———

I spent that pitch-black evening stuffing as much food down my gullet as I could hold. It was going bad quickly. I had to spit some of the gamier bits and pieces into my hand and toss them up and out. I hated to waste the food, but I would hate myself even more if I chanced trying to digest it.

My belly fully sated, I found myself in a stupor much like that mythic tryptophan-induced drowsiness everyone gets at Thanksgiving. It was sweet bliss to fall asleep for reasons unrelated to pain or nerves. Before I slipped into another dreamless sleep, I made sure my Bible was under my pillow, ready for reading in the unlikely event the clouds ever cleared and I could see well enough to read. As I gripped it, I felt something curious, a thickness to it that I hadn't bothered to notice before. There were things stuffed between the pages, pieces of paper someone had tucked away. *Maybe it's just my imagination*, I thought as sleep overtook me.

I spent the next few weeks eating off the Nortons' stash from the fridge. The sandwich meat held up remarkably well. I loaded up on the condiments too, and there were a few jars of pickles I snacked on mindlessly—a little too mindlessly I realized one day when an especially delicious jar of dills gave me the runs. Without a moment to spare, I sprinted up the steps from the Nortons' basement aboveground and evacuated into the billowing ash. The sound and smell of it were both so unseemly and startlingly putrid there in the quiet howl of desolation that it sent me to laughing fits that convulsed my body, thus exacerbating the immodesty of the situation. I was lucky, in fact, that when I fell over, I fell to the side rather than backward.

"Here's what I think of what you've done to my planet!" I shouted into the purple darkness. It was uncontainable catharsis. I praised God. I couldn't have taken care of my immediate emergency any other way. Without even thinking about it, I had run into hell and defecated on it, suffering no reprisal—nor had I even expected one.

But, oh! My guts were in a knot! I felt sick for the remainder of the day, remembering afterward what I wished I had before. My cousin Julia used to drink out of the pickle jar when her mom wasn't watching. Her pants would practically explode later on from the force of what followed. As much as Aunt Stacy admonished her for it, she didn't fully quit the habit until she was five and a half, by which time the rest of us had learned *never* to drink from a pickle jar. I guess I had never caught on not to eat so voraciously from one either.

Speaking of unmentionable matters, I rectified my sanitation problem at home. For two months now, I had been using the bathroom into two wastebaskets. You can imagine the stench. From now on, I would still use the wastebaskets as needed but dump them daily into a place a few dozen yards from the basement on the other side of the house, away from the Nortons. It was no way to live, but at least I was living.

I was still afraid to travel outside between the houses, but as long as I kept an eye on where I had just stepped, I knew I could make it back to my basement safely. It may have been my imagination, but it seemed that over the weeks my tracks didn't cover up as quickly as they had the first time I went out. The howl of the wind grew quieter but, again, very gradually, so that might have been my imagination as well.

I found a clock on the thirteenth of February. It was an analog type, run on a battery, one of those big wall-mounted wristwatches that were trendy in the late eighties and early nineties. I couldn't believe it was still running. It was under Katie's bed. I was searching there to see if there was something useful, something that cast light, perhaps. I pulled it out and saw dim sunlight glint on it. It was almost a quarter after twelve. The short day was at its brightest. It was glow-in-the-dark. I was surprised when three o'clock came and I could still tell time. It had gathered enough energy from the little light it had received to give me the time for another two hours. I smiled and thanked the Lord, wondering how Sara would receive such small but significant blessings in the middle of all this.

She'd have already lit out on her own and found other survivors by now, I thought.

I gasped in my sobs and said, more to myself than to the Lord, "But I'm not there yet. I'm not strong enough."

Don't be so hard on yourself, Dad said to me once. *You don't have to do anything for me to love you. Just* be.

When was that? I asked the Lord that afternoon as the clock's light faded away from me.

All the time. The response was immediate. Again, it sounded like Dad but then nothing like him, in between the familiar and unfamiliar. I don't have to explain where it came from.

The Bible was still under my pillow from the night before. I reached for it, felt that thickness again, things there that shouldn't be there. *Who put them there?* The answer suddenly struck me between the eyes with all the subtlety of a bullet to the brain. Why hadn't it occurred to me before? Had I been so delirious with hunger and survival that it didn't register? *We see only in part now what we will one day see in full*—another maxim from Dad, something he brought up when my adolescent mind couldn't grasp disappointment. I'm still learning. Regardless, I now realized that Dad had slipped his own notes into my Bible some time ago, and it was absolutely imperative I find a way to read *now.*

BREAD

My mind had been on other things—fantasies, the past, things that took me out of the moment. When I woke up at ten in the morning of the fourteenth—sunrise—I imagined the perfect Valentine's Day with Sara. It was based on the two we had had so far—dinner, a date movie, a medium–slow dance to our song, "When Did You Fall" by Chris Rice (her choice; I had never heard of the guy and never listened to anything else by him, but it seemed to work well enough). Then a kiss good-night, and she'd sign off as she did every date: "Just remember this, my love—I love you, but Jesus loves you more." I was so enamored with her that I just smiled at whatever she said.

As I began to increase in the knowledge of God and of his love, I began to increase in understanding about Sara, and the more I understood about her with my spirit, the less I understood with my mind. She loved me, and yet I didn't believe her Jesus. Sure, I believed *in* God, but that was lip service. I didn't believe in him the way she did, and yet she loved me like she wanted to spend her life with me. I had little doubt she'd say yes when I asked her to marry me. I thought, *But surely she knew the wisdom of marrying a believer as opposed to a nonbeliever, so why me?* She had fasted and prayed about me, and God told her to go for it. I wish I had thought to ask her—I think God told her more than she had let on. I think he told her that she'd be part of my redemption, that in the end, she'd win me over. I wonder now if that's part of what attracted her to me. Yes, she found me attractive physically, but even before I knew Christ, I had sense enough to know that Christians, at least the proper ones, don't dwell on externals. There would have been more to me than met the eye. I wish she were here to see what she'd done.

Now that I was a part of her fellowship, I pictured Valentine's Day going differently. We'd still kiss at the end of the night, but we'd also sit down and pray for each other before parting, and I'd repeat her beautiful send-off right back to her. I cried happy tears, for my faith that there was a heaven and we'd see each other there had grown exponentially as the God of my sufficiency continued to provide day after day. We would get our chance to whisper sweet nothings of the Spirit to each other in our true home. What unending joy!

But now a different matter pressed at me. Sara took our future with her, but my future in the Lord was still under development. I *needed* to read that Bible. Night fell, hours passed, and I lay awake in the blackness embracing God's book in my arms and longing for his light. I felt so ignorant, so soft, so *new*. I was weak. Even though Dad, Katie, Mom, and Sara had spoken God's grace into my life over the years, I had never sat down and studied it myself. It was time to drink water straight from the fount rather than the tap of my memories.

—✦—

I didn't get my chance until the next morning. I stayed up all night praying. I didn't want to miss the light when it emerged. The moment it did and I could make out my surroundings, I leaped out of bed and clamored over the wall onto the brief stretch of ground to the Nortons'.

The ground was cooler now and felt harder beneath my bare feet. The air was still warm and thick, but it was getting easier to breathe. I found that I could take a few deep breaths here and there without coughing. As I tried my voice out in prayer, I found it staying with me much longer than it had before.

My purpose was actually twofold. First and most important was to find something that would give off light. A flashlight would be ideal, and I thought for sure I'd find one. The second would be to see if there was anything I had missed in the refrigerator. I searched the workbench and found everything a man could ever want in a tool room except for the most immediate and essential item.

"Come on, Mr. Norton," I muttered. "You built a basement in tornado alley but didn't bother to keep a flashlight in it?"

Yeah, words to live by, right? I replied to myself. The lack of such an item in my own basement was apparently above my own reproach.

I couldn't just give up, though! Surely Mr. Norton had the foresight to keep one on hand, perhaps even a pocket flashlight, the kind that helped you find the keyhole when you needed it on a dark, late night. I cast about, trying to see something I had missed on the other several trips. I hadn't explored the basement much beyond that first visit when I went looking for Mr. and Mrs. Norton. And that had been just a cursory glance through the other rooms.

We see only in part now what we will one day see in full. It sounded like Dad and God again, then I said it. "Help me see, Lord. I need to eat your bread, not just little crumbs here and there but the whole loaf. Don't keep it from me any longer," I prayed.

My eyes were wide in the darkness, all pupils, taking in the little light there was. I wanted to see the things not seen. What was I missing? Then, there it was—a round object sticking out on the wall by the fridge. It looked like it didn't belong. I walked to it with my hands out in front of me. Distances were deceiving in the darkness. I hit it before I saw I was going to hit it, slamming it with the back of my left wrist and shooting pain up my arm. I ignored it. I'd felt worse.

It was a doorknob. Now that I was close enough, I could see the crack of the door. It was thin and tall. It could only be a closet. I pulled it open, and it fell from its weakened hinges. Objects like the refrigerator were one thing, but how I hadn't seen this closet above before I had no idea, but the Lord has a way of revealing little surprises along the way that makes me wonder if he isn't having a little too much fun.

I had found a food pantry. Cans of Chef Boyardee, corn, green beans, clams, sardines, peaches, pineapples, black-eyed peas, and on and on stacked floor to ceiling on shelves nailed to the inside wall. I also found a couple of loaves of bread there. Most of the slices were moldy, but I ate what was salvageable and thanked the Lord for the mold as it meant *something* was still alive out there. I also found boxes of cereal and Pop-Tarts, bags of chips, stuff for the kids and grandkids when they came to visit.

There were a few gallons of water in there, which brought me to the realization that some of this stuff was the Nortons' earthquake stash. They had probably started keeping so much stuff in hand after the scare of 1991, when some quack predicted that a big earthquake was going to happen on such-and-such a date. School was actually canceled for it. There was no evidence it would ever happen in our lifetimes, no seismographic readings, anyway, and yet this guy had everyone convinced the New Madrid fault was going to tear the world in half and drop Missouri into oblivion. In spite of that, here I was. The world had ended, and I had enough food here to keep me stuffed for months on end. I held my hand up to my mouth as I cried and gave thanks to the Lord.

And then I saw, on the fifth shelf up, eye-level where I couldn't miss it, a giant Maglite flashlight, and behind it a small Citizen's Band radio. It also had AM and FM. I thought my heart had stopped. I snatched them up, along with a can of fruit, tuna, some bread, some green beans, distilled water, and a hammer and screwdriver to open the cans. I had stripped the Nortons' bed and used their sheets for my new bedding while I used my own as clothing for my excursions. Before going back, I took it off and wrapped food and supplies up in one corner and wrapped the rest around my body. I had gotten skilled at it to the point where the supplies always ended up slung over my back. I could thus still use both hands to pull myself over the wall.

When I got back home, I could barely contain my excitement. I opened the tuna and chowed on it greedily from one hand while using the other to operate the radio. I could barely see the orange needle working its way across the numbers. This thing was *really* old, but it was also built to withstand practically anything. So long as I could find batteries down the road, I was free to get on it and search for a signal all I liked. It was a small hope, but hope nonetheless. I toyed with the CB as well, switching to each channel and calling out "breaker." I used my own name as my handle. There would be no danger in revealing my identity. Still, nothing but fuzz, but what glorious fuzz it was. I nurtured hope that somebody would broadcast something from the underground, and I would be there to hear it. *Lord, let me see the day.*

I set it aside and took the flashlight. In my excitement, I hadn't even tested it at the Nortons', but when I pressed the rubber button, it blasted into the darkness like a supernova. I shone it about, taking in the colors of my environment for the first time. To have artificial light again was a blessing beyond words.

Everything was coated in ash of an even, light gray texture. It looked like snow. The walls, furniture, and floor were of the same color, but I could see different shadings belying what was beneath. The ash on the wall was darker from the orange paint beneath than the floor, which was already carpeted in white. I walked around, shining it everywhere, relishing the freedom of sight. I found the places on the floor where I had made my messes. If I ever had the luxury and desire of using cleaning agents, I would get around to that. Fortunately, these piles were also covered with ash to the point that you couldn't make out what they were without knowing.

I walked to the bookshelves and saw *The Lord of the Rings*, *The Complete Sherlock Holmes*, anthologies of Dickens and Poe, *The Chronicles of Narnia* and *The Screwtape Letters*, volumes of poetry and myth, and on and on. *The Bill James Baseball Abstract* was also there, and next to it, Dad's complete baseball card collection bound in at least five notebooks. I saw something on the far left set of shelves, on top, that I had forgotten would be up there: photo albums.

I sat down and held my breath for a moment, my heart pounding like it wanted to come out and see. I could *hear* it thumping, and I saw my world through a slow-motion lens, seeing my perspective change as I stood back up and reached my hand across the universe to touch the leftmost volume. Mom kept them in order. This one would have been their wedding. I wiped ash off the spines as I had had to do with the books and saw the dates rise on into the late eighties and early nineties, the time Katie and I appeared on the scene. I thought about what would be inside—birthday parties, graduations, pictures of girlfriends past and the one present contained in the albums farthest to the right.

I felt a longing in my spirit to see my beloved and my family again, but I knew the grief of not being able to have them would undo me all over again. "I want to so badly, Lord," I said.

Eat first, he responded. I had already eaten, of course, but that's not what he meant.

In a way, it was a relief that he told me to hold off. I wasn't ready to cry at that moment, not like that. I stepped away, back to where I set this past trip's catch. The Bible was there. I took all the stuff off the blanket and wrapped myself in it again. I sat back against the couch and set the flashlight up on the cushion just over my left shoulder. It worked perfectly. My eyes filled with tears at the sight of the words jumping off the page. I skimmed through the prefatory notes and introductions, gleaning what I could about the authors and different historical periods when the Bible was written. It was all so rich and full that I couldn't digest it, nor did I feel I had to. I just let it move me, one page to another.

I had entirely forgotten about the extra notes slipped in there. When I flipped to Genesis, the first one fell out. I opened it and saw what I had suspected. Dad had written something and stuck it in there. Hands shaking, I opened it. I felt like I was looking at a ghost as I read.

My dearest Ryan,

I noticed you didn't take this Bible to school with you when you left. I saw it on your nightstand. I opened it up and took a look in it. It creaked like I had opened it for the first time. I sat down on your bed and cried a while. I was already missing you dearly. We'd had such a good summer together, all the fishing and nature walks, long talks over my pipe. I couldn't bear that you were gone, but I thought, *At least he has his Bible, doesn't he? Doesn't he?* When I came in here and saw it, I felt like a part of me had died before I was ready.

Mom found me that way and said, "Gary, give him a call. I'm sure he'd love to hear from you."

I just about couldn't speak, but I said, "And what am I going to say that he hasn't already heard me say a million times? He hated this Bible. He never did like it. What was I thinking, all those years, that I could be the one God used to bring Ryan to him? It was my job, and I failed at it."

"You didn't fail, Gary!" she said. "It's not like he's dead!"

But I knew what kind of pressures you are going to face in college, all that skepticism you are going to get pounded with day after day. I knew the mistakes I had made at your age, even though I came in as strong a believer as they come. I was knocked back on my heels. How much the worse for you if you don't know the Lord?

And I know that you don't. You attended our church faithfully your whole life, even over this past summer, when you turned 18 and didn't really have to do a thing I told you. Remember that conversation we had?

I did. It was another of what I called our "pipe chats," although he was the only one who smoked. He said, clear as day, "I can't make you do a thing you don't want to anymore, Ryan. I thought before about insisting that as long as you were under my roof, you would respect my authority, but what kind of legalism would that be? How would that bring you any closer to Jesus? So I prayed about it, and the Lord told me to let you go. If you don't want to go to church with us in the morning, by all means, stay home and enjoy your time."

That was Saturday night, after the dessert—Mom's blackberry cobbler. Dad and I liked to pick the seeds out from our teeth and spit them back in our bowls just to gross her out. I was so touched by the way he put all of it that I couldn't say no to church. I loved him too much to let him down. I wasn't sure I believed what he believed and thought, regardless, there was always time to change my mind, but I couldn't stay home tomorrow. So I went, but I didn't believe. I sang the songs, but I didn't feel them. I never had.

I could tell by the look in your eyes, your whole life, that you didn't know the Lord. I started to notice that look when you were seven. It was like a light went out. But I kept hoping, kept praying, that I'd see the day when you'd trust him and all that I ever taught you would go for something. Seeing this Bible here…I'm not sure that day will ever come.

But I decided to hope and believe anyway. I have spent your whole life praying for you. I can't well quit now, and as I prayed there on your bed, the Lord dried my eyes and gave me a project to do. I'm not sure if this is just to keep me busy and happy or if there's something more going on, but he wanted me to guide you through the Bible. I know you've heard and read Scripture before, but the word doesn't live in you. This can be a difficult and daunting journey if you trying to go it alone, and I have a strong feeling that without these notes, you will be doing just that.

See, the Lord gave me this feeling that something is going to happen that will leave you stranded. I don't know what, and it was just a passing thing, really. You know the old cliché "Somebody just walked on my grave"? He said to me, plain as day, "Ryan's going to need you, and as much as you'll want to be there, you can't."

It scared me, but like I said, it was a fleeting thought, like a whisper or a hint, something random and then silence. I wrestled over whether that was the Holy Spirit or just my frightened conscience, but in the end, I decided that writing these notes would be a good thing, for my own therapy if nothing else.

If you've opened this Bible and have started reading this note first, I should tell you that if you haven't accepted Christ yet, please do so now. It's the most important thing you'll ever do. That you've opened your Bible is a good sign. Perhaps you're on the verge. My abiding hope is that you're already saved. I also hope that you'll come home from college one of these weekends and snatch up this Bible and leave my project incomplete. I'm going to put it downstairs, in the basement. Maybe you'll notice it's gone and go looking for it. I pray the idea that somebody moved it would even anger you. Ryan, I love you and long for the day! Don't you see? There's nothing I have ever wanted in my life more than that you would know Jesus. I could care less whatever else you do or if you ever hurt me with something you said or did because if I knew he was in you and you in him, my joy would be abundant and complete, knowing that you were in his hands and no longer your own.

I tucked this note in Genesis, but that's not where I want you to start. It's the beginning, yes, but to grasp the beginning you must go beyond it. Turn to John, I beg you, and read through chapter 3. Don't stop, and read it out loud. Let his words sing to you. Trust me, they will.

Love always and forever, in his precious name,
Dad

My body was wracked with sobs, a deep, abiding grief at all those hollow years I walked in darkness. They came crashing down, brick by wasted brick.

"My Lord and my God," I whispered. I felt a presence in the room with me. It felt like Dad again, but it wasn't. It was him, the Holy Spirit, the comforter. He filled the room. His scent went into my nostrils, throughout my body, giving me a refreshing chill. I felt as if I was swimming in a deep, warm ocean, bathing in the arms of God. He didn't speak, but he loved. My tears were sweet and warm. I felt the wonder and joy of an eternity ahead of me, a passing phase behind. I'm sure that my father's death was sudden, and his will and testament no doubt had burned up in the fire, but because he purposely moved this Bible down here, he had left me a priceless inheritance.

"Thank you, Father," I said. "Both of you."

I picked up the Bible and opened it to John, careful as I flipped through the pages not to let the other notes fall. I was curious to read them. *But everything in due time*, I told myself. I found the Gospel of John's blessed first words, mirroring those in Genesis. I read them aloud, my voice suddenly booming past the foul blockage that continued to ache my throat, "In the beginning was the Word…"

<hr>

When I turned the page, just about to begin chapter 3, I found another note. It was folded twice. On the outside were the words "Finish chapter 3 first." I wanted to hear from Dad more than

I wanted to read the Bible, but I respected his command. After finishing, I opened the note.

Ryan,

Did you get it? Before I tell you, close the note and make a guess. Skim what you just read, see if it jumps out at you.

I laughed. This could be fun. I closed my eyes and considered everything I had read, what it might mean. I went back to that first sentence: "In the beginning was the Word, and the Word was with God, and the Word was God." What was the word? Was it the Bible? That would make sense. Dad used to talk about how God was really the author of the Bible, but he used men to write it, like the authors of the Gospels and Moses; therefore, the Bible was the inspired "word" of God. I had always believed men wrote it and they alone based on what they thought about God, but now that I had heard his voice too, I more easily believed it was as Dad had said. The Bible was really God-authored; these other guys were merely his ghost writers. So in the beginning was the word.

Wait a second…God wrote *the Bible. All this stuff that had happened came* later *than the beginning. He wouldn't write history that hadn't yet happened. If that was the case, Adam and Eve would have known all about their sin before they even committed it. The "word" John spoke about was not the Bible. But hadn't I heard the pastor at church say that the Bible was the infallible word of God? What was the word John was talking about?*

I looked at the text, read on about the word becoming flesh and dwelling among us. I skimmed through the whole three chapters and realized that this "word" was Jesus. Jesus was there in the beginning with God. Jesus *is* God! He is God's son, but he's not just that—John said that Jesus *is* God.

"No way," I said. I returned to the letter.

If you're still as smart as you always were, and if Jesus is in you, then you got it, and it's blowing your mind right now, isn't it? It took me a while to get it, too, and that's because nobody pointed it out for me. Well, now you know. I'm sure that when you accepted Christ, you accepted the reality that this son of God, with this mysterious and indescribable love, took the wrath of God's punishment on himself on the cross. I'm sure you felt how special that was, but now you know that Jesus was not just a man…he was and is the living God. Give him glory, son.

I did. Sweet, glorious praise. My heart took flight.

Go ahead and finish the book. Take as much time as you want. You can read a chapter a day or the whole thing at once, but make sure you're paying attention because the enemy is crafty. He'll try to distract you and turn your mind to other things, things of this world, to keep you from enjoying the rich blessings of what the Lord wants to reveal to you. So many people will tell you that God is mysterious and we can't fully understand him, that there's things about himself that he deliberately withholds from us because we can't handle the full weight of the truth of who he is. Don't you dare believe that. Jesus himself tells us that he is there to reveal the Father. Everything he knows we will know as well, and that's what the entire Bible is for. Soak it up, son. In your hands is the power of the ages. And if you haven't gotten it in your head, get it there now and see how the whole Bible reveals this—if you have put your trust in Christ, then you have been made the righteousness of God in Christ. You are no longer a sinner. You've been set free.

I thought I couldn't possibly get distracted and bored with what I held in my hands. Dad talked about being distracted by the things of the world. *What world?* I thought. *The world's over. This is really all I've got.*

Sure enough, he was right. I got through ten chapters before my butt started to hurt from how I was sitting. I tried to change positions, but I just got restless. I set it aside, trying not to feel guilty for being bored. But I did, and I spent several long minutes praying that God would forgive my weakness. When I finished, I felt good that I had done my part, but I didn't feel any less bored.

You've been set free, Dad said.

"Am I right to feel guilty for being bored?" I prayed aloud. The Lord didn't respond. "If I'm righteous, then whose condemnation am I under?"

I sighed and set the Bible down. I was disappointed that the excited energy had worn off, but I was even more perplexed that I could still feel accused when there shouldn't be anything more to accuse me of. Again, the words were in my mind: *You've been set free*. What strange, ironic comfort in such a time and place as this. I wasn't sure how to wear it, and I hoped I'd learn.

Days and weeks began to pass. I began to feel cabin fever, and even the twice-weekly trips for supplies from the Nortons couldn't suppress it. I had finally grown comfortable in my surroundings. There was nothing new under the dim sun, nothing to fear. Daily I tried to pick up a signal on the radio—AM, FM, CB. Nothing but fuzz. It didn't sound as hopeful anymore.

I needed exercise, so I began a daily routine. I started off easy—two sets of ten pushups, one in the morning, the other in the evening. Then, two sets of twenty-five crunches. They burned a bit, but they started to get easy. I started running laps around my house and the Nortons' in a figure-eight pattern. It sufficiently fatigued me and gave me a more satisfying rest at night. I wished I could run like I used to—up Grant, then on Roanoke to Evans, from there, all the way up to Woodstone and back—but even if I could conquer the fear, I'd easily get lost. For me, it was a significant achievement just to get out of my underground confines and bite my thumb at the darkness.

Over time, the purple began to fade into a dark gray. The sky took on that ominous hue of a supercell, a thunderstorm with a wall cloud from which a tornado would drop any moment. The random swirling was more noticeable and pronounced. I was reminded of that scene in *Raiders of the Lost Ark* when Indiana Jones and company were opening the chamber where the ark was and the sky overhead was boiling because God had shown up and wasn't happy. It was a fearsome sight, all the more frightening in that was the sky had been doing this the whole time above my head—it had just been too dark for me to see.

Increased sunlight meant longer days. I called the time the light first appeared "sunrise," although I knew the sun actually breached the horizon the same time it always had in March. Same went for sundown. But former rules no longer applied. Thus, sunrise by the middle of March was at 9:30 a.m., sunset at 4:00.

My biorhythms had begun to adjust as soon as I found the flashlight. No longer was I this lost, bumbling idiot in the dark. The day I cracked open the Bible, I began to slip into spiritual maturity. It was gradual. In fact, I didn't notice it was happening at first. I had started as a baby, soaking everything up, collecting, receiving, learning how to trust God to be my sole sufficiency, putting one foot in front of the other with painstaking deliberation. Each step forward was a game-changing victory. I had unchained myself from the walls of the cave and taken that first step out into the world.

With God's word in my hands, I began to think clearly for the first time in my life. The questions came on so fast that I didn't know how to put them into words, and I found the answer each time at the foot of the cross. Everything Christ's ministry on earth was about could be found at Calvary, and Dad was there to point out the markings on the trail. Over time, however, the empty tomb began to call me nearer. There was a hope there, beckoning.

I finished John in less than two days. At the end, Dad left a note telling me to explore the other Gospels. He explained what each author was trying to accomplish. *Why did there need to be four?* he asked me, standing in for my own inquiring mind. Each one, he told me, provided a different perspective on this man, each one focused on a particular aspect of his identity. It wasn't so that they could debate each other, as if one was more right than the other; it was to add depth and clarity to what the other three had said. It was called the "harmony of the Gospels."

But the entire Bible has harmony, Dad said. *And if you think you catch God's word in a mistake, that there's something in there that doesn't jibe with the rest of it, give it a chance to prove you're wrong. I guarantee that you'll find the problem is not with the Bible, but with your own understanding. Don't worry. God won't leave you in the dark.*

My journey continued. I didn't think Dad would ever let me get into the Old Testament. I'm a cover-to-cover reader, but that's apparently not how this was supposed to work. He knew I would be having difficulty at the end of my journey through Luke, the last of the Gospels I read. He wrote, *You're dying to go to Genesis, aren't you? I know how you work. You want to treat this book like any other book you read. It's killing you that I won't let you do your math, isn't it?*

"What does that mean?" I said. Then I laughed—loudly. I forgot he knew about that. I used to assign myself a book a week, making an ambitious project out of what other people do for pleasure. The schedule never wavered. I started on Sunday, ended on Saturday, reading an equal portion each day. This obsessive routine often kept me faithful to finish even the most boring, useless stuff I could pick up. It ensured that even if the book was horrible I would still get through it. Dad caught me doing my calculations on a sheet of paper one Sunday afternoon and asked me what I was doing. He had to goad it out of me, but I eventually told him. He laughed until he cried.

"You are an unending joy," he said when he had recovered.

But I couldn't do the Bible that way. This was "Choose Your Own Adventure," although the adventure had been chosen for me before the foundation of the world. So I finished Luke. Dad told me to read Acts through the Epistles, "but skip Hebrews for now. Trust me, you'll know why later."

"Okay," I said, hoping he—and I—wouldn't forget to hit it eventually. I hated doing it out of order, but he had his reasons, I supposed.

LEAVING THE CAVE

Earlier, I had mentioned unchaining myself from the wall and leaving the cave. Freshmen at Drury had a mandatory yearlong course called "Alpha Seminar." It was supposed to be our introduction to academic discourse, the fabled "marketplace of ideas." We read literature and essays that ran the gamut of all subjects, the objective being to turn us from mindless public school automatons into independent critical thinkers. We wrote our own essays and thought-pieces—reactions to our assignments, maybe. Research papers here and there. The class was occasionally interesting. Really, it depended on what we were reading. Our Alpha teacher was a business professor. Once, he had us watch the movie *Wall Street* and write a ten-page paper about it. I had a hard time finding the relevance.

One of our reading assignments meant a lot more to me than the rest, though—Plato's "Allegory of the Cave." The point of it was that humanity dwells in darkness, seeing shadows cast upon the wall, until one brave soul breaks away from the pack, goes exploring out there in the great beyond to see what's casting the shadows, and comes back to tell the rest of us what it's all about. We had to write a two-page essay on why we even read this as college freshman. I thought it was obvious, but not everybody in the class got it. My summation was that we have a choice: Do we remain in the cave, or do we choose to be the one to leave it and step into the light of truth?

On a day when many people would have been rushing to turn in their taxes, I had to leave the cave. It was a small step out to find a tiny sliver of truth, but my world was going to change. It was April 15, and my stash from the Nortons had finally run out. I had rationed the food to last me until May, but my appetite had increased from my exercising, something I hadn't counted on. Thus, I was back where I had been three months previous, wondering where my next meal would come from and fearing I'd never eat again.

How much more will he clothe you? I told myself, Luke 12:28 suddenly popping into my brain.

"How about that?" I marveled at my new ability to use Scripture. It was a proud moment, but it was fleeting. I was starving for something to eat. I thirsted, too. It was amazing how quickly those feelings set in when my supply was out, and they were magnified by the constant coating of ash on my tongue, drying me out. The distilled water was entirely gone, as were the supply from both toilets and the cases of bottled water. I hadn't brushed my teeth in a week, making the case pretty overwhelming again for a cavity.

But that verse gave me hope. The Holy Spirit had put it in my mind exactly when I needed it, and so I prayed, "Lord, you told me not to even worry about where my next meal would come from, that you would supply my needs in abundance. I take you at your word. Lead me to food and water as you have promised."

Walk down the street, he told me. *Stick to this side of it. Stop at the first basement you find. Bring the blanket to tote back what you find. You will not get lost.*

The sun had just come up—9:20 this morning, unless the watch-clock was getting slow. I had no point of reference, unfortunately, but I took cheer in the possibility that the day was getting longer. I wrapped the blanket around me, tied it off, and hopped over the wall.

I passed the Nortons' in short order, but after that it was like I had stepped right into the middle of the desert. The visibility had improved, but my view hadn't. I could see perhaps a half a mile in every direction, beyond Evans Road to my left, beyond the end of Grant ahead of me. In no way, however, could I see any distinguishing feature of the landscape but the subtle rises and dips of hills and valleys, miniscule in size compared to the Ozarks of Southwestern Missouri. I hadn't realized how bland this part of the state was before, and the sky was such a mixture of pale and dark grays that at times I wasn't sure where it ended and the land began.

"Just focus on what's immediately in front of you," I thought I could hear Sara say. She had begun to pop in and out, just her voice. I pictured the beautiful lower soprano of it, as if she would begin singing at any time. It was a comfort to me, even if it wasn't really there, much like picturing Dad's voice speaking to me in his letters. I had accepted that she was dead—in body, at least, but I could still hope that her spirit was alive and cheering me on.

"Yes, love," I said; to God, "I trust you."

I stepped away from the familiar confines of the Nortons' yard. I had a strip of sheet from home tied around my head as a bandanna to keep the dust from billowing into my mouth and choking me. I was very thirsty. I didn't want anything to steal the little spit I had at that time.

I shuffled forward at a slow gait, glancing back to see my footprints fading slowly in the wind. I pictured the street as it had been. After the Nortons' would be the Brents' house—no basement. I thought of that beautiful family of three in their final moments in the cul-de-sac. I hoped they didn't feel any pain. The fire burned so hot that if they did, surely it was only for a moment. Then, paradise. They were believers, praise God. They were home now, no doubt enjoying the perfect presence of the Lord with Sara, Katie, and Mom and Dad. My eyes were too dry to cry.

Past the Brents' was that new family I hadn't met. They moved in after I went to college. Mom said their name once, but I didn't catch it. I didn't care. I was too caught up in my new college life. The Codys used to live there. I had only been in the house once, when I was a little kid and had come over to watch *Teenage Mutant Ninja Turtles* with Chris. They said they didn't have a basement, and I thought that was weird because I thought every family had.

Next door, Mrs. George. She was ancient before I was even born, a very sweet old lady whose husband died in the Korean War. She had never remarried, never had kids, never even had other relatives that I knew of, but she came to every neighborhood gathering as the most honored guest. We were all her children and grandchildren. We dared each other when we were kids to sneak by her house without getting caught and invited to have some pie. While our parents taught us never to trust strangers, they said in her case it was always okay to make an exception.

I had never been inside her house. I had seen the inside from the front porch, but only to see a living room decorated with small hand bells from countries around the world and various figurines and old-lady knick-knacks. There was a kitchen beyond that, where all the good smells under heaven came from. But she was mindful to keep us kids out on the porch. She knew what we had been taught. Her house, then, was a mystery to me.

And on tax day, I almost fell into her basement. I caught myself and stared into its yawning opaque-from-above blackness for a while before taking the plunge. My heart beat rapidly, and I prayed for the bravery it was going to require. I imagined, as I had before, the monsters hiding out in there, ready to sneak out and attack from below. I had nothing on me to defend myself—

maybe I could throw the blanket on them and momentarily blind them as I ran back home. But they'd find me.

"Lord, I trust that you would not have sent me out here if you didn't mean it. You don't play games, you don't trick me, and you only have my best in mind. Dad wasn't a mean-spirited practical joker, and neither are you. I believe."

I hopped in.

I had the flashlight with me. It hadn't been very practical along the way. It shone for a few feet around me at times, but the light was quickly dispersed and scattered by ash, so I had shut it off. It came in handy again down there, however. I sent it around the room, saw closets, dressers, a sofa, some chairs, a card table, an old rear-projection television set. She had quilts and blankets that I could use for fresh bedding, and I found some toiletry supplies like deodorant and toothpaste in the bathroom. While the former was the feminine variety, nevertheless I thought it would serve me better than my own foul stench, which I still had not gotten used to. These all were tremendous pleasures but didn't serve the needs of the moment.

I was starting to feel a chill in my bones from my empty stomach, a dizziness to my head as well. I craved foods I had never before enjoyed—my last meal was a can of black-eyed peas from the Nortons', and it was bliss. I would take anything she had. I searched through every drawer and cabinet door I could find, but it didn't reveal anything. I reviewed where I had been and where I hadn't, recounting and recovering the tracks I had already made in the carpet of ash. I found photo albums, keepsakes, a couple of medals her husband had won posthumously, and the case that displayed the flag she received at her husband's funeral. These mementos were so eerie. I felt like I was exploring the *Titanic*.

"This is all nice and poignant, God, but I don't need memories and keepsakes! Am I to eat the furniture? Is that what you sent me out to do? 'Consider the ravens?' *They* don't even eat like this!"

Look! he said.

"What? What is it?"

I turned the flashlight back around the room and saw a door with a lever handle. It had one of those sweeping rubber mats attached at bottom that kept the room insulated. The door was so obvious that I couldn't believe I had missed it, but I hadn't been seeing clearly. *Right, Dad?* I asked in my mind. I sounded like I was seven.

Right, bud, but I don't always see very well myself.

I smiled and said, "Maybe you don't play tricks, but I still think you're enjoying yourself too much."

Unlike the rest of the basement, this room had been dug in so that the earth was its roof, so it was perfectly preserved. I had spent at least a half hour crashing about without seeing it. I had actually worked up a sweat in spite of the starving chill in my bones. I opened the door and found a walk-in pantry that would keep me well fed for another two months.

———

Over time, I would go out on excursions up and down the street. There were four other basements on my street, but the only ones with food were the ones I've mentioned. Mrs. Taylor, across the street and up one house from Mrs. George, was another ancient widow, kind of a batty old thing that we had all tried to avoid, although I got on well with her grandson, Jacob, most of the time. Once, when I was six, Jacob and I were playing too rough and I accidentally popped him good in the nose and made it bleed. My parents took me down there with them to apologize personally to Mrs. Taylor, and she softened after that. I was always welcome, but I didn't take advantage of the welcome very often.

Jacob lived there every other month. I don't know why. I never questioned it. I was a kid and thus took it for granted. He had a room in the basement. He and I lost touch in junior high, but as far as I knew, even after high school, he dropped in to stay a week every once in a while. He looked after his grandma when her

Alzheimer's set in, but eventually they put her in a nursing home two months before the blast. Mom told me that she thought he'd put the house on the market, but he hadn't yet moved anything out of it.

I hoped to find clothes in his room. He was six inches taller than me by the time we graduated, but I didn't care whether or not they fit me. I was just tired of hanging uncomfortably loose in my makeshift robe. When I got down to his room, though, I found that he had already moved out everything he owned except for a Cardinals pennant and signed Albert Pujols photo on the wall. *Wonder how much that would fetch?* I thought sarcastically.

I did find clothes, however, and I had to laugh. They were Mrs. Taylor's. She liked pantsuits, most of them blues, pinks, and purples. They looked *fine* on her. After I got to know her, they made her look downright fun and cosmopolitan, a social butterfly with a sharp wit who had no patience for children and childishness. Yeah, she wore them well.

But me?

Still, it beat being naked and overexposed. "Solomon himself never had it so good, right, Jesus?" I said as I began to slip them on.

I had grown so thin that I could actually zip up the pants around my waist. It was a snug fit, but they'd stay on, at least. I left the suit jackets behind and decided to wear the shirts only occasionally. The ash layered on the pants hid the flamboyant colors, to my great relief, and regardless, it was so dark most of the time that I soon didn't care what they looked like on me.

She didn't keep her underwear in the basement, a blessing in hindsight because I most certainly would have worn it for the added comfort. The pants were just a momentary comfort, something in passing. They kept me wanting better, which kept me willing to explore farther. A few days later, unable to stand the indignity of her wardrobe, I lit out and found a teenage boy's room in the basement of the first house around the corner from

Grant, on Roanoke. It was by any measure the farthest I had yet ventured from my own basement, a journey that on a normal day would have taken me only ten minutes round-trip if I walked fast. On that late-April day, it took me from sunup till sundown, and it was worth every dreaded step.

His wardrobe was a bit young and urban for me—baggy pants and sweatshirts, hats that looked like somebody had spray-painted some nonsense word in a Wingdings font on the front, Converse shoes that *looked* worn and old but weren't. I had to cinch the pants up with a bit of rope from Mr. Norton's tool bench. I wouldn't have ever chosen the clothes for myself in my former life, not even if you paid me. I liked short-sleeved tees in the summer, long-sleeved tees and sweaters in the winter, all tight-fitting so as to make me look much more muscular than I was. But now, when I found this kid's room (I think his name was Ricky), I felt as if I had discovered the wardrobe of the gods.

As I searched through his closets and drawers, I found that his clothes never changed from one season to the next. He had about a hundred sets of the same stuff I had just put on. Either he kept the other stuff elsewhere and was thus spoiled in particular abundance, or this was it. I figured this was it. I had grown up with kids who would dress this way in Tahiti if they ever happened to travel there. The look worked for them, I guess.

The temperature remained muggy and warm; the air, thick. The clothes got stifling, but I didn't want to lose them and wander about in any state of undress. Keeping my shirt on kept the semblance of normalcy and civilization. I wasn't going to give that up. I found a set of giant scissors in Mrs. George's basement that she used to cut fabric; there was evidence she made her own dresses as I saw yards of material on the top shelf of one of her closets. I used the scissors to turn my pants into shorts and cut the sleeves off a few of the sweatshirts. I didn't know if the weather would ever turn cold again, but I kept enough back there that I would be prepared if it did.

May 15. I had just finished reading my Bible for the day. It was two hours after sundown. I had a dinner of kidney beans and corn from Mrs. George's pantry. It settled well enough. I washed it down with soda. Mrs. George liked to have a bottle of Coke on her porch in the summer as she watched us ride our bikes up and down the street. I wasn't surprised to find two cases of it in her basement. I decided only to drink it occasionally. I valued my sleep and didn't want anything to mess it up. My dreams were weird enough without the influence. The caffeine sometimes wound me up enough to be in an in-between state all night where my dreams were more like hallucinations and random people and old pets wandered in and out of the room. I knew better than to believe they were really there.

That night, however, I couldn't convince myself of the caffeine-induced hallucination no matter how hard I tried. I woke up with my eyes still closed, so I heard it before I saw it, a crackling noise with a constant hum in the background. It sounded like the electric sizzle the spaceship made when it powered up and sent the blast. My body went numb immediately.

"God, no," I mouthed, too afraid to make a sound. "Don't let this happen, not again."

Somehow, they had found out. Above my bed and beyond my eyelids, perhaps even above the heavy cloud-cover of ash, I could hear them, poised to send a blast straight down and kill the one who got away. When I was a little kid and had nightmares, I'd wake up petrified, afraid even to move my eyes around the room because of what I might see. Eventually, I'd realize I was awake, the bad things were gone, and I was safe. What do you do when you wake up *into* a nightmare, though?

"Oh Lord," I prayed, "I don't think I'm ready to die."

And why not? Sara asked me. *What do you have to fear?*

I couldn't answer her. Do I fear death? I had been living with the possibility of certain death for six months now. It was just going to be a slow death—starvation, asphyxiation, thirst—take your pick. At least with a new blast from the alien ship, it would be sudden.

No, the real agony of it was hearing that horrid sound and anticipating the blast that hadn't come. It was irregular too, not a constant sizzling but intermittent (although the bursts were frequent, about one every two seconds). Even including the vessel, I had never heard anything like it. And beyond my eyelids, I could see flashes of light that accompanied each sizzle, like they were taking pictures. It reminded me of the cameras they had in period movies where the flash bulbs were these giant light bulbs that exploded every time they took a picture.

"Lord, if you mean for me to die, you would have let it happen already. If this is my time, I still believe you are God of all creation, sovereign over even that thing above me and whatever it's up to. Just remember your promise to me, that you would never leave me nor forsake me. I believe that I will have victory in you over the grave. I'm going to open my eyes. Keep me strong in the face of what I see."

I slowly opened them. For a moment, it was a view as through a blurry glass as my eyelashes and moisture in my eyes distorted the view. In that moment, I thought I saw the oblong object of my nightmares spinning above me.

"I will not relent," I vowed.

I opened them all the way. I didn't see any definite shape above me, but I did see the clouds roiling around in their hellish fury, lit up every few seconds by lightning flashes that spun spider webs across the sky from one hook to another, sizzling and popping each time. There was no thunder, however. It was beyond spooky. I suppose there wasn't enough clear air for the sound to travel. I'm not a science whiz. In fact, everything about this new, scary world flew in the face of common sense.

I smiled. "I shouldn't even be alive," I said to the Lord. I marveled at the natural phenomenon that I was seemingly alone to witness. There was no rain with it, and so far as I knew, the wind wasn't doing anything out of the ordinary. The temperature felt the same, hovering somewhere in the lower seventies, it felt like. If it had lowered or varied at all since the event, I hadn't noticed.

You may have seen the lightning, too. I'm sure it wasn't limited to my location. It didn't touch the earth or dip below the cloud cover much more than a mild swoop here and there. It was so quiet that the sound of it would have gone unnoticed in a normal world, with all the whirrs and whines of our machinery keeping us sedated. In that insufferable low moan of the wind, however, it stuck out.

I read an article once about the Mt. St. Helens eruption of May 1980. Such a fearsome spectacle, it spawned lightning storms minutes after the eruption in towns dozens of miles from the volcano. Witnesses could recall the lightning scorching the earth, the thunder clapping instantaneously with each flash. The phenomenon was the result of all the friction from the ash in the air, the eruption's own self-contained severe weather system. I would have to assume that our ash had also created a friction in the atmosphere that eventually led to the sizzling and popping lightning. But still, no thunder, no bolts hitting the earth. So very, very strange.

My environment lit up with light it had not seen for several months now. I could see the nightstand first of all, a spider with four long legs reaching down into the gray-white of the carpet. On the wall, a picture of some nameless ancestors from over a century ago, their gazes obstinate and stony. It created impish shadows under their eyes and along their chins—looked like fangs. I could see the vague floral print of the wallpaper underneath the ash, could see burn marks dipping down from the tops of the walls in strange, finger-like parabolas. The shifting shadows looked like greedy hands clawing at the clowns on the shelf, threatening to make them move. Their gazes turned maddeningly about the room.

The light bounced off and scattered from every conceivable surface, casting strange and unsettling reflections, and in the innumerable shadows in between, I could see eyes, squinting as if smiling in pleasure as they were about to feast, and I heard their voices: "The god you worship doesn't love you. He cares nothing for you. You're alone here, you have always been. Curse him and die." They were real.

"No, never!"

"And your loved ones, they're with us now. We came for them, we took them to their real home, and they curse you for leaving them to die by our hands. Sara's an especially tasty one."

"That can't be true!" I whispered. The lightning flashing, the spooky environs gave their lies weight, exacerbated them.

"Oh, but it is! All is death, don't you know? If God really loved you, they'd still be here. He wouldn't have let us take them. As it is, he doesn't care."

The prowling lion, seeking to devour, had found his meal. And yet hadn't Jesus told his disciples that they would cast out demons in his name? Had it not been said that Satan is the father of lies, that he speaks no truth? Usually so subtle, he was now showing me all his cards.

Holy Spirit, fill me up, I prayed. *In the name of Jesus Christ, give me courage.*

I was filled with righteous anger. It surged through me all of a sudden, and despite the paralyzing terror induced by the lightning storm and the eyes and glistening sharp teeth shining at me from all directions, I leaped out of bed and charged at the first pair I saw.

"In the name of Jesus, the lamb who was slain, the one who was there before the foundation of the world, depart, all of you. I command you to flee by the power of the one who shed blood on the cross freed me from sin. You have no ground here."

I heard shrieking. I *heard* it. I thought that I would see each pair of eyes blinking out as if I had imagined them, which I still halfway believed at that moment, but instead I saw their eyes close, their teeth gnash in pain. Then, one by one, they rose into the air, screaming. I could see their little dark shapes silhouetted against the light. They looked like cats—ferocious, mutant jungle cats—but it was dark, the light fleeting. They disappeared into the cloud ceiling, but that wasn't enough for me.

"God, give me a sign so that I know they won't return."

I didn't see anything specific, but God is a master showman who has a way of giving you what you want even though you didn't know it. After they went into the clouds, the lightning intensified, but it stayed within the cloud rather than bolts shooting out and around it like before. And I could see the feline silhouettes scattering about in the middle of the air and thought I could hear their shrieks way up there. I saw other shapes, vaguely man-shaped, with great sweeping motions of arms, chopping down, thrusting. Lightning blazed all around as if creation itself was taking place in there, and then I heard thunder, so loud I had to put my hands over my ears.

At this point, I was standing in my baggy, cut-off street clothes in the middle of the basement's main room, looking up and gawking. I was so overcome with the mighty and terrible sight that I fell straight back on my butt, giving it a bruise that would make it hard to sit for a week. Hands still over my ears, I watched as the last of the demons was put to death.

The silence returned and the lightning lasted for hours until a little while before sunrise, when the flashes finally became much more intermittent and dimmer. The sizzle and strobe faded to more infrequent bursts, leaving me mostly in calm silence. I had stayed awake all night, too awestruck to sleep. When I got around, I cracked open the Bible and read it for the next ten hours straight, stopping only to use the bathroom. I'm reminded of Romans 8:38–39. Dad had a note on that part: *Memorize this verse. There will be countless instances in your life where this truth will move mountains. Believe it.* This was what the passage said: "I am convinced that neither death, nor life, nor angels, nor principalities, nor things present, nor things to come, nor powers, nor height, nor depth, nor any other created thing, will be able to separate us from the love of God, which is in Christ Jesus our Lord."

"Amen," I whispered and laughed as I considered what I had witnessed the night before. I know it was weird. I'm tempted to disbelieve it, to pass it off as an especially vivid dream, but, friend, I couldn't. I know that God usually doesn't work in such visible signs and wonders, that he is a hushed whisperer, a gentle, kind God, but I saw what I saw. There was nothing subtle about it. I know there are invisible powers at work in an unseen realm all around us, but for that moment, God peeled back the layer a little to show me where the fight really is and where I believe it may continue to take place as we move forward. I wouldn't blame you a bit if you don't believe this episode really happened; I just hope your disbelief won't cast aspersion on how you feel about the rest of my experience. I *would* blame you for that (don't misunderstand me—I write this with a smile); look around you, friend. The normal rules for the real world no longer apply. *That* you should know by now.

⟶⇥⬥⇤⟵

Despite the tremendous victory over the enemies that night, I didn't want to be kept awake by the lightning anymore. I found a hacksaw at the Nortons' and used it to cut away chunks of their walls. I didn't measure but also didn't feel like it was that important. I intended just to build a rudimentary roof over the bedroom so I could sleep peacefully at night with no disturbance. Mr. Norton also had a hammer and nails, of course. I spent the daylight hours of the next day putting it up, the flashing of the lightning providing ample light to see what I was doing.

It gave me quite a fright to see the landscape lit up like that. The lightning provided far greater visibility than I had had so far, but it played with my imagination, too, casting strange shadows to make things rise, walk, and fall across the desolation. I thought I could see great black beasts lumbering on the plain, stalking and searching, and then they'd disappear. It also gave the appearance of holes in the ground opening and then closing. I'd wonder if they were basements that I should consider exploring only to see them close back up. *It's going to be impossible to navigate now*, I thought. I'd have to know *exactly* where I was going and what I was going to find once I got there.

Part of me also wondered if I was seeing more beasties along the lines of what I had seen the night before. They were silent this time, however. The fact that they were silent convinced me they weren't really there, that it was my imagination. But I also thought that, by their silence, they were perhaps speaking *volumes* at me.

I hammered away in spite of the distraction, looking forward to getting below the makeshift ceiling to see if it was going to work.

It did. That night, I slept the sleep of the dead. Vague, dim flashes crept in around the corners and through cracks in my crude construction, but I didn't hear that sizzling and popping, nor did I see anything lurking in the darkness. Something told me those little devils might be gone for good after what I sicced on them.

A MOST UNSEEMLY MEAL

I found a day-by-day planning calendar on Mom's desk in the growing light. It was a rather boring item—no words of inspiration or scriptural references in the whole thing, just the calendar date, phase of the moon, or holiday, if it applied. It was turned to December 12 when I found it, the day of the attack. Mom had written down her plans for the day. One of them was to make spaghetti for me that night when she got home, my favorite meal.

I flipped back through, found other things on her lists that would have been mundane to anybody else. They'd have been mundane to me too, but after the event, I longed for those chores. I flipped past each page, finding them woefully blank. She hadn't made any long-term plans, but she never did. *Sufficient for you are the things of today*, I thought.

I used the calendar to start keeping track of the days as they passed and forsook my antiquated tick-mark system. I also used it as a journal, writing in shorthand the events of the day, what I had learned along the way. I carry those pages with me now to remind me of where I came from. Hopefully they'll tell me where I'm going.

When I flipped over into May 30, a switch flipped and bombs exploded in my head. I sat down overcome in Mom's office chair. *Sara's birthday*, I thought, and I went to the bookcase. There was nothing else I wanted to do but look at photo albums and cry, and I did.

Under the Maglite, I relived the years and memories, even the ones that weren't mine, like my parents' wedding and Katie's baby photos. I longingly caressed my hand across their images. I could feel their smiles, the heat from the light in their eyes. Their spirits were still strong. They felt *alive*.

And they are, I told myself. *They're just not here.*

I spent the entire day at it. I laughed when I saw the pitiful pictures of me with chicken pox when I was two or when I wasn't even a year old yet and had managed to turn a bowl of spaghetti over onto my head. There were pictures of Katie teaching me how to roller-skate in the kitchen floor. A picture of my first black eye Mom had taken of me on a float trip. Pictures of me and my high school sweetheart Rachel on a band trip and at prom.

Then, that last album, the one I took my time with, crying fat drops that splashed across the Mylar pages. It was from the last couple of years, starting from when Sara came down to stay with us at Christmas the first year of our relationship. In the first one, she still looked green from the drive, but she was smiling, those sweet, beautiful, perfectly white and straight teeth brighter than the sun, her lips bee-stung and begging to be kissed. She had straightened her normally curly hair that week. I thought I had died and gone to my own personal heaven when I saw the results.

We had just walked through the door. Mom had her camera ready, and she snapped pictures almost before we had a chance to pose, so Sara looked a bit chagrined by it, but the smile was genuine. She was adorable. I wanted to hold her so badly. She never let me get *too* close to her, but there were a couple of times when her body touched mine. I remembered how soft she could be, how much life was just under that skin. I'll bet we would have made beautiful babies.

But what did it gain to dwell on something that no longer was? How do I take the best of something without feeling at my worst that it was gone and could no longer be? When I finally closed the last album and put it back on the shelf, I cried for hours and fell asleep in the floor.

Gosh, all this bawling! When I was a little kid, it always felt better after I cried when I got hurt from falling off my bike or some other inevitable accident. This didn't feel good. I only felt emptier. *I've got to quit on this*, I thought. *It's done.*

I left the albums aside and enjoyed some Chef Boyardee. It calmed my nerves; it stifled the sobs. It was the last of such food that I had gotten from Mrs. George. Ravioli. I had no idea why she had it. I amused myself with thoughts that the reason she was so sweet to us all those years was to try to entice us into her house, after which she would fatten us up with some of our favorite nutritionless microwaveable foods and then have us for dinner.

Either that or perhaps she just liked überprocessed foods. Such meals still wrought havoc with my digestive system. I forgot at times to supplement them with cereal or some other fibrous item. Mrs. George had some Mueslix and bran cereal in her stash. I kept leaving it aside because it was as boring to eat as watching paint dry. I'd learn my lesson eventually, I supposed.

At the beginning of June, I found myself with only a week's worth of food left from Mrs. George's. Unfortunately, I had not yet found another basement food pantry. Mrs. George had some distilled as well as bottled water in her basement. I had rationed it to last as long as my food, meaning I spent most of my days in uncomfortable thirst and with a parched throat. My voice came and went.

The days were getting longer, just a few hours shorter than they normally would have been with a clear sky. I could almost see a horizon. It was still tropically warm outside. It depended on how the wind was blowing on a given day. It didn't blow with the same constant gale force anymore; rather, it seemed it was starting to follow an irregular schedule, much like weather patterns used to do. Some weeks, it kicked up the ash to the point of total whiteout; others, it was comparatively still, ten miles an hour at the most.

There was no rain, and I began to accept the possibility there may never be again. The fire surely vaporized our planet's water with everything else. I couldn't be sure, but I thought the clouds above me and circling around me were 100 percent ash, kicked up by the worst extinction-level event of all time. It had put out the sun and boiled all of existence away. Were anybody to happen by our planet looking for a place that would support life, they would leave it be without taking a look behind.

I didn't even have a cockroach to keep me company. I would have thought I'd see at least that much. At least I had the mold on the bread from the Nortons' a few months ago to convince me there was still such a thing as life. If I had seen a bug or a mouse by the time I got to the third week of June, I'd have eaten it without a thought.

I had been up and down the street and to a few houses on Roanoke. To find another food source, I'd have to go farther, potentially far enough to lose all sense of place. I wasn't ready for that, but I knew it had to be done. I was thrown into an involuntary fasting. It was time to increase my prayers, and I did.

By this time, I had worked my way through most of the New Testament. I read further proof that in Christ, I have victory over sin and death, that nothing could separate me from his perfect love, that nothing could affect my standing with him.

If you've trusted, then you're a saint now, Dad wrote. *You'll fall short, yes, but that is no longer your nature, so quit apologiz-*

ing so much. I laughed. He knew I'd have a problem with that. Every time I got tired or somehow couldn't pay attention to the Scripture I was reading, I'd feel the need to repent and beg God's forgiveness as if I had somehow done something unthinkable. But Dad told me along the way to be careful I don't try to read too much for my own concentration. *Some of the food God gives us is very rich, and we have to eat it in smaller bites. You'll definitely get full quick in Revelation. Count on it.*

I prayed to the God who had promised to meet all my needs. When I got to Hebrews, Dad told me to mark my place and read the Old Testament. He guided me to the story of Elijah and a part when the prophet had to hide from his enemies in a cave. He didn't know where his food was going to come from, but he trusted God to provide and God sent ravens to him, bearing pieces of meat to feed him as he hid. I prayed that God would bring me my own ravens. I had no conceivable source of food; thus, I relied on the inconceivable eternal God to keep me safe.

But each day started to pass and I got nothing. The thirst and hunger began to increase, making me dizzy at first. Then, I began hallucinating again, seeing things that didn't make sense. My temperature rose and fell as my body started to exhaust all it had left, all the fat and then muscle. The thirst was exacerbated by the ash on my tongue and in my throat. The constant coughing burned calories I didn't have and couldn't replace.

A memory flashed through my mind: I was eight and wanted a Nintendo. I wanted it so bad it was killing me. The worst part about it was that every one of my friends had one and talked about their games, shared cheat codes and tips for passing levels. I was increasingly ostracized on the playground as they played their games together. It sounds silly now, but back then, it was a matter of life and death to have one of these things. Finally, in February of that year, I gave up on trying to play along. They told me if I couldn't name all the characters and what their special moves were, then I couldn't join. I didn't stand a chance.

"Please, I can learn!" I said.

Danny, the potty-mouthed, uncontested bully of the bunch, said something foul. Translation: "Buzz off!" Then he pushed me so hard that I fell down on my butt in the mud. The other kids laughed. The teacher on duty that recess didn't see. Sure, I could have told him, but that would have earned me only further, more enduring rebukes from my peers. I had no choice. I got up, dusted myself off as best I could, and went to sit on one of the railroad ties that bordered the playground. I tried my best not to cry. It was the hardest thing I'd ever had to do.

Thankfully, they played on the other side of the playground, at least a football field away from me. Every once in a while, Danny looked over at me and sneered. It felt like everybody in the whole world hated me. I took it in and turned it back outward as resentment against my parents for not getting me the Nintendo.

They eventually did, a year later when it wasn't such a big deal anymore. In fact, it seemed that I was suddenly ostracized for playing it *too* much. Now all the other boys were consumed with sports; some even chased girls in a phase of explosive prepubescence.

But I fell in love with the Nintendo anyway and decided it was a better friend than the ones at school. At least when I played it I could be master of my own destiny through the characters and avatars and wonderful stories I discovered. I started writing stories based on the games in a notebook. Those eventually inspired original ideas. Three years later, I took up a new hobby: reading. It didn't entirely replace video games, as the disappointment I suffered on my thirteenth birthday reminded me, but it slowly became prevalent to the exclusion of almost everything else in my life. Writing turned into a lifelong passion, all because God had faithfully answered my prayers for a Nintendo, but in his timing and for his own purposes.

I held on to that as my hunger pangs took on an unprecedented severity. I cannot recount exactly what all took place during that time. I do know that I tried to read my Bible, and certain things came through—stories of David escaping Saul and then practicing mercy with him in return, the wisdom of Solomon in Ecclesiastes and Proverbs, but it all came through in a fog. My fears of what lay out there, beyond our block, just would not succumb to the need for survival.

On June 24, for the first time, I went to the mirror. I had avoided looking at my reflection since the blast. Mercifully, it was as if a gray blanket had been draped over it, but I wiped it away to take a look at myself and couldn't believe the horror that stared back at me.

I looked like a concentration camp survivor. My eyes bulged, my cheeks were sunken, bones standing out like the points of daggers. I took off my shirt and saw my ribs practically on the outside of my skin. I breathed in slow desperate gasps through my mouth. Something rattled in my throat when I exhaled. My hair had grown out to considerable length over the past several months. I had a beard now—bushy, tangled, long. Were it not for the malnourishment, I would have thought I was John the Baptist, wandering through the wilderness, eating locusts.

I would kill *for a locust right now*, I thought.

I could see spots on the edges of my vision. I thought they were just phantom illusions, more hallucinations come to pay me a visit, but as I glanced around and tried to blink them away, I saw they weren't going.

I had thought they were gone for good after our first encounter, but Dad had written, *Be sure that you are ever wary about the presence of evil in this world. Yes, you have been given the power to cast it out, but the devil still reigns for a time over the earth and over the air because God has allowed it so that man may still have the choice. Yes, he will be gone forever someday, but until then, guard your house with a constant sense of alertness. He catches us in our moments of greatest weakness.*

"Ryan, you poor thing. Look at you! What's happened?"

I fell to the floor, and they followed me, surrounding me. I looked at them, could see them in better detail with the flashlight shining there underneath my bedroom roof. Their smiles were without deceit; they looked genuine. They still had that strange catlike shape, but I thought I could almost see kindness in their eyes.

How do I judge between good and evil? I prayed.

I tried to speak and tell them I was dying of thirst and starvation, but I couldn't get my weak tongue to move. It didn't matter. They intuited what I was about to say. They pretended they hadn't been watching me, but they knew what had gone on.

"He let you down again, didn't he? Told you he would provide and then left you to die. How often does this happen, really? How many disappointments have you had? He told you not to worry, that he was taking care of things, and you trust him and now this…"

"I can't trust you either," I whispered.

"No, you can't. Can't really trust anybody, can you? Nobody but yourself. But where's that going to get you now?"

"Nowhere," I said.

"Nowhere, that's right. But there *is* a way out, Ryan. There always is."

"The pills are gone," I said.

"*Yours* are, yes, but what about the other basements? You haven't looked in their medicine cabinets lately, have you?"

"Just for toothpaste, floss, and deodorant," I said.

"What about painkillers?"

"I haven't needed them since my healing."

"Aren't you in pain?"

Yes, I thought.

"Don't you want to die?"

Yes.

"Ryan?"

"Didn't you hear me? I said—"

Didn't they hear me?

I suddenly realized they hadn't. Dad wrote, *God is the only omniscient being that exists. The devil can't read your thoughts. He'll try, yes, and he'll definitely put thoughts in your head, but he never really knows what's going on in there. That's why you have to tell him out loud to bug off.*

"Wouldn't it be so easy just to walk over to the Nortons', see what's there, end your misery? You weren't meant to live, Ryan. No one was. You're just living on borrowed time."

Their voices sounded so kind, so soothing. One of them actually began to purr. Scenes from Job passed through my head where his friends offered comfort but really fostered malcontent.

"It would be very easy," I said.

There was murmured assent from the pride of demonic cats.

"But Jesus never said it would always be easy. Just that life was going to be *good* and abundant. And that he would send his Holy Spirit to comfort me, and that he would fight for me."

I found strength then, that curious fount of it from within that never absolutely went away but just lay dormant in my dark hours like it had until then. It was *always* there. It woke me up, just enough to speak a rebuke that would clear them out. I did so, out loud, in his name, by his authority, and the forces of good in the spiritual realm of this universe banished those rotten, foul beasts from my presence. As they fled, I heard their shrieking and smelled the stench of death. It was so overwhelming that it made me gag. There was nothing to throw up, though. The spasms passed, and I felt quieted.

And I was so very, very weak. As quickly as it had come, the strength was gone. My spirit was at peace, but my body was finished. No hallucinations, no voices, no dreams, just rest. I lay curled up on the floor, waiting to die and meet God face-to-face at last. It had been a good run, these six months. I did not consider the time wasted. It was a blessing to have had any time at all in which to learn about God and build upon the foundation of a right relationship with him. I had not made it through the entire Bible yet, but I'd learn the rest of the story and then some in eternity.

I stole a line from the Savior: "Father, into your hands, I commend my spirit."

"Ryan, don't you dare!" Sara shouted at me from somewhere far off. Actually, it wasn't quite like that. She sounded like a train coming straight at me going a hundred miles an hour, blasting its whistle. I snapped awake.

She wasn't alive. I knew that full well. But the God of wonders had used my best feelings and memories of who she was to minister to me in the darkness and keep me going, speaking through her voice. It wasn't her who was really speaking to me. It was *him.* Jesus really meant it when he said the church was his body because she was one of a handful of people I knew who represented him almost entirely without fault.

"Get up and walk," she said.

"Where?" I asked.

No response.

Dad wrote, *Sometimes it seems like God is silent because the answer is actually right in front of you.*

"In front of me how?" I asked as I slowly fought off the fog and vapor of death and sat up. *There's nothing here!*

"Walk, and do it in faith," Dad said.

I had been lying at the foot of the bed. I used the bedposts to pull myself up. It felt like I was climbing a thin strip of twine on the edge of a cliff, fingers straining to keep hold. Slowly, inch-by-inch, I was able to ease myself into a hunched-over standing position. I propped myself up with my hand on the bedpost. I stood there a while, tempted to fall back asleep as the downy comfort of the bed beckoned to me, but I knew I had to turn and walk.

I was scared to take that step, so sure was I that I was going to die, and if I was going to die, I'd rather it be here, under the ceiling, protected from exposure in the one thing resembling a normal habitation that I still had in this world.

Jesus called me to leave the boat and come out and meet with him on the waves. I remembered the story of him and Peter from the Gospels.

"Picture him in front of you, beckoning you onward," Sara suggested.

I did, and there he was. The image was my imagination, but the reality of his presence was not. I could feel him. He offered his hand. I took it. His grip was strong. His face was set and determined. He did not smile. He looked like he was preparing himself for a fight. I remembered the monster from my earliest memories, that beard, that smile, that reassuring voice.

I walked step by agonizing step into the hallway, then into the den. He gave me a hand as I stepped onto the sofa, which for the past few weeks had been my perch to go outside. I reached above to the ground and tried to pull myself up but couldn't even get my feet off the cushions. The Lord got behind me, put his hands on my backside, and pushed. Then, he was above me, pulling even as he pushed behind me. When I was prostrate on the ground, ash getting into my mouth and making me cough, he put his hands under my arms and picked me up. He turned me so that I was bent over and, facing the ground, gave me a tremendous slap on the back to get the ash out of my throat.

Through my weakened vision, I could see my toilet heap. The wind blew mercifully in the other direction, as I think the smell of it then, even if only slight, would have put me under. Jesus turned me away from it. I was still bent over, his arm still around me, but he nudged me to stand up straight and look. Like I said, visually it was only in my mind that he was there doing the things I'm saying, but I could feel him there with me every step of the way—my ever-present help in time of need.

As I lifted my head and my eyes, I looked across the street…I saw nothing. There was a dip in the landscape, but nothing more. But he pushed me all the same.

Walk, came the quietest whisper.

"The answer is right in front of you," Dad said.

I had nothing left but faith and trust. I walked in them both, step-by-step across the street. I stumbled as the hill descended more rapidly than it looked, for all around me, the concepts of distance and depth were a cruel joke my eyes played on me. I fell and rolled down the hill into what used to be the street. Thinking back on it later, I realized the incredible fact that not even the asphalt road remained after the blast. Nothing withstood it aboveground, absolutely nothing.

I hit hard on my bony hip when I rolled to a stop, but nothing cracked or broke. I had a bruise later but was gloriously spared of anything that wouldn't heal back unaided. The sharp pain sent needles to my brain. I breathed through my teeth and could feel the swirling ash coating them as I inhaled. It snapped me briefly out of my clouded mind. Tears of pain came to my eyes. I was surprised there was enough water there. I saw stars, but when they faded, I saw clearly.

It was brightening outside to the level of a wintry overcast day. The view was good but still disconcerting, as a whiteout may happen with a sudden gust of wind. I got back to my feet and walked on, and that's when I could see where I had been going. Although I had been up and down the street numerous times with the flashlight, I hadn't yet seen the basement the neighbors had across the street. I had completely forgotten they had one. I had never set foot in it. They were quiet folks who kept to themselves, never invited anybody over, never came to the neighborhood socials. I think the husband was in sales. He was gone most of the time. Their basement was hidden behind a hill. I remembered you had to get around back of the house even to see it. I hadn't because I didn't remember to look.

I thought I could see some papery objects scattered about the top of the hill; they were blown out from the basement. They were different colors, like construction paper. Upon closer inspection, I found them to be napkins for different occasions—Christmas, Valentine's Day, etc. I remembered then that the wife was a party planner. Mom always found that odd. She planned parties but never attended them herself. The napkins were a blessing, laying there as they were. They gave me something to fix my eyes on, something to walk toward and judge my distance; they also gave me hope there might be something edible in the basement, even if it was those awful mints folks have at parties. At least it would be something. My mouth was too dry at the moment to salivate, but my heart quickened.

In the brighter day and walking an uncharted path in that barren waste, I was scared to death by my exposure for the first time in a while. Thankfully, the lightning was gone that morning. There really was no hiding in a landscape like this. It reminded me of that dry lake bed in California where they shot car commercials and music videos, except that place had some mountains rimming it off in the distance. No such luck here. Even if there were mountains, they'd be the same dull color as the ground and the sky, and I wouldn't be able to tell the difference.

But I walked on, Sara's voice encouraging me, but this time, instead of a gentle platitude, there was a *challenge* that struck me to my core.

"Got to stay alive, baby," she said. "You're going to waste away if you don't move, and you'll never know what really happened to the world and all the people, never know if you could have been happy, all because you let fear lead you to starvation. That's not the man I fell in love with. You're only occupying the shell where he used to live."

Leave it up to my imaginary, now-dead future missus to goad me into motion. At times during that brief period of starvation, I really did think she was there. I even imagined I saw her, but as soon as I cleared my eyes, shook my head, or focused on something else for some perspective, she dissipated, broke up into a million pieces and blew away with the wind.

I pulled myself together and walked across the road, or what used to be the road, as she had told me to. I heard another voice. It wasn't hers. It wasn't Dad's. It wasn't God's. It was mine.

"I want to live, and I'm going to even if I have to die trying." I strengthened the force of my declaration with a mild swear and felt all the more determined for it. It's not the most quotable line, but things said in the immediacy of a dire moment rarely are.

At the end of a rough first semester at college, when I had papers heaped upon me with no idea of how to go about even *beginning* them, much less writing them well, I had a moment one night when I decided I was going to quit worrying about how I was going to do and just said, "Ryan, you do what you do because you have to." I had just returned from Aunt Stacy's funeral. She was killed suddenly in a car wreck. The grief nearly broke us all to pieces, but I *had* to put off my grief until later and focus on where I was and what I was doing. Again, it was a horrible line, but it worked. And the same kind of logic worked now.

To my left, at the dead end of the cul-de-sac, there used to be a line of trees that stood about fifty feet tall, towering over the end of the street and framing an entrance to a private drive as if concealed within was the house of seven gables. Now nothing, but every time I closed my eyes, even to blink, I saw something that should have been there and no longer was, like there was a strange world when we weren't looking at it where everything is still the same. Have you ever looked out a window into a bright sunny day for a few seconds and then closed your eyes and found images burned into the back of your eyelids like you were still looking at it? This was the exact same eerie effect.

The wind ceased to howl that morning and instead *shushed*. It was soothing, like being in the womb. I wanted to sleep, but I fought it. I walked down and around the hill to come up at their basement from below. It was built half into the hill, and the way the fire had torn it apart as it licked the hill created a slope at the upper rim of it that I would have spilled down, breaking my leg as I fell through the opening, if I didn't circumvent it like I did.

Their basement was simply a carpeted den. Not knowing anything about it, I had no idea if there would be any sustenance down there. The Lord had told me to walk here, though. It was my only shot at staying alive, so I counted on it.

There were a couple of couches, a coffee table, a desk against one wall with a credenza. There was a doggie bed in the floor that their Chihuahua, Angel, would stay in at night. She would have been aboveground when the fire happened and would thus no longer be with us. Even if she had been alive, she would have disappeared long ago in search of food, which would have surely brought her to me. I could have used a dog to keep me company, even though she jumped in my lap and peed on me every time she saw me sitting down on my porch.

My vision began to fail again from exhaustion when I saw that comfortable sofa, so I don't know how reliable my recollection is. All I can remember is that I didn't find any food down there. I randomly lumbered around like a zombie, searching every cabinet, cupboard, and drawer, finding nothing but papers, excess kitchen-related paraphernalia, blankets, towels, and on and on. No food in sight.

I made it into their bathroom and to the commode. Its lid had been left open before the blast, and inside was not water but a thick, mousse-like paste of wet ash about three inches deep. My stomach lurched at the sudden idea I had to eat the stuff, and I most certainly would have vomited if there had been anything inside me to get rid of. When my dry heaves faded, I felt the same emptiness and a craving to fill it with practically *anything*. I sympathized with desperate pregnant women who crave dirt and laundry detergent. My mouth was a hollow stone. I couldn't work my tongue enough even to moan through my hunger, and my throat was parched like the Atacama Desert.

I collapsed in front of it, unable to bear my weight anymore. I reached over with my left arm and landed my heavy hand right in the muck. I withdrew a fistful of it and managed to get it into my mouth. The moisture hit me like a waterfall of immeasurable strength, and the ash-water mixture slid down my throat like pudding. I didn't even have to flex my jaw to mush it around. In the haze, it tasted like gravy, but I knew what it was. There were dead things in there, dead *people*.

I immediately threw it back up, all over my stomach. My shirt had pulled up. It hit my bare skin. The sudden warmth of my own mess galvanized me and I sat up and leaned back into the toilet to grab another couple of handfuls. A part of me couldn't believe I was doing this; I still can't believe I did it. All I remember is that I buried myself in that sludge. I'm glad I don't remember the thoughts that passed through my mind. There was no way to know if the toilet hadn't been used and then left unflushed before the fire came, but I can't nurture that thought, even now. Some things are better left unknown.

I passed out at one point, and when I woke up many hours later, it was nighttime, and I discovered by feeling around that I had completely licked the bowl clean.

<hr />

I was afraid, however, being in that strange half basement, part of its den blown into oblivion. It looked as if it had been intentionally designed to be half unfinished, like Willy Wonka's office. I found it funny that the idea of a full basement like mine, in a world that had been blown completely to hell, was somehow like a little slice of heaven to me. What did it matter? Still, this baby missed his blanket. I needed to be back home.

My energy was greatly restored after eating the crud in that toilet bowl. Scared almost to immobility but unable to stay in unfamiliar territory one more moment, I jumped up, ran out of their basement, and bolted up the hill. There was no lightning that night. I ran into my basement shelter and was frightened at first to see there was a light on in there, but then I realized I had left the flashlight on before my excursion. I picked it up and turned it off. It had grown dimmer. I was going to need new batteries for it, and to my knowledge I had not yet found any D batteries, not even in Mr. Norton's tool area. I was going to need to find some, somewhere. I prayed God would lead me to them. I knew I was in good hands. He had sent me ravens, and I had eaten.

"But don't make me eat that stuff again anytime soon," I prayed. I felt fine, full of vitality, but very, very conflicted that I might have just committed cannibalism.

This is my body, take and eat.

"But this is different," I argued.

I heard silence on the other end and decided the matter wasn't worth pursuing. As I've thought over it, though, I've absolved myself of the thought that I committed cannibalism. After all, I wasn't eating actual flesh, and I've been comforted by the thought that when we die, our bodies nourish the ground, eventually giving way to the fruit we eat and the grasses to feed animals who give us meat. I had just cut out a few middlemen. And besides, I was *alive*.

I didn't fall directly asleep, although I was extremely fatigued. I had noticed that there was something different about the night as I hastily made my way back home from the basement across the street, something that didn't quite jibe. I sat up in bed and thought about it for a minute.

I pulled an all-nighter once my sophomore year of college, the only one I ever did. It wasn't out of necessity. I just did it because I knew other folks routinely did it because they had put off their papers too long, and I wanted to know what it felt like. I had some take-home essay finals to do, and I did them all in one shot in the computer lab on campus. I got home at six in the morning and crashed. I woke up a couple hours later to take a shower before my first class. When I stumbled into the bathroom, it was huge, easily ten times the size it had otherwise been, and I said out loud, "Am I in the right apartment?" Still, all my stuff was there, so I took it for granted and hopped in the shower. The hot water woke me up, and when I stepped out, the bathroom was back to its normal size. I thought I had briefly stepped into another dimension. It was the only way to explain what had happened. In reality, I had been half-asleep when I meandered into the bathroom and thus hallucinated the change in size. It wasn't a dream, but it wasn't reality either. That same strange phenomenon is the only explanation for how I missed the glaringly obvious fact on my jaunt from across the street back home—I had been able to see where I was going.

I slipped out of bed and stepped into the hallway, and thus under the open sky, I looked above. I could see the swift-moving ash clouds, lit from above. I remembered Mom's calendar said that it was a full moon. *The moon is out!* I thought, and I laughed and praised God that the faint light on the white ash gave me the evidence that *somehow* up there, all was as it had always been. Were I able to fly above it all, I would see the moon shining in all its bright glory. I considering bunking down on the couch that night and dreaming wistfully to see the stars and moon in full clarity, but the nightmares would most certainly come again with the exposure, and I just couldn't have that.

ANOTHER CAVE

———⟫●⟪———

I *did* dream that night, however, and it was wonderful. I remember every detail.

You know how they say you don't actually see colors in your dreams, that you dream in black and white and your mind makes the colors later as you're remembering it just before waking? Well, that wasn't true this time. I saw the colors as I dreamed. I know I did just like I knew the moon was above those clouds even though I couldn't *really* see it.

I was hiking through a tropical forest. There were trees and animals that somewhat resembled ones I knew, but they were different, the colors more vibrant, as if somebody had created a world based on the one we lived in, but left out some details here and added some in there, like an extra finger on a monkey, or a fruit that looked like a banana but tasted like almonds. It was still Earth, just tilted. It felt like Eden.

Eventually, the trees cleared, and I found myself on the edge of a deep, deep canyon. The flora didn't stop there, however, but instead grew and thrived right on down into the depths below and up to the water's edge at the bottom. Greens and reds and splashes of fuchsia burst forth all around me—wildflowers and fruits cast hither and yon with the careless abandon of a master artist's hand.

Beneath the calls of the primates' hollers and birds' sweet melodies was music. It sounded a lot like "Clare de Lune," one of my favorites. Again, as with the other details of this world, it sounded like some aspects of the music were left out and other aspects newly invented.

I stood at the beginning of a path at the top of the canyon. I felt like I was supposed to walk down it, so I did. You know how dreams feel like they go on forever, but when you really think about it, you can see how time skipped around because there are gaps? There was no gap here. I could remember every footfall.

The river became steadily louder as I got closer to it, and I could feel its coolness rushing up to me. It was a very calm river, but it gurgled softly as the current pushed it up against rocks on either side. Small waterfalls cascaded down the rocks to meet it.

I reached bottom after an hour of walking, and the brightness of the morning sun had dimmed as it gradually hid itself behind a wall above. The path led me to a waterfall that fell into a large pool. The fall came from a hole in the rock instead of a source tucked back in a crevasse. It wasn't runoff like the others; it was a spring. The pool slowly poured over a rock rim and fed the river. It looked like a beautiful swimming hole, and I wanted to take a dip.

I reached down to take off my clothes before realizing I was already naked. I looked at myself and saw myself clothed head to toe in the ash, and I felt on my back to find the burn scars still there. I could taste the grit in my mouth and could feel it burning my eyes and coating the inside of my nostrils as it had these long months.

I was the me I had been shortly after the blast, naked and exposed. I still had those shoes with the melted soles on. I reached down and removed them and stood barefoot on cool rock by the side of that pool. I could feel cool air from the water come over me with a gentle breeze. I wanted nothing more than to submerge myself. I didn't care how cold it was.

The edge was steep. I saw no danger in diving straight down, so I did, plunging into the depths of that coolness without a care in the world.

I normally have this fear of deep water, but in this dream, I felt only comfort, almost as if I had dived into a plush blanket. After the sound of the splash disappeared and ten thousand bubbles slid past and cleared, I began to hear something in the water…a voice, whispering. It was the most beautiful sound I had ever heard. It reminded me of being in the womb, if indeed one could recall being in the womb. I knew this is what it must have felt like.

The water was a degree or two above freezing, but my body was warm. I felt love in it, and that voice…it got louder the deeper I swam, and so I swam downward. I couldn't see the bottom yet, but as I swam deeper the voice got clearer until I could make out the words, and when I could, I stopped. It said, "To him who sits on the throne, and unto the Lamb, be blessing and honor, glory and power, forever."

I looked above me then, scared to death by how far I had swum, scared that I wouldn't make it back to the surface before my body went into spasms for lack of oxygen and hitched the water into my lungs to drown me. I saw the surface. It looked a hundred feet above me, and I began to turn to it.

The voice said, "Ryan, stay."

I quit my panic and remained still there in the depths.

"Turn back to me."

I didn't want to open my eyes. Still afraid of that deep water. It had looked pitch-dark from above, and I could feel that deep darkness around me as a palpable presence as I dreamed. But I turned and faced it all the same, eyes tightly shut.

"Please don't ask me to open my eyes," I said, the sound of my voice gurgly under the water, but the voice that answered me was crystal clear.

"You don't have to if you don't want to. It's up to you. It will always be up to you."

The darkness had lightened considerably, however, to the point where it seemed as if the sun was shining beyond my eyelids. My lids fluttered, but still, I couldn't bring myself to open them. I couldn't bear the thought of what I might see and almost wished for the darkness again because at least *that* made sense.

"You are safe," the voice said.

It was so calming and yet so authoritative that it gave me the push of strength I needed. I opened my eyes. I saw a city down there, at the very bottom of that pool. Perspective was difficult in such surreal circumstances. It may have been a thousand feet below me. It may have been a thousand miles. It was as if I was looking at it from the space station.

The city was Jerusalem. Again, it's something I knew without being told. But it was a new city, a holy city. Although I could breathe underwater as if it were air, no amount of swimming would get me down there. I wasn't meant to touch it, only see it.

"Hang in there," the voice whispered to me. "Now go, and walk."

Suddenly, my lungs began to feel the pain of holding my breath. I turned toward the surface, leaving that beautiful golden glow below me, and broke through just when I had started to black out. The air was sweet in my throat, and immediately the chirping of the birds and rushing of the waterfall hit my ears, twice as loud as they were before. The colors were more vivid, even in the dim light of the canyon shade. I swam to the rocks from where I had dived before and climbed out.

I took in the view of myself. The ash was completely gone. So were my scars. The mysterious water in that depthless pool had washed it all away. I looked for my shoes, but they were no longer on the rock where I had left them. They weren't anywhere.

I climbed out and scanned the surroundings for them. No tracks. The shoe thief had left behind no sign of his presence, and I struggled to remember if I had even had them to begin with. Dreams are funny that way. Even while you're having them, you wonder if you've been dreaming.

I sat down on the rock, wondering if I was ever going to wake up. I felt that it wouldn't matter if I ever did. I could stay in this place forever. Such *music* in the air, that sweet melody, both familiar and new. As long as it played on, it never cycled back around to the beginning that I could tell, like a CD on repeat. The melody returned, but it was different each time around, as if parts of the orchestra were added or taken away.

"What do I do now?" I asked the air.

There was no response. I wondered if I should take another dip and see if there was anything I had missed, but then I heard the singing. It was faint, like it was in my head as some distant memory or vague imagining to fill in the empty space. Was this real, or was I just yearning for something?

But I hadn't *felt* like I was yearning for anything. I was at peace. The singing occurred completely out of the blue; it was an outside stimulus, and I was meant to investigate. I stood up and cocked my head to the side to hear it better. It was coming somewhere along the path beside me, over the rocks and around the curve to the back of the waterfall.

I became more conscious of my nudity. If there were some-body actually there, I would be exposed to them. I looked around me for covering, perhaps the leaf of an elephant-ear plant, but there was no suitable foliage down here in the canyon bottom. It was all above me. The thought of a fig leaf ran through my head, briefly. If anybody was going to see me, they would have long since done so.

But I remembered this was just a dream; people dream about being naked all the time, and while such dreams may have been provoked by some occurrence in the real world, they would never have any bearing on it. Nobody was *really* seeing me naked.

"Screw it," I said and laughed at my own coarseness in the ethereal environment.

I walked along the path, trying to peer behind that curtain. The water cascaded in a thick enough deluge to obscure all but the most vague outline of the figure hanging out behind it. It was definitely human

"Who are you?" I called out.

They didn't answer.

"Are you someone I know?"

"You will know me, Ryan," she said. *It's a woman!* A soft voice that spoke barely above a whisper, but I could hear it clearly through that water all the same. Only it didn't sound *quite* clear; it sounded instead like a human voice layered with the sound of tinkling crystal.

I wanted to think it was Sara back there somewhere, but everything in me at that moment said it couldn't be. I had said good-bye to her already, and while God used her in my waking moments to comfort me, I had made peace that I would never see her again. This could not be her.

"I want to see you," I said.

"You cannot," she said. "Not here. Not like this. This is not meant to be."

I walked farther toward that blasted curtain, determined to go around the back of the falls and see this mysterious girl who knew my name and my destiny so well.

"Who *are* you?"

I walked into an invisible barrier. It felt like a hand that had been held up to stop me. I tried to walk forward, but it pushed back with just as much force as I applied, no matter how hard I tried. It kept me at a standstill.

"You will know," she said. "But not like this. You see through a glass darkly now, but soon you will see in full."

Is this a prophecy? Of what?

I squinted to see her. I could only see a form, a shape, and it drove me crazy. My loneliness in the real world transferred into my dream, causing me a deep inner pain and anguish. I wanted to cry and could feel my eyes tear up.

"Ryan," she said, and I could see her slowly shake her head. "Haven't you mourned enough? Dry your eyes and look up, look out, look around. You must leave so that you can live."

"I don't know how!" I cried.

"I cannot find you unless you come find me," she said. "There is no other way."

I tried to see her. The curtain cleared just slightly, and for a passing moment, a millionth of a second, I could see her in full—and I still had no idea what I had seen. But she wasn't wearing anything, and I felt a shiver cross over me in my dream and in my real-life body. It warmed my loins and lit a fire in my heart that had lain dormant. It wasn't lust. There was more going on here than primal urges.

"It is not good for man to be alone," I said to myself, softly, but she heard.

"And you won't be, but you *must leave!*" she shouted. Her voice pierced my ears, pierced my soul. It hurt, but it was still beautiful, enticing, a siren's song that wouldn't lead me to my death but to the rest of my life.

"Are you going to be my wife?" I asked.

She didn't respond, but I didn't need her to. She was, or at least she embodied the promise of a wife. She was divinely crafted, fearfully made.

"Wake up and go find food," she said.

And then I snapped awake. I was shivering uncontrollably.

My shivering came from hunger; I was starving almost as much as I had been the previous day when I ate that hideous sludge out of the neighbors' toilet, but I didn't feel like death was just waiting for me to catch up to it like I did then. There was a resolve there.

I went into the bedroom and pulled a blanket off. In the past few weeks, I had dusted it enough that I had almost gotten the ash entirely out of it. Of course, the stink from my sweaty sleep was so buried into it that I would probably never get it out even if I miraculously found a subterranean washing machine powered by a generator in somebody's basement somewhere.

I took it with me topside and wrapped it around myself and started walking. My clothes hung off me in such rags that I had removed my jeans and underwear. I had a sweatshirt with a hood draped around my torso. The shoes still fit, at least, but I could have walked barefoot across that smooth, burned-away landscape and not felt a thing. It felt strange to expose myself again like I did. I now thought back to the first several weeks of post-blast life when I had been naked for most of my waking moments with the perspective Adam must have had after the fall: *How did I get away with being naked all that time?*

With each step, I felt more exposed, more in danger. I had no directions to guide me, no voice telling me exactly where to step, to say, "It's okay, I've gotcha." Jesus dropped no hints this time because he knew I didn't need them, and I knew he was right. There was nothing like the voice of a mysterious and enticing bride-to-be behind a waterfall to keep a boy on track to become a man.

I kept Dad's maxim in mind: *Sometimes God seems silent because he's put the answer right in front of you.* Walking straight ahead had worked well enough yesterday morning. There was no reason why it wouldn't today.

The wind whipped around something fierce. Ash billowed in giant clouds and twisters that towered a thousand feet above me. Ten steps into the trip, I was knocked down by the vicious vortex of one of them. I hit the bruised hip when I fell. I cursed through my teeth and shook my fist at the twister. It didn't make any difference, but it made me feel better.

"You do what you do because you have to," I said then. "I want to live, and I'm going to even if I die trying."

The toilet-bowl feast had worn off like of a shot of adrenaline, leaving me more drained than before for lack of nutrients. I didn't want to do it, but like Paul said in Romans, we do what we don't want to do, and what we don't want to do, we do. So I gathered up my nerve, took a handful of ash, and threw it in my mouth. I had enough spit to slowly dissolve it, like eating flour milled from your grandma's ashes.

It wasn't like some sort of magic powder that gave me instant life. I wasn't stupid enough to believe that. Instead, it had a strange placebo effect. It energized me at least to be doing *something* with my mouth and stomach. I stood back up, reoriented myself. I was only a dozen yards from my basement. I looked across the way but couldn't see a blessed thing.

"Be still!" I shouted from around my bandanna.

And it *was*! I would have never thought that we'd have faith strong enough to control the weather. Although Jesus had said with only a mustard seed of faith we would be able to cast mountains into the sea, I had believed then that he was speaking metaphorically. And perhaps he was, but had Paul also said we could do all things through him who strengthens us? Regardless, when I spoke, my conviction was set. I had not a shred of doubt that the elements would obey, and in an instant, the wind ceased to blow for the first time since the blast. The ash fell where it was, the twisters disappeared, and I could see clearly to the farthest horizon, miles and miles away. I could see basements pockmarking the landscape, an endless sea of ash filled with islands of hope, so many to explore I didn't know where to begin. But closer than them all, perhaps only a quarter of a mile away from my house and directly in front of me, was a cave.

I was so shocked by the sudden appearance I had to sit down. I had seen some strange things so far, some imagined, many of them real. I had seen enough to convince me there were forces going on beyond this visible world that could not be explained by anything but spiritual means. I had learned to trust God implicitly to guide me and keep me safe and well. Even on the edge of death, his hold on my life was secure. But each new strangeness took me back out of myself, back out of the security I had felt. That cave had never been there before, shouldn't be there now. *What's going on here?*

I stood back up and walked toward it anyway. Each new basement I had found carried with it the possibility of life. If there weren't humans there, perhaps there would be mice, bugs, or even small pets. Anything with a pulse would have been akin to finding life on Mars. If this were truly a cave, carved out of limestone, there may indeed be people in there, eking out their existence, getting along as I have by what they could scavenge. *Oh, Lord, let it be so*, I prayed.

But still, why was it there? Had the blast carved it out somehow? Had it always been there, cut into that strange hill that rose so abruptly out of the surrounding flat plain? Was the entrance cut off for thousands of years until the blast burned it away?

My pulse quickened. I wanted to *see!* I felt like Indiana Jones all of a sudden, ready to plunge in despite the certain death that lay ahead. This was not the first sense of adventure I had felt at a new discovery, and it would not be the last. I carried my flashlight with me. I had checked it before I left. It appeared as if it still had enough juice to get me by for a couple of hours. I couldn't wait.

When I was only a couple hundred yards away, I saw shelving inside the entrance in neat, orderly rows, and floor tile, all lit just barely by the dim light coming through.

Eh? I thought.

When I realized what I was looking at, I couldn't *believe* it had taken me so long to remember. This place should have been my first order of business, but I had been so terrified for so long, able only to reach out and grab what was right before my eyes, so scared to leave my own cave that, on the occasions when I did so, I didn't stay out long enough to wonder. This place, wow. *This* place is where the rest of my life *finally* would begin.

Let me explain.

There was this very strange sort of neighborhood grocery store on Evans road called "Frank's," originally owned and operated by a man named Frank Edson. It was *crazy* old school. He first opened it back in the late forties, and it was a classy joint. My folks hadn't grown up in Poplar Bluff, but they knew about it even as kids up in Jackson—envied it, in fact. It had a soda fountain and served burgers to kids just after school let out in the afternoons. On cold winter days, those rare occasions where the temperature midday would dip below freezing, they gave away hot chocolate for free. They had a jukebox and permitted dancing, so long as it didn't get out of hand.

Mr. Edson was such a wholesome, delightful man that kids and their parents alike loved him. They called him "Pop" and thought of him as the cool dad everyone wished they had but secretly knew would spoil them rotten if they did. He had kids of his own, and when Frank Jr., his eldest, got old enough, he entered into a partnership with his dad and brought the place into the postmodern era without losing its charm.

They managed to keep the soda fountain from going out of vogue. When I was in grade school at Odem Elementary, I used to go two blocks out of my way on the walk home from school to spend two dollars' worth of hard-earned allowance on a chocolate milkshake, and there was nothing like it in the world. If I was in the mood for something hotter, I'd get hot chocolate, or sometimes some Tater Tots if I was hungry. While I was certainly a regular, I wasn't the only one. There must have been ten of us from Mrs. Clarke's fifth-grade class alone invade the place on Fridays. Business was always booming.

They updated the jukebox with music we liked, but we still couldn't get over the retro value of the thing. They kept comics on racks up front, always the latest—no vintage stuff of any real lasting value, but that was to be expected. They probably got shoplifted enough as it was. We never much ventured farther into the store than the entrance, but I remember it was always stocked with fruits and vegetables as well as nonperishable canned goods, boxes of cereal, bags of chips, and other things you'd expect to see on a grocery store shelf. They had cold cases where they kept milk, frozen dinners, and ice cream. So much stuff packed into a small space, but it never felt crowded, and a lot of folks in the immediate neighborhood did their grocery shopping there. I'm not sure what lay beyond the grocery section. An office area, I think, maybe a restroom. It wouldn't have interested me, regardless.

Evans is a long, long road, much used. Not your cookie-cutter nuclear-age suburbia, but Frank's offered competitive enough prices that it did well despite its more off-putting location on a major thoroughfare. It would have worked better on a corner somewhere, but the Edsons liked to keep the business close to home, which is why they lived just next door to the store.

Many times, I had thought of places that may have survived the blast and came up short. It seemed all the landmarks, places people would think to gather, were aboveground. No subterranean shelters in the lot of them, not even a church basement somewhere. Perhaps I just didn't know enough about my hometown, but I should have remembered that there was a guaranteed place that would have almost perfectly survived the blast.

Frank's, you see, was built completely inside of a hill.

That had been the charm of the place. The sign and any other identifying markers like a front door and newspaper rack were now burned away because the facade of the building stuck out maybe ten feet from the hill, but the rest of it was set perfectly into it. There was no other place like it in Poplar Bluff, and it was certainly the only grocery store of its kind anywhere. Folks went there because they always felt like they were walking into a cave, and you didn't see many caves until you got up around the Big Springs area in Van Buren. The hill it was set into was unique, too. Poplar Bluff was a hilly area compared to the flat plains around it, but these hills were all looming and rolling, not very big or dramatic. Inconsequential. Hardly any steep ones, except for this one.

And it was steep because Pop had had it made. Dad told me. It happened before my parents were even born. Apparently Mr. Edson paid some folks to build up a huge mound of dirt and seed it with grass and plant a few trees to make it look more naturally like a part of the landscape. It was supposed to appear organic, but really it was pretty obvious. Actually, the building came first, and then he built up the mound of earth around it. It was pretty strange, and neat.

That's what had drawn us all in and kept us coming back. It was just so *weird*, and I remembered asking my dad about it— what in the world was the point of such a place?

He told me Pop had been pretty alarmist about the communist threat and didn't take it lightly. The store was supposed to double as a bomb shelter when the imminent nuclear war started. The front of it, in fact, was reinforced steel, made of the same strength as most underground bomb shelters of the day. Dad said it was never a matter of *if*, but *when*, even for the most lackadaisical, devil-may-care types. The end of the world was *going* to happen; they were just all waiting for somebody to make the first move.

In fact, Pop Edson closed the place during the Cuban missile crisis. Folks were welcome to come in and take shelter, of course, but he didn't operate the business during that time. His earnings took a hit, but he was safe, at least.

I considered the possibilities. Sure, there was probably enough food in there to get me through at least the next few months, even if I completely pigged out on it, but in spite of my irrepressible hunger pangs, that wasn't at the forefront of my mind. What if Mr. Edson, Mrs. Edson, Frank Jr., and the kids had used the store for its other purpose and taken shelter from the blast?

I was giddy with anticipation. Above me, lightning started to flash high in the atmosphere again, triggered by I don't know what. Could have been solar wind from a sun storm and could have been just heightened friction between ash particles high in the atmosphere. It was so far above me that I didn't hear the sizzle and pop, but I couldn't have cared less one way or another. The phenomenon was far less a miracle than if the Edsons were still alive.

If anybody else survived this blast, this was going to be my best chance of finding them in the whole town. Pop and Frank Jr. never stopped believing the commies would come for us, even after the wall came down and the Soviet Union collapsed. There was still Cuba, China, and North Korea, not to mention Iran and whoever else. If it wasn't the commies, it would be *somebody*. They were patriots to the core. I wouldn't have put it past them to have a secret gun safe in the very back of the store. If that were really the case, I would definitely need to be careful in how I approached.

I chided myself for such fears and foolish thoughts, though. They would remember me. They'd be happy to see me. They might have been eking out their existence this whole time just like I had, staying close to home and praying for a miracle. Their supplies were probably running low as well. Hopefully they'd have enough to at least feed me a spot of dinner while I was there.

I considered that I might soon leave my basement shelter for good. I had come to depend on the basement, especially that little hovel in the bedroom, a safe sanctuary that allowed me the luxury of a good night's sleep after a day of exhausted exploring, reading, writing, ruminating, and praying. I would be lying if I said I didn't shed a tear in that moment; I also seriously considered staying in that room and curling into a little ball and wishing all of it away, like it might yet be a bad dream that would end with a sudden phone call waking me from my slumber at the apartment, perhaps from Sara herself.

But it was foolish to nurture such a fantasy. I could hear the quiet wind start to blow again, could taste the ash on my tongue constantly, could see the dense dark-gray sky swirling above and the endless gray expanse below. Nothing would happen ever again unless I made it happen. It was going to be my choice. That's how God had left it; that's how the mysterious young woman in my dream had left it. I continued toward destiny.

———⇒•⇐———

Frank's was less than half a mile due west from my front porch. When I was a kid, after me and my buddies would finish our milkshakes, burgers, and/or Tater Tots there, I would cut across the field behind my neighbor's house to get home. It saved me at least a mile's walk. Sure, I was trespassing, but who would really want to have pressed charges against a ten-year-old boy just passing through?

I began to feel the panic of overexposure out there, but I crushed it by throwing caution to the shushing wind and began to walk briskly. I felt a fire come into my legs, the last vestige of strength in my body spurring me forward. I began to run, and as I ran, I began to smile. The smile felt good. It did not turn into laughter. Not yet, but it was a beginning.

I stopped my running just thirty yards shy of the shelter and gaped at it. It was so weird to see that indestructible steel facade just *gone*. Sure, I could understand the glass and other weaker elements of the construction just whisked away by that consuming fire, but *steel*? The framing material of it had been designed to withstand nuclear winter. No such luck.

And yet just beyond that doorway, the place was entirely intact. There was some ash sprinkled on the floor and on top of packages of food and medicinal items, but it looked as if nothing had even touched the establishment. And *there* was the rub.

If nothing had changed at all, if they hadn't even so much as tried to put a new door on their shelter, then they couldn't actually have been there. The shelves looked fully stocked, as did the beverage case. Everything was as it should have been without any sign of human intrusion.

I muttered a curse and sat on a barstool, just looking at it. The room was pretty dark, the only entrance for light being the open doorframe. I listened for the sound of anything rustling in there and just heard dead silence. The wind didn't penetrate to whistle around my ears as it had done almost constantly back at my basement. At moments, I thought I heard a tapping sound somewhere in that darkness, but it was just my imagination.

I was still afraid, however, of what might be in there, so afraid, in fact, that I didn't call out to see if anyone would answer. Dejected, I just turned around and walked back out without exploring anything or even taking any snacks with me. I had failed to make contact, and I saw no point in sticking around any longer. It was sad to look at this place I had grown to love and know so well, a place that had been entirely preserved by its location within this hill, preserved against the ash that kept covering everything up outside and billowing around across the desolation. It was a thing that shouldn't be, especially without the presence of its owners. I felt like my presence was defiling that place somehow. I began to make tracks back home immediately.

But the hunger wouldn't let me go. I darted back in real quick, took the blanket off from around my shoulders, and used it as a knapsack to carry the entire contents of the first shelf. All tuna. Then, I headed back home and swore I wouldn't return. I didn't deserve the luxury of a place so well preserved.

In fact, I decided it wouldn't do to remind myself so much of what had been, there or in my own basement. I had nurtured these romantic notions that I would read through Mom and Dad's library in the endless time I had at my disposal in the basement. I would go through their stacks of *Time* and *National*

Geographic and *Discover*. I would read Dad's collections of literature by, about, and concerning ancient Greeks and Romans and his baseball books from Bill James and Ken Burns. I was looking forward to reading through the David Baldacci books he had liked so much, so I kept them on hand, dusted them off, and looked through them without actually reading them, planning on doing so someday when I was perfectly resolved that the world was forever and always going to be this way and I may as well get comfortable with it. I found I could no longer nurture such aspirations; they weren't doing me any good. I hadn't read page 1 of any of them, and I can't say that the dimness of light filtering through the clouds was any excuse. If I had really wanted to, I would have just used the Maglite. I didn't want to.

But I couldn't just burn them and have done with it. These were historical relics now, symbols of a lost culture, and they should be preserved. I begrudgingly decided that it would be best to take them where they would best be protected from the elements, so I began carrying them in knapsacks-full over to Frank's. This seemingly mindless and stupid project actually gave my day a purpose. I found a nobility in it. I liked it. It kept me occupied, gave me exercise, and proved that I still cared about something. I began setting them down just inside the entrance, careful not to enter the tomb, careful not to desecrate this place that had become a cathedral in my mind.

"Ryan, don't be stupid," I heard Sara say.

"I'm not being stupid, Sara. You didn't grow up with this place. You didn't know."

"You can't live the rest of your life off two weeks' worth of tuna. Eventually, you're going to need more than that. Tuna isn't enough to live off of and you know it, so stop it."

"You really think it's okay?"

"Ryan, was I *ever* a bad influence on you?"

No, you weren't, I thought. *It's a wonder I didn't drag you to hell with me, in fact. But you were always above reproach.*

I laughed at myself and prayed. It went something like this: "God, forgive my foolishness. I came here by your strength alone. It is not up to me to decide what I deserve and what I don't. If you want me to drink from this cup and enjoy the abundant blessings here, then don't let my delusions of modesty get in your way." So for each trip, I carried back another knapsack full of food to enjoy at home. And as I got the books, albums, and various unneeded clutter out of my basement, my anxiousness to escape the doldrums of my own refuge began to build. I knew the time was coming. I just didn't know what was going to kick it off.

As the days started to go by unheeded, I continued exploring the neighborhoods around me and pilfering for goods and luxury items. I actually managed to sleep in other beds, growing gradually more accustomed to the unchanging open sky. After six and a half months of living in this empty world, I realized that nothing was ever going to happen to me. If it did, it wouldn't amount to anything more than an abrupt change of scenery.

Food remained plentiful, although I was growing tired of not having anything warm to eat. So tired, in fact, that I knocked some loose bricks from a basement fireplace to build my own fire pit on the path between me and the Nortons'. I found some matches and used some loose scrap paper to start a fire. I held various canned foods like vegetables and processed meat over the fire with a pair of garden cutters from the Nortons'. I had begun to build an immense supply of food from Frank's, and among those various goods were marshmallows, Hershey's bars, and graham crackers. It takes no stretch of the imagination to figure out what I did with those. I sang songs around the fire, told myself stories, but no scary ones. The time for scary stories was over. Instead, I did the opposite. In my stories, I spoke of heaven and happy tears. The warmth of the fire couldn't match that which was within.

In spite of Sara's admonition and the confidence I had felt at first, my decision to continue to take from Frank's didn't come lightly. Since the place was in such good shape, I treated it reverentially, like somebody's home they were still occupying. I felt like I might have been at somebody's final resting place, and that by taking Twinkies, soda, and chips from it, I was somehow taking flowers from the grave. It was silly, but something about that place had an aura that I needed to treat with respect, like there was a spiritual presence that hadn't left with the owners.

I found more flashlight batteries there. Now every time I went back to Frank's, I didn't need to squint in the dim light trickling in from outside to see exactly what I was doing.

BATTLE

I had a new lease. Life was good. I put weight back on. My ribs
went back in their cages. I gave thanks with more enthusiasm
than before. I read my Bible, getting through the rest of the Old
Testament. Dad guided me the entire way, teaching me how to
look for Jesus in everything, starting with the part in Genesis
where God tells Eve that one of her descendants will one day
crush the head of the serpent. It was like I had been given sight.
I *knew* I had read that before, but I had never *seen*. I looked for
other patterns, like when Shadrach, Meschach, and Abednego
were in the furnace and there was a mysterious fourth person
who was in there with them, too. Get a load of *that*—Jesus, just
hanging out in fellowship with these saints when they should
have been roasting. Then there was Ezekiel, Isaiah, Malachi, all
the minor prophets, doing their thing, and underneath it all was
the implication of grace, the promise of a deliverer. I returned to
the New Testament, read Hebrews, saw the litany of heroes of
the faith recorded in Hebrews 11. I was touched especially by the
story of Abraham. He lived before God gave man the law, and
his faith alone was reckoned to him as righteousness. All it took
was for him to believe. That was all it took for me now. The entire

massive Bible itself was a recorded history of God's love story with man. I felt like the communion of ancient saints surrounded me, instructed me, encouraged me.

I was going to need it.

In September, I heard a noise. Sounds silly, I know, but if it's happened to you, you know the shock it can bring when something random and unexplained comes out of the stillness. Keep in mind that there were only three things I had heard with constant, monotonous, and expected regularity since the blast: myself, the steady drone and howl of the wind, and the sizzle of the lightning. On September 13, I heard a knock coming from the back of Frank's.

I was in the middle of putting new batteries in the flashlight when I first heard it. It came on suddenly, and I squealed and jumped back.

"Wh…wha…?" I said.

I felt a warmth spreading, and I couldn't believe it—I had peed my pants. Fortunately enough, I had been back repeatedly to the teenager's room on Roanoke and had ripped off his whole wardrobe. My weight had varied greatly, but with that one great exception in June when I almost starved to death, they always fit just fine. Thus, I would readily have a fresh set of clothes to change into, but I chided myself for the impropriety because I had no ready means anywhere to wash myself and wouldn't dare waste a bottle of water just to rinse off. These clothes would probably end up on the dung heap.

I found it in me to back out and run away, not stopping until I got to the basement and safely within the bedroom shelter. I had left my flashlight at Frank's and thus couldn't see a blessed thing when I got under the roof, but still I felt safe, as if the bedroom shelter had been consecrated as a panic room and nothing could reach me in there.

Ten minutes later, I was laughing at myself and praying that God would have patience with me and forgive my fear.

I took off my clothes and stepped unadorned out of the bedroom. I climbed up on to the ground and let the open air dry off my soiled body. It actually helped. The ash collected and stuck to the spot where I had wet myself, creating a thin paste that dried to mud after a time and could be scraped off. Strangely, I found myself somehow cleaner underneath than I had been even before I wet my pants. Ash baths just might be the way of the future.

I sat on top of the southern basement wall, legs dangling over the floor seven feet beneath me, and looked north. I couldn't see far enough to Frank's, but I squinted and peered as best I could anyway, hoping and fearing equally to see somebody or some-*thing* step out of the gray either to greet or claim me.

I must have sat there for a full hour before deciding it wasn't going to happen. I hopped back down into the basement and put on a set of fresh clothes. I set the soiled clothes out into the hallway to throw back up on my dung heap when I went back out. While I was in the bedroom, I took stock of what was in that closet again. I had done so before, mostly finding sets of Mom and Katie's clothes that wouldn't fit me no matter what—although I would have preferred them to Mrs. Taylor's if I had had the choice. There were also various holiday decorations, useless to me, of course. I considered storing them at Frank's so I wouldn't have to stare at them and get depressed that it was meaningless to celebrate anything anymore because there was nobody to share it with.

I could barely see anything in there and cursed my missing flashlight. The dim gray light from the basement corridor, out from under the makeshift ceiling, wouldn't penetrate far enough for my satisfaction, but I could tell that there was something in there I hadn't noticed before. Perhaps I had been too hasty when I checked it the first or even the fifth time. There hadn't been much in there to interest me anyway. Until now. The item was a steel-reinforced rectangular box sitting upright in a corner. I gasped.

Dad's gun cabinet.

It had a combination lock, and unfortunately I had never memorized the combination after Dad told it to me. I wrote it down and kept it tucked away in a keepsake box somewhere, but I didn't feel like I had much use for it. I had rarely even shot a gun, something I was embarrassed to admit to anybody, but Dad and I had never gotten around to it. I blame myself more than him. He was always available and even asked me once when I was fifteen if I'd like to go hunting. At that time, I was already hot and heavy with my high school sweetheart, and I wanted to spend that weekend on the phone and/or on dates with her. Idiot that I was, I didn't realize I was missing a prime opportunity to get to know my father on a much more personal and spiritual level.

I looked at that cabinet as a symbol of lost time that would never be regained. I wanted what was in there now just as much as I had always feared it. I didn't even know what kinds of guns Dad had. I'm sure he told me one time, but I had let it go in one ear and out the other. I was always so anxious to go off and do something useless that most of what he said didn't register to me when he said it. Well, it registered now. I began crying as I realized how much I really missed him.

I let myself have it out and then repented for time lost that would never be regained. It felt better.

"So now what are you going to do?" Sara said. "Can't keep crying. Got to move forward, baby."

"Darn straight," I said, only it was much more coarse. At an early age I had learned how to cuss good and proper from a friend, and it's an old habit that dies very, *very* hard, especially when there's nobody around to offend.

I wiped my eyes and looked closely at it, could barely make out the numbers. It helped me to talk out loud. I said, "It's got to be three sets of double digits. He probably used a date. Something important to him."

I began trying it out. It looked like a standard padlock, and I started putting in combinations the way I would on any other. I tried their wedding date. It didn't work. Same went for his birth date and Mom's. I remembered off the top of my head that they had used their first date as a code for the keypad on the van door, so I tried that. Nothing. I began to try various world events of some significance, like the bombing of Pearl Harbor. Dad was somewhat of a World War II buff, especially since his father had fought in it, but that didn't work either.

"Dang," I said. I was starting to sweat with anxiety and breathless anticipation. I knew that, as long as the food and water held out, I could keep this up for the rest of my life, but I didn't want to. Having a firearm suddenly felt urgent to getting on and doing what I had to do to go out there and find another living soul.

I slumped my shoulders, about to give up, and then I got an idea of which date it might have been, and it hadn't occurred to me because I didn't want to go there. It would be too much. I bit my lip against the tears about to come over me and entered my birthday. I heard a magical click, and I turned the crank. As the door opened, so did my tear ducts, torrents sweeping over my soul.

Inside were four guns—symbols of the life Dad wanted to have with me, but I never gave him the chance. Three of them I didn't know; the other one I was pretty familiar with. I only found out what the other three were because Dad had boxes of their shells on the shelf above. I pulled each one out into the small basement corridor under the sky so I could get a look, but I got the feeling that I needed to be extra careful not to let the dust get on them, just in case it jammed them up. I didn't know much about what I was doing, but I knew I needed to be careful.

The first was an M1 Garand, a World War II rifle that I vaguely remember him telling me he got from a friend of his; this guy reportedly had a collection to rival the Michigan Militia, about 100 various guns. This one was a gift, and Dad told me it still fired perfectly, like new.

The second was a .22. I had actually fired one of these before, when I was twelve. I was so tiny then that I could barely hold the thing up. My grandpa was present at the time, and he kept yelling at my dad to "tell that boy to be careful, he's screwing around with it and not respecting it."

Dad appeased him, but then leaned forward and said in my ear, "You're doing great, son. If he gets on to you or me again, I'll tell the old man to take his .22 back and stick it."

I started laughing so hard I almost dropped the gun, which set grandpa off all over again. Dad gave a startled shout but then started laughing, too. He and I couldn't stop laughing for the rest of our target practice, and Grandpa finally said, "Give me the dern thing back, both of you. Ornery little turds."

He stormed off with it and would never let us touch it again. I thought for a moment that this particular .22 may have been the same one, but then I remembered Dad telling me that Grandpa sold it because every time he looked at the thing he got mad about the day we wouldn't respect the firearm and take it seriously. Grandpa was a good guy, but he was too sensitive and serious sometimes, especially when he was sure it had something to do with a lesson Dad and I both needed to learn. Good times, though. Having Dad there to help me laugh kept it from being a tarnished memory over the years.

The third gun was when it started getting hard for me. It was a Daisy air rifle. I got that one the Christmas after I first fired the .22. It *almost* served as a turning point for me from boyhood to manhood. I had opened it up and loaded it and then went out in the snow in my pajamas like Ralphie in *A Christmas Story* to take some target practice on an empty two-liter bottle of Mountain Dew in the backyard. I didn't shoot my eye out. I did manage to put a few holes into the hard plastic, and when Dad saw how many times I had hit it out of 20 shots from 150 feet away, he said, "You're actually a real crack shot, son!"

We went inside and he bragged about me so ebulliently with Mom and Katie that I just knew I could get into this and perhaps even graduate to something bigger; we could go deer hunting the next fall. My head became full of hopes and dreams that, finally, I'd get out and do something with my pop just like the other boys I knew did, a real rite of passage that would transition me properly to genuine, godly manhood. Dad suggested I bring it with us to Grandpa's that afternoon, and that's when my first-cousin Doug showed up and opened his big stupid mouth.

I laughed as I thought about how mad Doug could make me. He was a bully in a way that was passed down through our family over the generations, going back to the old country, and I'm thankful that the tradition ended with Dad. Doug was ten years older than me, and with him, his dad, and grandpa, working with firearms seemed to be all about cussing at the youngest among them to be careful with them, that you could kill somebody with them. You'd think I'd know that by twelve years old, and besides, it's a BB gun.

I shook my head and grimaced sourly at the memory. I examined the thing lock, stock, and barrel. It was so light compared to the previous two as to feel weightless, but it became pretty heavy the day after Christmas, back when I was twelve.

We had all loaded up in the van and gone out to the old Sterling farm to walk about and explore, and I brought the gun along, spare BBs in my coat pocket, just to shoot at random stuff I saw. I took some time out to shoot at a tree stump while the rest of the gang walked on ahead to talk and reminisce about growing up. I remember the stump was maybe thirty yards away and sitting at a ninety-degree angle away from the family, due east while they were traveling due north. Nobody in their right mind would have ever thought I was firing at my family, but all of a sudden, frightening the living daylights out of me, Doug walked up behind me and said, "Careful, Ryan, you're firing in the direction of people. You better give me that."

He took the gun out of my hands, walked back to the car, and tossed it into the backseat. He then walked back by, looking completely past me, to catch up with Uncle Chester and Grandpa and be the favorite grandson as usual. I got so steamed I actually managed not to talk to him at family functions for the next couple of years. I knew if I got demonstrably mad at him he'd find a way to turn it into a joke—with the constant exception of Dad, the Sterlings tended to think it was funny when I got mad. They only laughed when he wasn't around, though. Dad defended me as if I were as infallible as Abel for the duration of my life.

When the group caught back up with me, Dad asked me where my gun was. I thought about calling Doug out, but I took a look at Grandpa and Uncle Chester and knew the cards were stacked against me. I said, "Just got tired of carrying it. I put it in the car."

He gave me a long, hard look. He knew how I struggled around his side of the family. I think he struggled too. He knew what I felt, and I think he actually knew what had happened. He looked over at Doug and then back at me and said, "I sure hope you're being honest with me." His gaze lingered, and I broke eye contact. He didn't believe me, but he left it up to me.

I only fired the BB gun once or twice after that, and then it was gone. I had meant over the years to ask what might have happened to it; I knew they wouldn't have gotten rid of it but would have had packed it away where it wouldn't have been in the way—i.e., this gun cabinet. Seeing that Dad had held on to it all those years kept my waterworks flowing. Two large packs of unused BBs sat on the top shelf.

And then there was the last one, a gun I had never seen nor heard about before: a 700-model Remington rifle. It used

.308-caliber bullets. Again, I only knew what type of gun it was from the information on the box of shells above. It was perfect, not a spot of dust on it, no sign of aging whatsoever. It had a beautiful scope mounted on top. I took a couple of peeks through it and knew that it could easily take down a buck on a well-aimed shot from a thousand feet away. Why I knew this, I didn't know, but something about the presentation of this gun, the feeling I got hefting it in my arms and putting the butt against my shoulder, made me feel its power and potential. It was special, and not just for the kind of gun it was.

In the corner of the cabinet, I spied an object barely poking its head out of the dark. It was an envelope. It had been resting against the stock of the rifle before I picked it up and had fallen back diagonally against the wall. I picked it up and opened it. The paper of the envelope was old and stained a bit by humidity and weathered from changes in temperature. I opened it gently and peered inside. It was a card, of course. I could tell as much before I even lifted the flap, which was unglued. It had been opened before.

On the front was a picture of an old man, a middle-aged man, and a young man, their backs to the view, walking into what looked like a sunrise. They were in a clearing in the middle of a wooded area, and the light was shining in a brilliant pink-orange beam onto the ground in front of them. The trees were monstrous; they could have been redwoods, but it didn't matter. They were mythic giants, symbolically flanking the path the old man was leading the middle-aged man on, just as the middle-aged man was now leading the boy.

Their postures were different from one to the other—the old man was doubled over by the years but still pressed on; the middle-aged man walked confidently, head high and proud; and the little boy kept his eyes glued to the ground, eagerly looking for tracks and adventure.

The words on the cover and inside the card were in golden italics. They said,

> *Train up a child in the way he should go, when he is old he will not depart from it.*
>
> —Proverbs 22:6

Then, in my grandfather's handwriting beneath that:

> *Welcome, baby Ryan, to a life of fun and adventure. When you get old enough, I'm going to take you and your daddy out hunting, and I want you to bring this rifle along. I can't wait to share the fun and adventure of Godly living with you and show you how special you are in Christ.*

I thought Doug was your favorite grandson, I thought.

I heard a voice speak, so gently. It sounded like Grandpa, but the Eternal One's signature was all over it: "Each one of you is my favorite. Give me the chance now to show you."

I set the rifle down and read the card over and over, crying fresh tears all the while that ended up caking the ash between my feet on the floor into mud.

When my eyes had dried, however, the questions started coming to my mind. How come Dad had never given me this gun or even talked about it? Why didn't we go hunting as Grandpa had intended? Did they both just get too busy? Was it me? Was it because I had never been interested in guns? I had been scared of the noise they made for several years. Did they give up on me during that time? That couldn't be why because I had handled myself with that .22 all right. I was angry, but not outraged. Sure, very saddened that somehow I had been cheated, for whatever reason, out of the rite of passage so many of my peers had had when they went hunting with their dads for the first time. Why was I denied the fond memory of stepping out quietly into that predawn stillness, the air frosty and cold, the sound of your footsteps through wet leaves the only thing around because the birds hadn't woken up yet, either?

"I know why," I said, very slowly. It seared my heart, and the memory clouded my vision with fresh tears.

Dad was a very strong-willed, positive, godly man. He had a determination in life that couldn't be squashed. It was a fire that almost literally burned in his eyes, like you could see the flames. But the first time I turned down a weekend fishing trip, something I had *never* declined before, I saw it diminish.

I was studying for a chemistry test, sitting up on my bed with the book spread out before me, snacking on Soft Batch cookies while I pored over it. He knocked softly at my door. He always did it that way so he didn't to startle me or catch me in the middle of something. Dad understood that I concentrated on my work just as hard as he concentrated on his own. It wasn't kosher to make a hardworking man, or young man, jump out of his britches. So it is written, so shall it be done.

Still, I was so immersed in it I couldn't help but jump. "Come in," I said, setting my pencil and calculator aside. I had been reviewing significant numbers and was figuring up a few problems for practice.

"Hey, bud," Dad said, poking his head around the door. "What'cha up to?"

"Just studying for a chem test tomorrow."

"Having any problems?" Although he became a contractor, he was a whiz at chemistry in high school.

"No, not this time around. I think I get it. We'll see when I find out how I did on the test."

"Is it okay if I come in?"

"Yeah."

Dad came in and sat down on the bed at my feet, folding his hands on his lap. "What's going on?" I asked.

"Oh, nothing. Your mother and I were just watching some TV, but I wasn't all that interested in what was on. You know, on

Tuesday nights it's her shows or nothing at all. You've been up here a long time. You sure you don't want to come down and hang out with us a while, maybe share your cookies?" Dad reached over and took a few cookies out of the package, the monster and his dinner. He could never resist.

"Yeah, I think I'll just finish studying and call it a night. Besides, if you're not interested in what Mom is watching, I doubt I will be." I began wishing he would go. There was silence between us, just for a moment, but I let it stretch out and get uncomfortable, leaving it up to Dad to fill it.

"Oh," he said, coming to and remembering his real reason for stopping by. "I was wondering what you would think if we went down to the river this weekend, just you and me, got us a room at the Gravel Bar, got ourselves a canoe, and went fishing? You know, as cool as the water's getting, I'll bet the bass are really getting active, and then maybe on Sunday morning we could go out to the woods on Keith Stewart's property, poke around some. He said we're always welcome, but we've never taken him up on it. There's a clearing in the bottoms there that's just gorgeous." It was late September; activity on the Current River was beginning to die down. It would just be the two of us out there again. *More sex talk?* I wondered.

This conversation had taken place on a Tuesday night, and I knew Dad was telling me in advance of the weekend to give me plenty of time for thought.

"No, Dad," I said without hesitation. "Rachel and I have plans to go out Friday and Saturday night."

"But aren't you only supposed to date one night a weekend?" he asked.

"Mom said it was okay to do two nights in a row sometimes, just not to make a habit out of it." I had now turned a potentially friendly conversation into a semi-hostile appeal to a higher authority. I was on the defensive. I couldn't believe Dad would actually try to come up with something that would take me away from my girl—at least, that's what I thought his motives were.

"Okay," he said, the mood calming down a bit. "Yeah, if that's what you want to do. I just thought, maybe, you know, I hadn't been spending much time with you, and, uh…you know, I thought this would be a good time to do that."

"Dad, you don't have to worry about it," I said. "I'm fine. I don't need you to plan anything out to get us together." The words came out of my mouth without me thinking first about how they sounded. I had completely misinterpreted the reason he asked me to do this with him. It was a nonverbal plea for me to take some time off and develop a relationship that, looking back, I could see was much more important than Rachel. I was rejecting the most intelligent, valuable source of wisdom I had in my life.

Dad lowered his eyes after what I said and nodded. He sucked in his lower lip, something he did either when he was thinking or matters didn't agree with him. He stood up and walked for the door. He turned back to me and said, "Good luck on that test tomorrow. Remember, if you need help, just call me." He shut the door softly behind him. It would have been better if he had slammed it. At least then I could actually tell that I had upset him.

Katie and Mom discussed the matter that week. After I broke up with Rachel, I discovered that they regularly talked about her and about how our relationship kept me away from the family. Katie called me from school on Wednesday night just to ask me how things were going. I told her fine. My test went well. How were things with her? Good, good.

"How are you and Rachel doing?" she asked me. Her voice sounded less than enthused, as if she really could care less what my response was.

"Oh, Katie," I told her, my voice suddenly waxing romantic. I then went into a long story, most of which was too unimportant to remember now, about something sweet that happened between us that week at school. It had to do with a note I had written Rachel, something full of wishy-washy poetic love metaphors.

When I had finally finished, Katie, blunt as ever, said, "So I guess things are good enough with Rachel that you don't really need Dad anymore." Katie always knew exactly which buttons to push.

"What are you talking about?" I said, my voice growing volatile.

"I know you turned him down for that fishing trip that he took time off for." Her voice was emotionless. She always sounded very matter-of-fact when she knew that the weight of the words she used were enough to drive the point painfully home.

"He took time off for it?" I asked.

"Yeah, he was planning on getting a lot of paperwork done this weekend, but he got a better idea and wanted to take you fishing. He got some new gear and everything. And then he was going to take you down to Keith Stewart's deer stand and see if you wanted to go hunting soon."

"How do you know all this?" I asked. I thought if I put her on the defensive, perhaps I could turn things to my advantage. It never worked. Katie knew what she was doing. She was my big sister, and if she had to put things in a very unpleasant way just to get my attention and tell me something she thought I needed to know, she would without hesitation. She saw it as sibling upkeep.

"Mom and I talked about it. We talk about everything, Ryan. Honestly, I don't like how you've changed since you started going out with Rachel. I mean, she's nice and all, but she's not for you, kind of an airhead. What do you see in her anyhow?"

I said, sharply, "Katie, now that's not very nice. You be nice to my girlfriend. I've been nice to every guy you've ever dated, even if I didn't like them."

"You're younger than me, Ryan. You don't know how to criticize my choices. I have hindsight, so I can tell you that this relationship isn't good for you or the family, and you've hurt Dad's feelings."

I didn't like hearing about my faults, especially when what I heard was true. Rather than address what she just said, I simply told her, "I'm hanging up." And I did.

When I came home from my Friday night date with Rachel, I found Mom awake in bed and reading. She was the only one there. Dad had taken off earlier that evening to go on the fishing trip anyway. I felt infinitesimally tiny.

Dad invited me to go fishing with him a few more times, not ready to give up. I turned him down each time, citing that I needed to be with Rachel. He wouldn't say a word. He would just leave the room and go about whatever business he had to take care of, leaving me standing there wishing he would fight for it. I was perpetually of the attitude that the world was against me following my impulses.

I was so blinded to the truth of a father's love that only now did it hit me what could have been. He was going to take me out to shoot that rifle at Keith's place, I'm sure of it. It was our moment. He was going to see if I took to that rifle, and if I did, he was going to get me enrolled in hunter education, but as with everything, it was my choice to make. I either wanted to hunt or I didn't. He couldn't make me. I chose Rachel, fleeting puppy-dog love.

"But why didn't he *fight* for it, God? Why didn't he *insist*?" I called out from that closet floor.

"He didn't want to make you mad. It wasn't his way."

"He could come down on other things, why not this?"

"He wanted *you* to choose who you were going to be. He had done all he could do. You were almost out of his hands."

"But what about 'train up a child in the way he should go'? What kind of training was that, to give up so easily?"

"He asked you several times," God said, gently.

"But that wasn't *training*," I replied. "Training means you don't ask, you just do. How *dare* he leave it up to me! I wasn't ready!"

My father's voice came out of the gray: "You're ready now, son. Search what you remember of me, what you remember of everything I told you, and consider how far you've come. My legacy lives on in you. You *are* the man I always hoped you would be. I'm proud of you. Now, which way will you choose?"

I took all the shells out of the safe and stuck all the guns back in but that Remington. I sat down and looked the rifle over. It had a cartridge that would hold five shells. I put them in. Then, I locked the cartridge into place. I got out of the shelter and stood up with it. I looked it over to make sure there weren't any outward signs that it would get jammed up and explode in my face, but I also thought, *Well, if I'm going to die, it would be nice to go out with a bang.*

I'm not sure if I'm saying this right, but the cocking mechanism was a bolt action. I pulled it and pushed it back into place, which loaded the first round into the chamber. I brought it up and held it at the ready. I looked through the scope and surveyed the landscape around me. Nothing but gray, the clouds, the air, and the ground, the view broken only by the basement holes. There was also the dung heap. I had begun throwing bits of food gone bad onto it as well. If I was going to need to make a mess, I'd rather do it all in this one spot, which pleasantly and unpleasantly broke the dull horizon. I had considered using it for target practice, but I decided it was best not to. Instead, I detached the computer monitor from all its connections and took my shots on that.

I only did about five shots. I remember a mantra I had heard: "Squeeze, don't pull." I had thought that was easy enough advice to follow until I tried using it myself. The noise of the gun is so startling that it's nearly impossible to steel yourself against it and gain control over your reflexes. You don't pull because you don't know better—you pull because your body feels it doesn't have a choice. I wasn't able to squeeze—and only squeeze—until that final shot, and I knew it would have to do. No use wasting ammo when I wasn't sure if I might need it soon.

The echo from the shot was deadened much like sound is muffled in a snowstorm. I had no idea how far away it could have been heard.

Confidence crept in. I could at least handle the startle reflex and overcome my fear of the loud noise in the stillness. That was a major victory.

I went back to the store and heard the tapping the moment I stepped inside. The gun didn't have a strap or any other way of carrying it on my person, so I had employed various and safe means of transporting it: cradling it in my arms, holding it in one hand or the other, or over my shoulder with the muzzle pointed behind me. Now, I held it in both hands, strongly within my grasp, ready to turn it toward anything that would come against me.

"Hello?" I called out. My voice was absorbed by the different products, furnishings, and surfaces in the store, but still its suddenness startled me. I never talked above a whisper except on those rare occasions when I prayed out loud or held conversations with Dad and Sara.

The tapping continued uninterrupted, so whatever it was, it hadn't heard me—if it was something with ears, anyway.

I walked toward the back of the store, sound of my breath in my ears. I prayed quietly for strength as I bent down to the flashlight. It lay undamaged where I had dropped it a couple of hours earlier. The batteries I had slipped in were lying beside it, haphazardly scattered from its impact on the floor. I held the rifle well within the grip of my left hand while I managed to put the batteries back in with my right. Very gently, I laid the rifle on the floor, pointed toward the back of the store, while I screwed on the cap to the flashlight with both hands.

I stood up and held the rifle in both hands while also holding the flashlight against the barrel with my left. I knew that, if I had to, I could aim and fire the thing without having to lose the flashlight at all. I thought it might be a good idea to attach the flashlight onto the stock of the gun with duct tape or electrical tape, like Ripley in *Aliens*.

I felt empowered. I trained the flashlight against the back and peered into the partially lit darkness. I could see the wood paneling of the back wall of the store, and then there was the corridor, leading to office space and who knew what else. I checked my peripheral vision and around behind me. I frequently saw things out of the corner of my eye wherever I went, feeling a mixture of wishful thinking that something might be there and fear that something definitely was. Of course, there never was anything, and there wasn't this time either.

I stepped into the corridor. There was an office through a door on the right. The tapping wasn't coming from anywhere in there. It was very surreal to walk into another room with a ceiling after all this time. It had no windows, of course, just a desk lamp and an overhead fluorescent lamp, neither of which would ever work again. The contents of the room had been undisturbed by the violence of the flame, save that the desk had moved a couple of inches, as there were holes in the carpet where it had sat for decades. I knelt down and examined these marks. They weren't just indentations but actual tears in the rug. If they had been the former, I would have been much more on guard because mere indentations from the moving of furniture would pop back out over a period of a couple of months and would no longer be there. I was both relieved and disappointed to see that this phenomenon could be explained by non-artificial means. The tears meant that somebody had scooted the desk some time ago without lifting it.

But then there was the door at the back of the hall. "Employees Only," a sign said in red lettering against white background on the front of the door. There was a small window at eye level in the door. I peeked in and couldn't see a thing. I shone the flashlight through the window and could see shelves with grocery products on them. I became excited that there were more foodstuffs and essential goods in there, but I could listen hard enough to tell the tapping was coming from somewhere in there, and it scared me too much at that point to venture any farther. I made a hasty exit back outside to the refuge of the wide open space, my heart racing. The gun may have been adequate protection against the source of that sound, but I was too afraid to test it, for the moment at least. Something was in there, and I didn't want to know what it was. I had a bad feeling that it was an actual physical presence and not just spiritual.

So the next couple of months were spent living off the stuff in the front of the store. I spent one full day carrying loads of everything I could tote with a satchel. It took twelve trips to get all the food and beverages back with me.

I plunged myself constantly into God's Word. I actually got to the point where it calmed me down enough to get me interested in reading other things to keep my mind occupied, so I retrieved books and magazines from where I had packed them away at the store and began to flip through them. I read a book and a magazine a day, on average. I read about the ancient Romans and Greeks, their history and mythology. I read some of Dad's Ian Fleming and Robert Ludlum novels. I flipped through the pages of *Time* and smirked at how irrelevant their social commentary was now. I whiled away the hours educating myself about a world that no longer existed.

Every time I went back in the store, there was that same rhythmic tapping. It would break about every ten taps for a couple of beats and then start up again, almost like there was a mind behind it. I pictured some gigantic, otherworldly spider-like creature, crooked legs stretching out across the storeroom floor, its feet razor-sharp points that tapped on that surface every time they came down. I pictured it wandering around the storeroom looking for something to eat. Perhaps it found mice in there that sated its hunger until I got bored enough finally to open the door and see what it was all about.

The spider was the least of the images that came through my head, and when I went to bed at night, I not only imagined what other things it could have been but also pictured it coming down to find me. Surely, if it were hungry, it would probably have smelled me by now and come looking for me. I could even smell myself. It wasn't pretty. Perhaps I stank too much for anything to want to consider me dinner.

My one hygienic blessing was that I had found much in the way of bathroom toiletries around the many basements I had explored. I could cover up my stink with deodorant and colognes as much as possible, and brushing my teeth, an absolute necessity, kept me from waking up mornings with a taste like somebody had pooped in my mouth.

But as I continued imagining what might be in that store-room, I became increasingly antsy. I couldn't let it go for much longer. Two months had passed since I first heard it, and it was getting old. I prayed over it, yearning to hear that small voice that would tell me what to do, but it didn't come. I knew better than to think God wasn't listening. Even though his world was gone, he was still there. I knew he had to be. The past year has taught me a lot about the importance of believing in things not seen, especially since there really was nothing to see anymore.

I also hoped that he wasn't going to let humanity die this way. If I really was the last person on Earth, God would not let it end this way. He would not let the story of his creation end with whatever I encountered in that storeroom. That woman behind the waterfall was out there somewhere for me to find. I was meant to find her, and my first step toward getting to her would come with whatever I met in that store.

I gathered my guns, forsaking the Daisy because it was use-less, and all the ammo. I loaded the M1, the Remington, and the

.22 as full as they'd take, and I tucked the rest in my knapsack. I made sure I had plenty of water just in case the battle raged on and I needed sustenance. I also made sure I had high-carb foods—mostly Chef Boyardee, which I would open with a Swiss Army knife I found in a basement down the street.

As I made sure I had it all gathered, I found myself *aching* for a fight, practically wishing that I found that spider-monster or worse there in the darkness. I wanted it because it would mean at least something was happening, and I was an integral part of it. No longer would I be a little dot moving about in this gray wilderness, eking out my survival. Instead, I would be a warrior, a soldier whose every move had brought him to this point. This was the moment where legends were made, even if I was the only one around to document it. No longer was I going to live one foot in front of another, praying the fight away. I was going to go out there and get it.

I fixed up a strap from the cotton bed sheet material that I could put around my shoulder to carry all the guns. I had them secured in such a way that accidental discharge would be impossible or at the very least highly unlikely. I took a laxative and let it run its course to make sure I wasn't carrying any excess weight. In my various improvised workouts and runs over the past year, I had developed muscles and endurance in all the right places. Sure, I had the moments of starvation, but my athletic shape had held up. If this turned hand-to-hand, I'd be ready. I carried two large kitchen knives as well. I used electrical tape to secure one of the knives to the top of the M1 as a bayonet, and I finally decided that would be the rifle that I carried with me on my journey past this place if I survived the fight.

With all my weapons and gear strapped to me, I knelt in the basement and prayed for strength, courage, and safety. This was the great battle of my life, something the entire year had been leading up to, as if the fire itself was meant to break me so the rebuilding process could begin. I took a look at myself in Katie's bathroom mirror. I saw in there a man I didn't recognize at first. I hadn't looked at myself since June. I had been too afraid to see what I had turned into. I didn't even use the mirror to brush my teeth. Now I took in the man this boy had become.

I was covered head to foot, as always, in ash. I could see how it might work as a kind of camouflage should this fight be brought outside the store. My hair had grown long. It actually reached in oily strands down to the small of my back, colored almost pitch-black from the ash that had stuck to it and gotten wet with sweat and bodily oils.

My beard was thick too. I had the means to shave and cut my hair that year, but I just hadn't felt like it. Perhaps it was because I knew there was never going to be a reason, and I certainly didn't want to waste whatever water stock I had just to soak my razor in. Anytime I brushed my teeth, at the risk of a possible stomach-ache, I would swallow the toothpaste-filled water entirely rather than spit any of it out. I'm not sure that was ever a very wise procedure, but it made me feel good not to waste it.

I put on my fiercest gaze. Opened my eyes wide, bared my teeth, and growled. My voice was raspy because I had never used it with such force as I did then. There was hardly a voice there at all, but I spoke past the thick blockage of disuse and found it much, much deeper than I had ever before been capable of. Feeling confident, I threw my head back and roared at the sky. It was the loudest sound I had heard, including the gunshots of my target practice several weeks before. It filled creation with its fury.

I went back to Mom's calendar and made a notation of what I had planned to do that day. I anticipated it being my last entry, but I kept it brief: "Encountered destiny today, and I won." I did not know for sure whether I would live, but I was confident that, either way, the outcome would be gain. It was December 31.

When I got out of the basement, I heard a fly buzz. A moment later, there was a tickle on the back of my neck. On impulse, I began to raise my arm to slap it, and then stopped. It remained there. I didn't see it, but it was *there*, the first sign of life beyond the mold and bacteria that I had seen growing on spoiled food and the dung heap. I laughed at the tickle as it skittered around a moment back there, then it left.

I turned quickly to catch sight of it, but it had gone on, probably to the dung. I smiled. "Eat and be full, buddy," I said. Sometimes, God uses the lowest forms of life on Earth to lift us up. Sometimes, he uses houseflies instead of butterflies.

The trek across the half-mile expanse felt like a hundred times that length, but I soldiered on against the fear that threatened to overwhelm me. Every man needs a battle, and I felt like survival wasn't quite it. I was still alive, true, but what kind of life had it been? I hadn't met another living thing in over a year now. And my vague imaginings were a poor substitute for what I really craved.

I pictured myself standing over that beast, crying my victory cry, then saying thank-you to it as it breathed its last because the beast brought purpose. On the converse, I pictured ascending to my heavenly Father and seeing a proud smile on his face and hearing from him, "You fought the good fight, son. Come into the Kingdom."

And even though there had been that promise from that ethereal womanly figure in my dream that someday we'd see each other, as I stepped toward certain death, I felt that what had been promised me was really to get me to the inevitability of this moment, where I would die not in a horrible, unfair cleansing fire I didn't see coming, but in a fight with the only other fearsome living thing on Earth, a fight to determine the future. It felt good to know that something was coming to an end.

I stepped into the store and heard the tapping immediately. I'm not sure if it had gotten louder or my fear made it louder.

Previously, I couldn't hear it until I got closer to the back of the store. I didn't care. I had prayed hard enough, steeled myself enough for this moment, that I found the strength to simply charge right on to the back, bypassing the stacks of stored books and various other nonessentials and the remaining groceries, the supplies of which I had almost exhausted.

I stood before the door, hearing that tapping now as a pounding. The creature knew I had been coming. Even though it couldn't have known for sure, it had intuited this moment was coming too. Behind that door was our executioner sent down here from the ship to make absolutely certain we were completely wiped out, and I was the only thing that stood between its kind and annihilation.

I stood off to the side of the door and peered around the corner of the window, that small porthole into hell. The scant light from the front door didn't reach. I couldn't see anything, but still I hoped to see some flash of movement there in the darkness that told me where it was. I considered shining the flashlight in there, but I didn't want to give it a target. Not yet.

I heard the tapping grow louder, then quit. It started up again, beating about ten pulses, then stopped. The thing was just circling around the room, wandering, probably feeding off whatever it found to eat in there, keeping itself busy while camping out and waiting like a trapdoor spider for something to fall into its hovel. I silently wished I had a grenade.

To bait it, I pushed the door gently. It swung open a couple of inches, just enough to catch the creature's attention, but the tapping continued, starting and stopping as before. It hadn't noticed. Perhaps it didn't even know I was there. But I knew it was just toying with me, pretending to be unaware but keeping an eye on me all the while.

"Be strong, Ryan," Sara whispered to me. "This is it. I believe in you."

I believe in you too, I felt that still, small voice say inside of me. It told me everything I needed to know. God was here, and he was not silent.

I shouted through the door, "Hey, this is your last chance. If you're human, speak up. Otherwise, I'm coming in, and I'm ready to shoot." The tapping stopped for a moment and then began its rhythm anew. It had heard me, and it wasn't human.

I readied my flashlight, finger on the button, and held it between my cheek and the stock of the M1, ready to aim wherever I sensed danger. I listened again for the tapping. It would be at my right once I opened the door. I assumed the danger to be eye-level. If it was anything lower than that, I would stab downward with the bayonet and then fire. I kicked the door open with my right foot so hard that it broke off its hinges and clattered off to the left. I roared, spun to the right, and fired.

The shot was deafening. I wasn't ready for it, and it startled me so much that I instantly fell backward into the darkness behind me. Gun and flashlight fell out of my hands. The latter went spinning across the floor somewhere. The gun fell off to my left. I couldn't see a blessed thing.

I scrambled for the gun, trying to get a grip on it. In my haste, I ran the tips of my fingers into the blade of the knife and earned myself painful cuts on my left hand. The pain burned into me, and I cried out in both pain and panic. But at least I had the gun. Heedless of my bleeding, I snatched up and turned back over onto my back, thrusting that bayonet into the air. The tapping had stopped. The creature was so close that I could almost smell its breath.

And then I heard the tapping again, away from me. It had not attacked me, hadn't even come close. Now that I was in its territory, I had no idea where it was, and the tapping continued its average length of about ten beats, building a crescendo and then stopping. I was safe for the moment, long enough to stand back up and ready myself for the next lunge. But there hadn't been a first lunge. *I* was the one who lunged.

Is it afraid of me? I thought

I didn't let my guard down for a second. My eyes were wide in the dark, mouth open and taking in short, quick, soundless breaths. I was covered in sweat, and I could even smell my own fear. I don't know how long I stood there, crouched with the bayonet pointing out from me. I spun in a circle, sure that it was going to attack me from behind, but the tapping continued to resound from the far side of the room, as it had before I even opened the door. The creature was pacing back and forth, from the sound of it, almost as if there was something back there it was protecting.

Its young?

Where is that flashlight? I thought. I prayed I would find it, and I began to take tiny steps around my side of the room, taking care not to bump into shelves and somehow startle the beast into action. I tapped around with my toes before I stepped down. I hit something soft that then crunched under my feet. I whispered a curse as it almost scared the life out of me and wondered what strange creepy giant insect I had just crushed. *One of its offspring?*

I nervously stuck the bayonet down there and poked around at it. I heard sort of a crackling sound as it scooted the remains around the floor. It took me a full minute of fearful hysteria to realize that I had just stepped on a box of cereal that had fallen off from the shelf.

Nevertheless, fear overtook me, and I fled out of the room, down the office corridor, and around the corner in front of the refrigeration units and their spoiled dairy items, clutching the rifle for dear life and praying against whatever was going to come after me. I needed to get out of there, to go back home and never return, to hide away, try to cover my scent somewhere and pray it never found me.

But that would only delay the inevitable. I had to get back in there. I would never forgive myself if I didn't. What good would the rest of my life be if I was only going to live in fear of the monster that had not yet even attacked me? Man was not meant to live this way. I was a child of a light that shone even in the worst pitch-black darkness. In that room, I faced both physical and spiritual darkness, and my faith would never be what it could have been if I didn't put it to work.

I turned around and charged back in. The light shone in from outside just enough for me to get my bearings straight. It only penetrated in a three-foot radius into the room, but it was enough. I walked heavily toward that tapping.

"Hey!" I shouted. I hit the flashlight with my left foot and sent it spinning off again, but I knew from hearing where it had gone. Holding my bayonet out from me against the creature, I stooped over and picked it up. It had hit the floor on the button and turned off. I picked it up, turned it on, and shone it toward the tapping.

There was nothing there but drywall.

<hr />

"What?" I shouted. I shone the flashlight once around the room to make sure I was alone, and then I set my guns down. They had suddenly grown very heavy.

The room was a lot smaller than I had thought, about the size of the basement. Three rows of shelves, each ten feet long, spanned almost the full length, with just a few feet of clearance on either end. The ceiling might have been about eight feet high, the width of the room fifteen feet, its dimensions practically square. The floor was bare concrete. I had imagined the walls to be concrete as well—they *sounded* like it when the noise of my rifle fire bounced off them, but much like our eyes, our ears can deceive us when we give our mind free reign to play.

I was still scared. That hadn't stopped, but added to that was complete confusion. The tapping continued. It made a sound that our pipes used to make in the dorm during the winter when the heat would kick on. But it couldn't be that, could it? Was there still heat radiating through their pipes? Would it make that clanking racket that had kept me up so many nights in school?

It was coming from right behind that far wall. I shone the flashlight all over it. It took me several passes before I caught the hole I had made when I fired the gun. I saw some small chunks of drywall on the floor. I stuck my finger in the hole. It was hot around the edges. I stuck it all the way in and felt the slug. It burned, and I had to withdraw my finger quickly and plunge it into my mouth to cool it off.

As I said before, I don't know much about weaponry and ballistics, but that slug had stopped cold against something and flattened instantly. There was something behind that drywall. I stepped back from it and looked all over. In the right-hand corner of the wall was a crack. The wall was painted with a candy-stripe pattern, so the crack was well hidden in one of those stripes. I never could tell what color it was in the dim light I had, but I could only assume the stripe was dark, perhaps even black.

The crack went straight up from the floor to the ceiling. Close inspection showed that three feet down the wall to the left, there was another crack. *A secret door!* I thought. I pressed my ear against the wall and heard the tapping coming straight from behind that door.

I looked for a switch or lever in that room and saw nothing. I pressed against the wall at all points in case there was some pressure-activated mechanism that would open it. Nothing. I searched the offices for some kind of clue, something in the paperwork or file cabinet, perhaps, that would tell me how it operated. I looked for switches, a button. Nothing. Even if it were electronic and thus defunct without power, I would have felt the comfort of knowing that *something* had worked, at least.

My mind became consumed with the possibilities. Did the Edsons have an underground habitation? Were they down there? Were there others? How deep did it go? How many people could it hold? Had they been living down there the whole time? What had I missed?

Or did our destroyers set up their new civilization down there?

I fled straightaway. I ran back to the Nortons'. They had had a splitting wedge in their basement workroom. It had never been of any use to me over the year—no wood to split—but now it looked like the Holy Grail. I ran as hard as I could back to the store with it, so hard that I was just sure I would trip and fall on the blade at some point.

I made it, however, and went straight to the wall. I had my guns at my feet and was ready to pick them up again in a heartbeat. I held the wedge over my head and brought it down as hard as I could against the wall. It cut deep. I could feel the blade glance off the hard undersurface. When I pulled it back, it brought a generous chunk of the wall off with it. I swung again, and again. I got to a point where I could grab chunks out with my hands and pull them down.

I held the light on it to get a better view. I saw that the real walls were made of steel. Hard, impenetrable. The cutout of the drywall *had* been a door. Hinges poked out of the remaining, hanging pieces of the wall I had knocked away, and on the other side of the opening was a doorjamb. It had been shut securely but could only reliably be opened from the inside by pushing out.

There was another door underneath the false one. There was a small square set into the door at eye level. *A window*, I thought. It was covered, but I suspected I could slide it open if I could find the mechanism. There was a small handle on the bottom of it, to the right. I grasped it and pulled to the left. It felt rusty and old, and it squeaked loudly, but with strong effort, I got it to budge. It slammed open, and I passed out from shock when I saw through to the other side.

I woke up shaking. The room was a bit brighter than it had been before. The extra light was coming through the new window, of course. I could hear the tapping more loudly, and there was now no doubt at all what was making it.

The door opened into a panic room. It was so obvious now that I have no idea why it never struck me that whole time I was investigating it. Pop Edson was sure his whole life that the commies would come for him eventually, and he'd be ready for them. Even though there was no longer a communist threat, there was *always* a threat. When the fire came, he knew the threat he had waited his whole life for had finally arrived. He gathered up the entire family, his wife, son, daughter-in-law, and their kids, and they retreated to the panic room inside a shelter that was already well-fortified against any attack, even extraterrestrial annihilation.

Apparently, something had jammed in that door, and they couldn't get out. Maybe they had a backup generator that powered the mechanism. I didn't investigate enough to see what had happened with the door. I didn't care to. They were all dead. All five of them. I could make a pretty good guess how they died. A body, a man's, with a long-sleeved, white-collared shirt on, sat on a bench on the west side. He was mostly decomposed now, but I think it was Pop. He held a pistol in his right hand, which had fallen slack and then stiffened at his side. The back of his skull was against the wall. I could see from the graphic evidence splayed on that wall that he had shot himself through the mouth. Everyone else had died by gunshot wounds too. I assumed they were dying of hunger and thirst. There were food wrappers all over, some from MREs that Frank Jr., must have had left over from when he had served in the Army and smuggled them home. That would have held them for a while, maybe a couple of months. I could see off in one corner that there was a small water closet with a toilet, and while the light was too dim to tell for sure, I could see its potential had been maximized. The plumbing had long since broken down, and the toilet had backed up to the point that some of the sewage had crept across the floor. The smell must have been awful.

The source of the light in the room came from a corner up against the ceiling, about ten feet up. It was small, too small for escape or even to chuck the sewage out of, which they must have desperately wanted to do, and their anguish at seeing the light but not being able to do anything about it must have crushed them. The walls were made of steel too but it had been proven quite destructible.

I inspected the back of the hill outside and saw the hole. That corner of the structure had poked out above the ground, but just barely. I could smell the decomposition and waste even out there, and it was horrible. Hidden around the back of that large hill, where I hadn't yet ventured, the wind had blown the smell away from me always before. Either that or my own stench had always been strong enough to counteract it. I couldn't stand it and quickly got away from it.

While it was tiny, the hole still let in a stiff wind, and that's where the tapping came from. Frank's right hand bounced against the side of the bench whenever the wind hit it. It came in gusts that blew strongly and then stopped, allowing the gun to tap the metal of the bench about ten times with each swell. It pulsed with a steady regularity. I suddenly couldn't bear to listen to it anymore. Crying tears of absolute sorrow for the Edsons, I left.

THE BEGINNING

I spent New Year's Eve in agony. *I could have saved them*, I thought, over and over. If I had only known—the only danger the entire year was my own petrifying fear. It had kept me immobilized for so long that they had died long before I even set foot in the store. If I had managed to reach them, they could have directed me to some sort of release button or lever to let them out before their supplies ran out. I could have tossed food in to them through that hole, kept them sustained. The despair they must have felt, as they began to waste away, their hope of salvation diminishing, while just beyond that steel door was sustenance that would have carried them at least for several months—it was a pain too heavy to bear. What must Pop have felt, watching his sweet grandkids dying before his eyes and knowing his only course of action was to put a bullet through their brains and end their suffering? And they may have thought that whole time, as I did, that they were the last people on Earth and that this is how it all ended.

My prime directive for the year had been my own survival. I fantasized about Sara and grieved after my lost family. I lifted up so many selfish laments to God while the greatest of tragedies was taking place only a half mile from my shelter. The mourning that night was matched only by that moment I had had several months previous when I saw my cell phone had died and realized fully that all my loved ones were dead.

But this was different. This time, I cried for the loss of somebody I didn't know so well, and it was good. It was cleansing. The longer I did it, the healthier it became, and when I could cry no more, I prayed from the deep inner pains. I prayed that I could live with myself after what I had allowed to happen, then I realized I could admit it was not actually my fault.

Quit on that nonsense, God said to me, and so I did.

"You *lived*, Ryan," Sara said. "And I'm proud of you." That wasn't to say there was shame in what Pop had done. I was in no position to judge the right or wrong of it. I only knew that I had also had the chance to kill myself, the aching need within to end it all because I thought there was no way out, and I held on because I knew there had to be a ghost of a chance that I was here for a purpose.

I sat down to read the rest of the Bible that night. There was one last book I hadn't gotten into, the rich food Dad told me might take a while. *Says who, Dad?* I thought and smiled as I finished it in one night.

Along the way as I was reading the line, I heard the voice say in the water about the one who sits on the throne and the lamb. I read of the New Jerusalem that God showed me at the bottom of the pool. I marveled that God had used Scripture with me before I even read it. He did it not only to impress me and fill me with wonder, but also as a sign so that I would be encouraged. Yes, I still would have believed because there were moments of desperation over the course of the year during which faith was the *only* thing I had. In fact, I would argue that it was *always* the only thing I had.

As I read, I also learned something that for some reason hadn't stuck before. My dear friend, if you have not yet heard, hear now and believe: the blast was not the end of the world. *Far from it!* God has plans for this world, and they *do not* include being killed off by aliens from some far-off planet hundreds of light-years away. Our story is not over. I feel, in fact, that we may have reached a new beginning. This is the dawn of a glorious era. Let's claim it now, and live.

I thanked God for this hope, then prayed for direction. I had centered my life around that store for the past several months, especially around the mystery of that tapping. Now that the monster was slain, I could go back to living just in order to live. I've learned, however, that survival is not an end in itself, just a means.

"You shall have life abundant," I said to myself.

"If you mean it," I said to God, "then make it so."

Walk, and don't stop, God responded, so I did.

I'm going to leave my handwritten manuscript at the store. It took me a week to write it. I managed to sit still that long, but I'm glad to be striking out now. Although it may have been poignant to leave on New Year's Day, like I was making some statement about new beginnings and such, I felt I needed to tell my story, if only as a history to encourage you that, yes, there are other people alive out there, and while some of them may have gone the way of the Edsons, still others have discovered how to live. I'm proof.

I certainly couldn't take all of the food with me, and I only kept one of the guns, the Remington. It meant the most to me because it spoke of the man Dad and Grandpa knew I could be. I took the card and will keep it tucked away. I'll look at it from time to time. The other weapons I've left here. You can have them if you want, although I don't think you'll be needing them. God didn't let us live just so that we might kill each other in the aftermath; I don't care how bleak it all looks. Those stories are foolish, nihilistic, and wrong. We are capable of tremendous evil, yes, but I now know the One from whom tremendous good can spring too. In him, we can be good for once.

I do have a lot of food with me. I found a rolling pallet, seren-dipitously enough, back in that storeroom. I loaded it down with all the bags full of food I could gather and tied it down with some rope I've found in my scavenging. There is still some extra food in my basement from my restocking trips. You're welcome to it. I'm going to pull that pallet behind me as I go. The wheels work pretty well, but I wouldn't be surprised if I have to stop every once in a while and pick ash out of the axles.

I tried the CB again, one last time before setting out. Couldn't hear a blessed thing on it, and I've decided to leave it here. Toy with it if you must, but I'm not going to put my hope in it any-more. It's let me down. I think all our devices will, eventually. If we're going to talk, it's going to be face-to-face, and I plan on hugging you and never letting go.

I've left a note telling everyone where to go to find us. Please leave it after you've read it, but like I said, take the manuscript and find me. I would very much like to have it back when you arrive. I left a few reams of paper there on the counter beside it. As you travel, you might want to write your story as well. I hope you know that yours is important too. We must keep a memory of how far we've come so that we can *learn* and never stop.

I found a map of Missouri in the store. There are dozens of them on a rack by the comics; I advise you to take one but leave the rest for whoever follows you. Look for Van Buren. It's about an hour's drive, maybe sixty miles. I think it will take a week of careful walking and navigating to get there. Pop Edson sold com-passes as a novelty. They're next to the maps. Take one and *use it carefully* to get to Van Buren. That's where I've gone.

I know it sounds crazy to go back there, where it all began, but you remember that dream I spoke about? You remember the spring coming from the rock? There is a place in Van Buren called Big Springs. It fed into the Current River. I'm sure the river and its little dead-end offshoots are gone, but the spring came from underground. It was a loud and raucous place, that ice-cold, clear-blue water coming from underground, gushing out, fields of watercress flourishing on the riverbed from all the nutrients. The fire only touched what was aboveground. As the preponderance of basements has proved, it didn't penetrate below. The spring is *still flowing*, and I know that's why I dreamed about it. I know that's why it was so beautiful in my dream. There's *life* there. That's where our rebuilding will begin. Come, and come *quickly*. Perhaps you'll find your own lady of the waterfall. Perhaps you *are* that lady. I think we will find our brightest beginning at the site of our darkest end, and there are *caves* on that river, lots and lots of caves.

And let us remember, let us carry with us, what we have learned in the absence of our dearest loved ones. The greatest thing we ever did for each other and the thing that will carry us on is to touch each other and leave behind the fingerprints of God. It's what has gotten us through this year. If you don't yet believe it, I don't see how. It's by his grace through our faith that we were saved. If that applies to you only physically, I pray what I have said here will influence you to make the right choice. Our future is entirely in his hands now. All our former comforts are gone, and you know what? In a strange way it excites me. What's he going to do with us now that we know he's all we have? I trust that great things await us.

It's brighter today, growing brighter every day, so much now that I can read by it easily. I have a feeling the sun may come out today, if only for a moment. My heart is overwhelmed just thinking about it. I'm bringing a handful of books. You can grab some too to keep you entertained. Dad wouldn't mind. I think he'd hate to see them go to waste. I'm going to read *The Lord of the Rings* on my journey because it's also about a great adventure—the heroes cross into lands unknown and unencountered, and at the end, they get their reward. We will, too. I *know* it.